PARTNERS

HARRISON YOUNG
PARTNERS

Partners by Harrison Young
First published by Jane Curry Publishing 2013
This edition published by Ventura Press 2015

PO Box 780 Edgecliff
NSW 2027
AUSTRALIA

www.venturapress.com.au

Copyright © Harrison Young, 2013

All rights reserved. No part of this book may be reproduced or transmitted in any form or by any means, electronic or mechanical, including photocopying, recording or by any other information storage retrieval system, without prior permission in writing from the publisher.

National Library of Australia Cataloguing-in-Publication entry

Author: Young, Harrison.
Title: Partners: love is a law unto itself / Harrison Young.
ISBN: 978-1-925183-60-3 (print edition)
ISBN: 978-1-922190-67-3 (Epub edition)
ISBN: 978-1-922190-68-0 (Kindle edition)

Dewey Number: A823.4

Cover images:
NYC skyline – Getty images © George Marks
Naked woman – Fotolia Photo Library © Maksim Šmeljov

Printed in Australia by McPherson's Printing Group
Cover design: Deborah Parry Graphics
Editorial: Siobhan Cantrill and Barbara McClenahan
Typeset and eBook conversion: Midland Typesetters, Australia

About the Author

Harrison Young has been writing fiction in airports and on weekends since 1981. Graduating from Harvard University in 1966, Young has been a journalist for *The Washington Post*, a captain in the U.S. Army Special Forces, a government advisor and an investment banker. He has done business in twenty countries and has advised a dozen governments on financial system issues. Young helped establish banks in Bahrain and Beijing and as a senior official at the FDIC in Washington he managed the resolution of 266 failing banks. A dual citizen, Young retired as chairman of Morgan Stanley Australia in 2007 and became a director of Commonwealth Bank of Australia.

Alice in Wonderland

The firm had a gym, and one day Alice, who they'd made a partner because there was no way not to, came in and took her clothes off. The men were frightened. They wanted to kill her.

Alice knew this. Her mother was a politician in a small way, and she liked to quote Lyndon Johnson to the effect that if you couldn't walk into a room and know by instinct who your enemies were, you had no business in Washington. Alice lived in New York, but she was good at walking into rooms. "Very self-possessed" was a phrase that was sometimes used.

The gym had been constructed on the (perhaps unconscious) principle that, as they shared liability, partners of a law firm should have no secrets from each other, might share offices or even desks. So it was just one big room, with exercise equipment in the middle, doorless wooden lockers and benches around the sides, and a large door into a big open shower room. When they made Alice a partner they just assumed she'd "understand" and never even stick her head in.

And the other women partners? Well, the short answer is they didn't go to the gym. Neither did a majority of their male counterparts, in fact. There wasn't any explicit rule that said who could use the gym. But working in a high-caste New York law firm is a form of self-mutilation. At some level most of the partners assumed they weren't *supposed* to be healthy, or have time for exercise. The three dozen or so who did use the gym on a regular basis were the powerful ones—the alpha males. There weren't any alpha females.

As word began to get around about Alice, some of the men who'd never spent much time in the gym developed a sudden interest in personal fitness, but most evidently decided it would have been a bit obvious to do so. Or maybe they were too modest. In any case, the firm's existing pecking order was largely preserved—except for the presence of Alice.

The first way the alpha males tried to get rid of Alice was to recommend her for a job in Washington. "Assistant Secretary of Something," said Oscar. "Or ambassador to a small country."

"Far away," said Henry, who was senior partner.

"What's your problem?" said Charles. "Good-looking woman on the next stairmaster. I personally find it quite motivating."

"Charles, it's awkward and you know it," said Henry.

There was a new President in residence in the White House. Several of the firm's partners had been important donors and, therefore, had "access." And being political junkies they knew that the appointment and confirmation process now underway often uncovered secrets. They sensed that Alice had some. Probably a lesbian, they said. Serve her right, behaving the way she had. And if she did get confirmed, she'd have to move to Washington, which would get her out of the gym.

When Alice heard about the plan to have her nominated she put a stop to it. "I couldn't stand the scrutiny," she said a trifle loudly as she dried off after her shower, facing the middle of the room to give everyone a good look. "And I know what you're up to" was the subtext, though she didn't have to say it. The plotters gave each other meaningful looks.

Alice *was* hiding something, but it wouldn't have caused a problem with a Democratic Senate. Her family was working class. She hadn't exactly specifically kept it a secret that her father had been an ironworker, up in the sky with the Iroquois who don't mind heights, or that her brothers were both firemen, or that her mother had been one too until she temporarily became a local celebrity for saving a little kid on television and someone powerful persuaded her to let her name go on the ballot—but a fair-minded person might have described her reticence that way.

Some improbable strand of DNA had given Alice a skinny upper-class body, with breasts that when she was naked were quietly perfect, rich black hair, pale skin and an aristocratic capacity for self-deception—whereas the rest of the O'Malleys were red-haired and freckled and as forthright as fire plugs—and she'd accepted the role destiny seemed to have designed her for. When she was fourteen, Alice's voice began of its own accord to acquire the neutral accent of a television newsreader, and she decided to become a lawyer. She'd seen lady lawyers in television shows and they seemed to live their lives in Armani.

No one at the firm knew Alice's "come-from," as Charles put it—or about her younger brother's decoration for bravery, or her mother's victory over the bureaucrats in keeping open an effective if old-fashioned high school in an unfashionable part of town. All her partners knew was that clients liked her, and asked for her, that she billed two thousand hours a year (which was a lot) and didn't make mistakes. Alice was proud of her family, but silently proud. And if her last name excited curiosity, she would respond that "all O'Malleys are related." That probably wasn't a mortal sin.

The next thing that happened to Mrs. O'Malley's daughter was that a partner she didn't know very well, named William, sat down beside her in the gym and said very quietly, "I know what you mean about scrutiny." Alice didn't know where he was headed, so she just kept on tying her gym shoes. The man had finished his shower and had nothing on but a towel, which added to the confessional quality of the situation. "I have a problem," he said finally, in a carefully non-alpha tone.

If a partner of a high-caste law firm has a problem that relates to his professional expertise, the firm has a problem. William was a tax partner and he'd cheated on his taxes. Well, not cheated exactly—taken an aggressive position. So as to improve his cash flow at the time of his divorce. And maybe simultaneously had been ultra-conservative about the value of his illiquid assets, which the State of New York would have expected him to share with his former wife. These two (in retrospect) errors of judgment interacted in subtle ways that reminded Alice why she had not become a tax lawyer, but the net result was that if he was unable to deliver some cash to his former wife within two weeks, she would make a fuss that would probably provoke scrutiny of his returns. And he continued to be short of cash. All this while gripping the towel and looking down at Alice's shoes. Most of all, he was mortified to be putting the firm's good name at risk.

Alice knew—and William knew she would know—what he was saying. If William's partners didn't help him, they would regret it. It wasn't a threat—just a reminder of the realities. The firm could beat up on him if they wanted to, and he was prepared to act embarrassed and grateful, but his former wife was a ticking time bomb and they better get on with it. He needed about seven million dollars.

Alice felt within her a flicker of alpha anger. She didn't look forward to telling her partners that each of them needed to kick in fifty thousand dollars to bail out someone who billed a lot but wasn't very popular. She didn't want to part with that kind of money herself. But most of all she resented William's assumption that she would be "good about it"—would be sympathetic and efficient and discreet, the way girls who joined high-caste firms were supposed to be, the way even former wives were supposed to be.

"Stand up, William," she said quietly. "Drop the towel and show us your dick."

William obeyed.

"And stay out of the gym for a while."

Alice got right to work, starting with known curmudgeons, which made it harder for the rest to waste time being outraged. She made William sign a loan agreement that obliged him to live on an associate's pay until the seven million dollars was repaid. She negotiated a settlement with William's former wife, staying professional and distant despite her curiosity about the woman. She got another tax partner to review William's back-year returns, the conclusion being that, well, he hadn't broken the law. And when William, whose sense of entitlement was nothing if not resilient, happened to return to the gym at the precise moment Alice emerged dripping from the shower, she just looked at him, and he backed out of the door. "Part goddess, part border collie," said Charles—just loud enough for Alice to hear him.

But along with this brutal triumph, something soft and spooky was going on. As she went around from office to office, soliciting checks from her partners, Alice realized that being clothed made her gym companions shy. And not being gym-goers made the rest uncertain. It was as if they all now knew that the selves they presented in suits and ties (or in her case a skirt and blouse and very expensive cardigan) were fraudulent. I know that you have clumps of hair on your back, she found herself thinking as she settled into the chair Frank offered her. I know that you have a pretty impressive body, Oscar, even if having been bullied as a little boy or guilt about something has forced bad posture on you. And you both have proof that I am a woman. It has become impossible any longer to see me as a sexless striver, which was such a safe and comfortable arrangement.

As the weeks passed, more and more of Alice's partners made cautious visits to the gym, but not to spy on Alice. As far as she could figure out, they wanted her to have seen them. They liked it. Their shoulders relaxed. The stress of self-presentation dissolved. It was like having been to confession at the age of nine.

Alice liked it too. Examining and being examined constituted acceptance. You have a sunburn, Paul. I have a bruise, Peter. Count my moles, George, if you like. There are six on my front and two on my back. I would gladly let you touch them, but lightning would strike you dead. And yes, Henry-pretending-not-to-look, when I stand up straight, you can see that my quietly perfect breasts are very slightly asymmetrical. Same as *your* wobbly bits.

Alice knew that there was endless speculation about what she was up to, what had given her the idea of walking into the gym and stripping. "She thinks she's being modern," said Frank. "She thinks she's being clever," said Andrew. Charles composed a haiku: "Alice be a frog. Work here twelve years, and never blink. One day she jump."

Alice adopted a strategy of not thinking about it, which was presumably how her father had coped with working fifty stories above the sidewalk. She pushed her own questions aside with words like "thrill" or "mischief."

The answer was ambition, of course. But what settled over her was calm. She had control. She liked that.

She began talking to Sandra, who'd made partner four years ahead of her, and whom she'd made a point of not getting to know, on the theory that it would be politically unwise. A woman had to make it on her own, really. Somehow that didn't matter any more.

"Come to the gym some time," said Alice when they ran into each other in an empty corridor. And I don't care if you're a lesbian, she added silently. I want to know where you buy those fabulous suits you wear.

"So the boys can look at me?" said Sandra.

"It isn't what you expect. It's... freeing. It's like being baptized."

"The sin of being a woman washed away?"

"Up to you how you think about it," said Alice.

Sandra did come, briefly, though on a day Alice happened to be seeing a client in Chicago. "Sandra peak in and Sandra run away," Charles told her with perfect political incorrectness. He spoke "fluent black person" (his phrase) as well as "oriental" when he thought he could get away with it. Sandra wasn't exactly African-American in appearance, but there was general agreement that it was hard to say what she was. Other than a scarily good litigator, that is.

Charles was a problem, Alice knew. She probably had a crush on him, though she'd kept that admission at bay for many years. He came from Nebraska, which he told you immediately. "I should have been a Southerner," he'd tell clients, "but I didn't have the poetry." What he did have was the body of a man who had worked on a farm as a boy. He liked to roll his sleeves up, and the muscles on his forearms *were* poetry. When he was in a drafting session, intensely concentrating on the task at hand, he made Alice imagine young Abe Lincoln straightening up from his rail-splitting and letting his eyes rest on the horizon—an Abe Lincoln who looked like Gary Cooper, that is.

Charles never hit on the female associates. He dated women in more glamorous professions like fashion and the theater. Armani wasn't the half of it. Alice had seen pictures of him in magazines she flipped through at the hairdresser. He had never even sniffed at Alice, though they'd worked on some long, complicated deals together. But he engaged her right away when she started coming to the gym. She'd be mostly undressed and he'd sit down beside her, straddling the bench with his (so to speak) manhood between them and start chatting away about nothing, studying every square inch of Alice that was available for study. The other men, Alice learned later, dubbed this "the battle of not being embarrassed."

Long, complicated deals could also be a problem. Alice knew this instinctively, but some of the firm's children evidently did not. So an associate named Mary had stepped out of the hotel elevator on the wrong floor, and a partner named Fred had mistaken her intent. They were coming back from dinner after an unexpectedly successful day of negotiations. He'd kissed her right there in the corridor, and Mary had thought—or so she claimed—this is cool. And now, she was pregnant.

Fred asked Alice to talk to Mary. He suspected she was pregnant but she wouldn't talk to him. "I don't know what to do," said Fred. "It was an accident. I didn't have a condom. I never take them on business trips."

"Too much information," said Alice.

Alice wasn't ready to admit she'd intended to acquire power but she seemed to be doing so. She had supplicants. As her mother would have said—maybe it was another of Lyndon Johnson's principles—she kept putting favors in the favor bank. She said she'd talk to Mary.

"Thirty-five days," said Mary.

"Everyone misses a period from time to time," said Alice.

"I've been to the doctor," said Mary.

Mary didn't want an abortion, and she didn't want to make any trouble for Fred, who *thank God* wasn't married. She just wanted to keep her job and maybe get a raise so she could employ a live-in baby-carer. She had a friend whose Ecuadorian had a cousin who was looking for work . . .

Alice didn't know what the answer was. She needed someone to talk it over with, so she made an appointment to see Charles in his office. She figured he could talk about sex without getting flustered.

"Just look at them," said Charles. "Individually and when they happen to pass each other in the hall."

"And?" Alice was lost.

"They're in love," said Charles, "and if they didn't have the misfortune to work in this cathedral of virtue and over-achievement, they would have started dating three years ago. They've avoided working on anything together until this last deal, even though they both have public utilities experience. You got eyes, girl?"

Alice didn't answer. "Evidently not," said Charles, eventually. He'd turned in his chair to watch the stream of well-dressed lawyers flowing past the glass wall of his office.

"Thanks," said Alice. "I know what to do."

Fred and Mary were married in City Hall as soon as the results of their blood tests came in. She kept her last name, and announced she would work until she had to leave for the hospital. Fred was so pleased he blushed any time someone looked at him. Since he was a partner, and hadn't fiddled his taxes, money was not a problem. It was agreed that Mary should probably move to another firm, but that could wait. Alice's one condition was that Fred and Mary *both* take some maternity/paternity leave. "This being in love is fine, but you ought to get to know each other," she said.

Alice was not a virgin. Climbing the skyscraper of her ambition included dating presentable men—required it, sometimes, when you needed to take an escort to a black-tie dinner raising money for a client CEO's wife's pet charity—and in order to do that you had to be responsive to their needs. But nothing had ever clicked. So the ballad of Mary and Fred, as Charles called it, made her a bit unsteady, some evenings, when she got back to her apartment. It was a small but attractive apartment, with a view of sorts. She'd used a decorator, and she kept the place immaculate—almost as if she expected a visitor.

Charles came to see her. In her office. "Nice painting," he said. He hadn't come to her office before.

"You want a diet Coke?" Alice kept a dwarf refrigerator under her desk.

"No thanks," said Charles, settling himself into a chair across the desk from Alice. Then, "You solve any more problems they'll make you senior partner." He picked up a pencil from Alice's desk and began playing with it. He could twirl it round and round his hand as if it had a life of its own. She'd watched him do it in drafting sessions.

"Henry's senior partner," said Alice. "The President of the United States returns his phone calls."

"Well, managing partner, then. Lawyers generally aren't too good at managing their own affairs, as you are progressively discovering." A smile passed over Charles's face for a moment. "And the President would get back to you too if he'd been in our gym."

Alice shrugged. That had sounded like a compliment.

"Comfort zone," said Charles. "I admire the way you've gone outside yours. Managing partner's just the next step. We don't even have one, if you think about it. The departments run themselves. Henry decides what we all get paid and every year he fires someone so we won't think he can't. Some of his decisions are . . . peculiar, though. He's in his own world sometimes. Having his friend get elected will make that worse, of course."

"Do we *need* a managing partner? What would one do?" Alice laughed. "That is, aside from managing Henry?"

"No idea," said Charles. "Probably do need one. Management's not my field, but I'm confident that once we'd elected you, you'd find useful work. But that's not why I'm here."

"You want to ask me out," said Alice, suddenly laughing.

"Comfort zone," said Charles, ignoring her outburst.

He manages rejection well, said Alice to herself. And then less clinically, Jesus, why did I say that?

"Like you," said Charles, "I have always pushed myself. I joined the Marines the day I turned eighteen. When I was thirty, I ran a marathon. I have called up glamorous women I didn't know and talked them into going out with me. One of them had won an Oscar the previous month. 'What do you want from me?' she said. 'I'll probably want to sleep with you,' I told her, 'but that's hardly original. How about I try to make you laugh?' Which she did, right then on the phone, and we had a drink, and it was clear as a trout stream that we would never be more than good friends. But I did pump a bit of adrenalin giving it a try."

"I've pumped a little adrenalin in the gym," said Alice.

"You have that shower with Sandra yet?"

"You are a very bad boy, Charles."

"Well, that's what I wanted to tell you about."

"As opposed to the supermodels you've had?"

"Some years back—I won't say where or when—I decided I was getting complacent. I'm physically fit. I can do what people who work here are supposed to be able to do. I can generally get a date. I wanted to go outside my comfort zone. I wanted to do something irrevocable. So I went to bed with another man."

Alice didn't breathe.

"As I'm sure you realize, that's kind of the third rail. Touch it and you're electrocuted. No do-overs. Or if you know about Native American culture, it's like the ordeal young men go through, being hurt and hungry until they have a vision. Afterward, they are not the same person. And I'm not either."

"So you're bisexual?"

"No. Not in the least. That's the point. I'm completely heterosexual. I didn't like kissing someone who needed to shave. I didn't like . . . doing the things we did. But I did them. I lived in the horror that homosexuality represents to a normal kid from a farm community in the Midwest. I did it for a whole weekend, in a very expensive hotel suite in a city where no one knew me."

"And?"

"Two problems," said Charles. "It was incredibly sexy. I hated it, but part of me liked the horror. I suppose it's like the first time you eat an oyster, only your whole body is involved."

"You're sure this doesn't make you bisexual?"

"I don't want to do it again."

"That's good news. So what's problem number two?"

"He fell in love with me."

"In another country."

"Oh, I was anonymous. All he knew was that I could afford an expensive hotel and famous wine with room service. But it wasn't fair of me to have let him fall in love."

"You didn't fall in love with him?"

"No. But I pretended. That was, in fact, the essence of the ordeal. And I pretended too well."

They were both quiet for a while. Someone looking in the glass wall of Alice's office would have concluded they were wrestling with a difficult legal issue, and might even have had the thought, how nice that partners of this firm can consult each other.

"Is that why," Alice said finally, "you never chase the female associates? You're afraid they'd fall in love?"

"Basic self-preservation," said Charles, shifting his tone. "I don't want to be Fred. But listen, Alice, the moral of the story is this: you can do whatever you decide to do. And you can survive it." He stood up, put the pencil back where he'd found it on Alice's desk, looked at her framed law school diploma as if he'd never seen such an object before. "High Honors," he observed. "Very impressive." The energy had gone out of the room. Whatever had just happened, they were on the other side of it.

"It got me this job," said Alice.

"Same as me." Charles put his hand on the doorknob but lingered for a moment.

"You did make all that up, didn't you?" said Alice.

"That would be a safe assumption," said Charles. "That is, if you want to be safe." He closed the door behind him.

If you don't know where you're going, it doesn't matter how you get there. Thus said the White Rabbit to another Alice. This Alice decided she needed her own ordeal, with or without visions. She needed to toughen up. I'm afraid of being hurt, she told herself. She didn't know whether Charles was flirting with her because he found her attractive or simply because he could. She'd seen a documentary on one of those nature channels, sitting up in bed at 2 a.m. eating popcorn, trying to become sleepy after a difficult day, in which it was explained that lions kill leopards "because they can," and maybe that was all Charles was up to: keeping sharp his ability to make women melt.

Whether his tale was true or not, the message was clear. With me there would be no limits. You can have anything you want.

So that night instead of popcorn Alice got in bed with an alligator clamp she'd brought home from the office and thought about letting it close on one of her nipples. It was about an inch wide—not one of the biggest but she assumed its grip would be sufficient. She approached the matter slowly because it was her reactions rather than the pain that she cared about. She'd never tried this sort of thing before. She wanted to study her fear. How did it differ from what she assumed ironworkers felt on their way to work each morning? She looked down at her perfect breasts, which were being particularly quiet. We're in this together, she told them.

"Ouch." It was, yes, exactly. She'd read that what you were supposed to do with pain was focus on it. Panic made it worse, let the pain achieve dominance. You had to stare right at the pain, decide what color it was. Pale yellow?

Alice removed the alligator clamp. It wasn't actually a decision. She just suddenly seemed to have the little nasty in the palm of her hand again, having endured at most thirty seconds.

She went for the other nipple right away, and then stopped herself. How does it feel? Is there excitement, and if so, in respect of what, as a lawyer would say? Invisible fingers did seem to be tracing patterns on her shoulders and thighs. It was cold in her bedroom and she was warm. Was it the prospect of pain or the fact of misbehaving that was doing that?

She let the alligator clamp squeeze her other nipple. We'll go for ten minutes she said to herself. She'd been thinking five and changed her mind at the last second, which shoved a little shot of adrenalin into her blood stream. The surprise of her decision made her gasp.

So if focusing on the pain was the recommended approach, what would happen if she thought about something else. Would the pain be worse? She called up images of saints being tortured for their faith. The alligator clamp was nothing. Well, not exactly nothing. Three minutes. Seven to go. Or maybe she wouldn't stop at ten. Could a person learn to fall asleep with one of these things on?

A person could not. And going beyond ten minutes hadn't in the end seemed necessary. Nor did whipping herself with a leather belt, which reminded her of a baroque painting when she caught sight of herself in the mirror on her closet door. It wasn't as satisfactory as the alligator clamp, despite the dramatic welts flagellation left on her backside. The thing about an alligator clamp was that you made the decision but then the tension in the metal did the work. The clamp didn't back off the way she found she did with a belt if the tip end caught her with particular viciousness.

I hope I don't develop a taste for this, Alice said to herself as she undressed the next evening. She'd kept the alligator clamp in a little velvet box that some earrings had once come in. She dropped in a second clamp. I've brought you a friend, she said.

Alice had always been a diligent girl. She practiced for two weeks. Not because there was anything to practice really—the alligator clamps were good at their job—so much as to not quit too easily. Living with the knowledge of what would happen when she got to her tidy apartment each evening was, well, part of it. Some days the ache in her nipples made her proud; some days it made her sad. She persevered, as she'd promised herself she would.

Alice told herself there wasn't anything mystical about what she was doing. Just hard work, with an occasional erotic tingle. On good nights, though, potential insights did present themselves for inspection.

Charles's disclosure wasn't an offer of sex but an offer of friendship. Or maybe of both. Alice didn't claim to be an authority on men, but most of them got pretty skittish about homosexuality, so perhaps the message was that Charles was prepared to trust her.

Or perhaps it was simply a confession, and he wanted to be forgiven. He was another supplicant. As for so many of her partners, Alice fulfilled a role that had little to do with Alice the person. It occurred to her that if absolution was what Charles wanted, she hadn't provided it. Again the thought occurred to her that he handled rejection well.

Sex, she decided, and devotional practice and, for that matter, growing up, all amounted to the same thing: finding a blend of mastery and submission that matched a person's resonant frequency. Charles had been willing to go down into the subway of his self and contemplate the third rail. Would it kill Alice to stop pretending she didn't have a family?

The thing that was embarrassing, actually, was not that her family lived in Brooklyn but that, at thirty-seven and wildly successful, she needed to keep that a secret. It was childish, like still sleeping with a teddy bear—which Alice definitely didn't do. It was evidence of the fierce ambition she had learned to hide, not least from herself.

On the final Saturday she let the alligators feast on her for half an hour, and afterward began to cry. I am not an admirable person, she said to herself. I am alone and I don't like it.

So at noon on Monday, Alice went into the gym as usual, undressed, spotted Charles under the towel he always put over his head when he was recovering from the rowing machine, and sat down next to him, astride the bench. Then, looking around to be sure no one could see, she fastened one of her alligator friends to her right nipple. It hurt as much as ever.

After a bit, Charles pulled the towel off his head and sat up. He saw the alligator clamp. "Don't do that, sweetheart," he said. He gently removed the device and attached it to one of his own nipples.

"I think you should marry me," said Alice.

"Good idea," said Charles.

"Why don't you ask me?" said Alice.

"I think I just did. Do I need to ask your father?"

"He's dead. Heart attack at fifty. Stress of the job, I assume."

"Same as my father. What did yours do?"

"Ironworker. Up in the sky." It wasn't that hard to say it.

"Farmer," said Charles.

"What's stressful about farming?"

"When there isn't any rain."

"You have relatives back in Nebraska?"

"Dozens."

"They don't mind about the rain?"

"They don't have a choice."

"Why did you?"

"Ran away. Joined the Marines. Saved money for college."

"You feel guilty about that?"

"Of course," said Charles. And then, "It's going to be quite a wedding."

"So the answer is 'yes'?" said Alice.

"Yes." And then, "Where does your family live?"

"Brooklyn. Fire Department."

"Figures," said Charles. "Courage gene."

Alice began to cry, and was very glad to have a towel to hide her face in.

"You know," said Charles, "if we're going to do the whole backstory, perhaps you could take this do-dad off me."

Alice started. "Of course, darling." She removed the alligator. "It's alright if I call you 'darling,' isn't it?"

"Very distressed if you didn't," said Charles.

Conquest

A change came over Henry—and this was some years earlier—right after they made him "senior partner." He began to notice the fragrance of the women in the office. Sometimes it was their perfume. Sometimes it was their shampoo—or he assumed that clean smell was caused by shampoo. He'd be standing in the elevator coming to work in the morning and crowded in in front of him would be a young secretary whose hair wasn't even completely dry. Why did so many of them leave it that way? Was it so men would imagine them in the shower? Henry certainly did.

"Senior partner" was, as Charles so delicately explained it to Henry over the brandy at a firm dinner, "a technical term—like 'asshole.' There's nothing in the firm's constitution. You get called that because you are. And everybody knows it."

Henry wasn't, actually, the longest serving partner of the firm, and he was careful never to refer to himself as "senior," but he understood what Charles was telling him, recognized the useful nudge he had been given. The following week, he forced two under-performing partners to retire. And noticed Veronica's perfume.

The process by which Henry had become senior partner was quite interesting. Charles liked to claim it was proof every serious law firm should have a social anthropologist on staff. He didn't say it to Henry directly, but word had gotten to him. Word now did that. He was waiting for the elevator and one of those fearless young women they seemed to employ just asked him. "So, Henry," she said without any preliminaries. The firm had adopted a "first-names rule" a decade earlier. "So, Henry, is it true you're getting us a psychiatrist like Charles says?" *As* Charles says, thought Henry sadly—and what in the world was this ungrammatical young lady talking about. "I mean, quite a few of us think it would be a good idea," she said. "The woman who writes the markets column in the *Financial Times* has a doctorate in anthropology, after all."

Henry started to formulate a sentence, but the young woman's elevator came and she left without waiting for an answer. Astonishing manners, said Henry to himself, fighting down the thought that he was being pompous. On the train home to Rye, he found himself speculating what a girl like that would be capable of if you met her in a bar.

But returning to tribal custom, the firm had a practice of meeting on the second Friday of each month at five o'clock in the afternoon—which once upon a time had been the end of the working day—to review its financial situation and discuss any issues that were on people's minds. The meeting usually took an hour and a half, and afterwards they had drinks. This struck the chief executives of the giant corporations the firm advised as a startlingly informal way to manage a business, but the firm had a wonderful franchise, and competent accountants, and that seemed to be enough.

On the second Friday in September, some years back, it had developed that Henry was tied up on a call and one of his younger partners had to be sent to get him. When they returned to the meeting the chair at the head of the table was empty and Henry sat down in it. "I'm sorry to keep you waiting," he said. "I was on the phone."

"Many of us do business on the phone, Henry," said Andrew archly. "But we finish up before five."

"I was on the phone with the Attorney General," said Henry. "I didn't think I should cut him off."

No one said anything.

"Well, what's first on the agenda?" said Henry. From then on, he chaired "Second Friday," as it was called. And at the end of the year, a couple of his partners came to his office and suggested he "take a first crack" at the always difficult business of dividing up the profits. He'd responded by inventing a formula. He wasn't foolish enough to be seen to have made the decisions himself, and have every single one of his partners angry with him. But it was his formula.

Henry didn't actually care very much about being senior partner. As he explained to his wife, Elizabeth, he wasn't power-mad. What he cared about was the firm's reputation, the quality of its work—and the work itself. That was presumably why his partners had put him in charge. "It takes a form of madness to make partner at a firm like ours," he said. "In some, this involves a failure to attain maturity. They don't need a king or a dictator but they do sometimes need adult supervision."

"And who supervises you?" said Elizabeth.

"Why you, my dear," said Henry.

Elizabeth smiled when he said that, in the mysterious way that had captivated him when they were both undergraduates, and he might have tried to demonstrate that fifty-five wasn't all that old, but a client called from Los Angeles and when Henry finally got back to the bedroom, Elizabeth was asleep. So Henry patted her on the shoulder, rolled over and thought about Veronica's perfume until he went to sleep himself. That didn't take long. Henry worked himself pretty hard.

Veronica was Henry's secretary. Now that he was senior partner, and had to address "gender issues," he'd asked her if she wanted to be called his "executive assistant." She hadn't. "I'm old-fashioned," she'd said. Whatever that meant.

"Gender" was of course a misnomer, Henry said to himself on the train back to Rye, where they lived so his wife could have a garden. "Gender" was a grammatical term. Nouns had genders. A human being had a sex. But that word made people uncomfortable, so the human resources people had replaced it with jargon. Henry disliked jargon. I'm old-fashioned too, he told himself proudly.

Part of old-fashioned, in Henry's view, was being courteous. So every so often, when Veronica was very busy, he took something to the copying machine himself. There were often younger secretaries there. Please let us help you, they would say. And he'd let them, because he enjoyed being fussed over, and also because he didn't completely understand the copying machine, which paused at unexpected moments and made strange noises. "I remember when there was carbon paper," Henry would say. And because he was senior partner, none of the young secretaries ever said, "I'll bet you do." Which was nice.

It was clear to Henry that he liked being treated like a small child, which Elizabeth did very well, by the way, so long as the small child in question was sufficiently important that allowing himself to be treated that way was his choice, could perhaps be regarded as a form of good manners. Henry reckoned that upper class Englishmen who stuttered were playing a version of that game. Their disability gave them control of the conversation, if you thought about it.

Part of being senior partner was having sandwich lunches with small groups of young associates. Henry would tell them about the history of the firm. Some of the associates would ask him questions about politics, his Washington connections being common knowledge, and some would essentially ask for career guidance. "Honest ass-kissing," was how he thought of it. "Nice young people" was what he said to Elizabeth.

The fearless ungrammatical girl eventually showed up. He'd been wondering about her—wondering if she was an associate or just a paralegal. There were so many young women in the office now.

"What's the deal about sex," she asked.

"I'm for it," said Henry, and was gratified to get a laugh from the group. Small boy was not the right persona for this group.

"At the firm, I mean," said the girl. "Are we not supposed to go out with each other? I can't get a straight answer out of human resources."

"Ah," said Henry. "We don't have a rule."

"That doesn't mean there isn't one," said the girl.

"You will go far," said Henry, and then looked down at his sandwich because he was suddenly afraid he was blushing.

"Because I asked or because I knew I needed to?" she said.

Henry realized that her contemporaries were enjoying the show, and that the girl—she must have a name—was probably already famous among them. "I'm sorry, what's your name again?"

"Millie," she said. "Short for 'Millicent,' if you can believe it. And be sure you remember it."

Back in Rye, Henry explained to his wife that he had tried to give Millie sound advice.

"I'm sure you did, dear," said Elizabeth. She said it with deadpan seriousness, which was her way of being ironic.

"Number one," he'd told Millie, "Life is easier if you keep things on a professional basis at work. Number two: that requires that you have a life outside of work. Number three: what you do outside of work is none of the firm's business, provided you don't draw attention to yourself or the firm."

"Thanks, Henry. We figured we'd have to take you out for a drink to make you talk about romance." She gestured to the others around the table, several of whom nodded agreement. Millie paused and then shrugged. "Can we take you out anyway?"

So that very evening, Henry found himself with six associates at an expensive bar being prevented from paying for the drinks and telling stories about the first time he argued a case before the Supreme Court, and about an unidentified United States Senator of his acquaintance who had "zipper trouble," and probably other things he shouldn't have mentioned.

Henry supposed that qualified as talking about "romance." The Senator himself referred to it as such. He was one of those charismatic politicians with a good deal of sentimentality in his make-up. The objects of the Senator's serial attention didn't always see it that way, however, as Henry knew from "coping" with one of them for the Senator. "It's not the '60s anymore," the young intern had said. "All I want is a good reference and bragging rights." Conquest. Henry skipped that part of the story. The young associates would probably think it was normal behavior, he told himself. It would just prove he was old-fashioned. Henry only enjoyed being old-fashioned when it was his choice.

Millie walked Henry to Grand Central, gracefully preventing him from stepping in front of several taxis, and delivered him to the platform the train for Rye left from. "I hope you won't hold it against me, being so direct," said Millie when the train was announced. "I can't help myself." She kissed him on the cheek, gave him a little hug and walked away.

It had never occurred to Henry in his life to keep things from Elizabeth, so he admitted to the "too many Scotches" that would have been obvious to her, and also to the kiss. "I think that's just what young people do now days," said Henry. He and Elizabeth had never had any children.

"So I understand," said Elizabeth, as if young people were an undocumented species.

The very next day, Henry was sitting at his desk pondering the ways of the young when Veronica came in. She'd been at lunch longer than usual, which wasn't an issue because she typically worked many more hours than she was paid for. "Can I do anything for you?" she said. Her perfume washed over the desk like foam from the sea. He had a sudden vision of her as a mermaid, coming out of the water onto his desk.

"What?" said Henry.

"Sorry," said Veronica. "You looked like you needed something and were waiting for me to get back."

"I was just thinking," said Henry. "But what I do need is the file I had yesterday, if it's not too much trouble."

She was back in a moment and so was her smell. Henry reckoned that if he objected to human resources substituting "gender" for "sex," he ought to say "smell" instead of "fragrance" —at least to himself. And there were several smells, actually. There was soap. She must have washed her hands when she got back from lunch. And it was just possible she'd had a glass of wine with her meal.

Henry wondered briefly about the life Veronica lived away from the firm. At forty and a bit she would have made a very presentable mermaid.

"I had lunch with Elizabeth," she said, as if reading his thoughts.

"Really?"

"Spur of the moment. We do it a few times a year."

Henry knew that his wife and his secretary had lunch from time to time. What was interesting was that Veronica thought he didn't.

"She was in town to get something repaired," Veronica went on. "A leather purse, I think."

"Elizabeth can get anything fixed," said Henry vaguely. She knew all the artisans in New York, it sometime seemed. She knew Manhattan inside out. Henry had a brief vision of Manhattan as a leather purse, with Elizabeth turning it inside out to show the mayor what needed to be stitched up. Henry though his wife had decided to throw that purse out, but evidently not. She was old-fashioned about not wasting things.

Elizabeth had grown up in the city of course, but didn't for some reason want to live there. Her father had been a professor at Columbia Medical School and they got faculty housing, a grand apartment on West Side Drive. Henry remembered picking Elizabeth up for a date and being growled at by her father about when she had to be home. She'd been serenely beautiful that night. They'd kissed in the taxi. A really good one. She hadn't wanted him to see her upstairs. "My father will be there," she'd explained. "It would detract from the pleasure of the evening."

Veronica broke into Henry's thoughts. "That cheeky associate wants five minutes of your time, by the way."

Veronica belonged in a 1960s movie. Early '60s. She hadn't gone to college, though she clearly would today, clearly had the brains for it. She had a gone-to-a-good-public-high-school-in-New-York style about her: clever, proud, cynical, defensive maybe. She also had an aged parent she took care of, somewhere on the Upper West Side of Manhattan. Henry's recollection was that it was her mother, that Veronica was the last of five children, that her brothers and sisters all had families of their own, had moved away, hated their mother, loved their mother but couldn't be bothered, had plausible excuses.

On reflection, Henry decided Veronica probably liked the situation she was in or she wouldn't have put up with it so long. "Old-fashioned." Every day she could tell herself she was the responsible one.

The thing about mermaids is they can't have sex. All they can do is be desirable.

"By cheeky associate I assume you mean the one who asked all the questions at the sandwich lunch yesterday?"

"And got you drunk, as I understand it."

"Just . . . cheerful," said Henry. "Word travels fast. Has she announced that she kissed me when she put me on the train for Rye?"

"I doubt she remembers," said Veronica, walking toward the door.

"Well, if you'll do the same, I'll buy you a drink tonight," said Henry. "Get me on the train for Rye, I mean." Omigod, he thought. "Oh, but wait. Is Second Friday today?"

27

Veronica stopped and turned around and nodded first no and then yes. "It's not," she said. "It's the first Friday of the month. And . . . 5:30. You have to be on the 6:42 for Rye."

The main thing about mermaids is their breasts. Henry had avoided noticing Veronica's for years. But standing next to her in a crowded bar, and then sitting on a couch when another couple got up and left, it was impossible not to brush against Veronica once or twice while reaching for the peanuts or paying for the second round of drinks.

"We've worked together for how long and never had a drink before?" said Henry, by which he possibly meant that their relationship was changing in some unspecified way and that that was fine with Henry.

"Sixteen years," said Veronica. Her smile was eager, nervous.

"Is it really that long?"

"It is," she said. "And it is time for me to get you on your train. As I promised."

It was, as Henry told himself all the way to Rye, "foreordained" that he kissed her on the lips when they parted. He chuckled. I have to stop doing this, he said to himself. Two nights in a row. At least Elizabeth seemed to be in a tolerant mood. He told her he'd kissed Veronica. "Of course you did," said Elizabeth. "Just don't get testosterone poisoning." The phrase was one he hadn't heard before but it reminded Henry of Elizabeth's father so he didn't question her.

It seemed to Henry, waking up slowly, as he allowed himself to do on Saturdays, that there had been a lot of "New Age" conversation in the bar with the young associates. It also seemed to him that all the young associates had been women. Could that be true? Maybe there were boys at the start but they left early. Anyway, the young women the firm now recruited seemed to put a lot of store in having lime juice with hot water when you got out of bed and finding time for daily meditation.

"As if you could," one of them had said.

"Do it on the subway," said another. "And it works best late at night."

"Oh, right," said the first one. "I'm happy to meet Jesus but not on the A Train through Harlem."

It had been important not to be dismissive of his employees' beliefs but also not to be taken in. These girls could easily have been trying to make him agree to foolish notions, just to see if they could, just as they'd conspired to get him drunk. So Henry avoided signing up for the detoxifying benefits of going barefoot or the importance of chakras, despite how pleasant it might have been to have Millie reach out and put her hand on his arm and say, "Henry, you get it. Listen, guys, Henry gets it."

Or maybe that had happened. Would Odysseus, having heard the sirens sing, have been able to remember accurately, or would their song have become a dream? And maybe he had been kissed. On a train platform as if in an old movie. Yes, that had happened.

In this haze of pleasant and embarrassing recollections, one phase kept beckoning: "going into the forest." It had to do with a group of Buddhist monks whose rule was particularly severe. "Forest monks," they were called, even though they seemed to live in places you would have expected monstrous flowers and hanging vines. Henry had a brief vision of "the Buddha," as the girls all called him, meditating among the pines and birches of New Hampshire.

Henry sat up in bed. There were no sounds downstairs. Elizabeth had presumably gone to buy muffins at a local bakery, as she did most Saturday mornings. The thing about these "forest monks" was that they introduced the notion of unfamiliar terrain. Which had some resonance for a man of his eminence who has allowed half a dozen young women to get him drunk, and the next night kissed his secretary of sixteen years. If Buddhists could go into the forest, presumably Presbyterians could go into the jungle—and undertake the transformation "going in" was a metaphor for.

Henry had never done that. He'd never meditated "as such." He'd certainly thought deeply, if that counted. As a younger man he had worked hard enough with little enough sleep to expect hallucinations, but they never came. His whole life, in fact, had been organized to avoid unfamiliar terrain. That was why he'd married Elizabeth. At 22 as much as now, she looked and behaved exactly like someone who could be married to a senior partner.

Up the stairs came the sounds of Henry's perfect wife, now back from the bakery, making the coffee, talking to the cat. He reminded himself of his intention to actually buy her a birthday present this year. He usually forgot—and she always turned out to have gotten herself something practical, something she actually needed, and they'd treat it as his present. "More efficient," she'd always say.

Veronica called in sick Monday morning. She'd called the services supervisor before Henry arrived. Henry hoped he hadn't suddenly made her uncomfortable working with him. Someone was assigned to fill in who had no idea how to find the files he wanted or even how a senior partner's telephone ought to be answered. He was quite dependent on Veronica, he acknowledged to himself. Shouldn't have kissed her, though.

Henry decided to take advantage of Veronica's absence to go see his doctor. He pleaded an unspecified emergency and Dr. Thompson said she would squeeze him in. Making doctor's appointments—and for that matter seeing that he went—was one of those matters Veronica looked after. Veronica in collaboration with Elizabeth. But Henry wanted to make this a private visit. He wanted to ask about this "testosterone poisoning." He'd taken a hard look at himself while he was shaving that morning and decided he was losing his grip.

And then Millie had shown up for her "five minutes" and it felt like she'd propositioned him. Maybe he'd made it up. But that didn't matter. What worried him was how much he liked her suggestion.

What she'd actually said was that as they seemed to get along, she thought he should make her his "private secretary—in the British sense." She probably had him pegged for an anglophile. "Better term is probably 'special assistant,' or plain 'assistant.'"

"An assistant to the President is essentially the top rank you can have on the White House staff," said Henry. "Special assistant is a lower-level title, at least in Washington." Was he showing off or stalling? Why hadn't he just said "no"?

"Can't be 'executive assistant,'" Millie continued, "because that's what important people's secretaries get called now."

"Veronica doesn't."

"Good for her. And I don't particularly care what you call me as long as you work me hard."

What was that supposed to mean? Henry said to himself. Inappropriate answers immediately presented themselves in his brain.

"I could travel with you," said Millie, "which I assume Veronica couldn't without it causing a stir."

"Travel isn't part of Veronica's job description, and anyway she has a bedridden mother she takes care of." Why was he telling her this?

"Mostly what I'd do is manage your in-box, read memos and tell you what you needed to read, read legal journals you can't possibly have time for. And I could tell you what was happening on the shop floor—in the firm I mean. I'm extremely good at finding out what's going on in a place." She paused. "See, I think you probably could be a lot more efficient with someone quite junior but very discreet as your 'maneuver element.' Sorry, that's an Army term. My father was a career officer. That's probably why I'm not shy. We moved so much, I had to get good at making new friends, and look, you and I are friends, now, sort of, and none of the other associates will have the balls—sorry, another Army expression—to suggest it . . ."

"What's in it for you, Millie?" said Henry.

"Well, if you get appointed to the Court as everyone expects, I will have worked for you. It will look good on my resume even if you don't. I'll need a good resume in a few years when someone takes me out to lunch and tells me I'm unlikely to make partner. But mostly, I kind of think you're . . . interesting, and I'd like to sit at your feet for a year or two. If I embarrass you, you can fire me. And I won't ever kiss you again in public."

"Um," said Henry. "This is a very generous offer, Millie. I don't know whether it is a good idea, for you or for the firm. Give me a couple of weeks to think. I will need to consult a few of my partners. Meanwhile, don't talk about it. You might embarrass yourself." As if that were possible, Henry said to himself.

The entire conversation had taken even less time than the five minutes she'd asked for. Millie had barged right in when the temporary secretary was away. Henry was still at his desk and Millie was standing on the carpet in front of him like an audacious schoolgirl, except that she was wearing what Henry assumed was her best dress. When he said he'd think about it, she did a little pirouette. "Oh, goody," she said. "You're going to agree." She turned and strode to the door. "And no gossip," she said over her shoulder. "Scouts' honor."

Having Dr. Frances Thompson as his doctor was something Elizabeth had insisted on.

"But I'll have to take my clothes off," Henry had said.

"Yes, exactly," said Elizabeth. "And you'll be embarrassed, and because you are you won't mind telling Frances everything you should, which you never will with Dr. Morton, who was two years ahead of you at Princeton and captain of the varsity crew, as you regularly remind me."

"Frances?"

"Yes, Dr. Frances Thompson. Varsity internist."

"You know her?"

"We went to kindergarten together."

"And why does it come up now that I should take my pants off for the benefit of your childhood friend?"

"Not her benefit—yours. And I read an article in a magazine at the hairdresser about how hopeless men doctors are."

Henry had done what Elizabeth wanted, as he always did. And Frances had inspected his totally exposed surface with the eagerness of an astronomer given four minutes to view the back side of the moon—as she always would, she assured him—and had found what proved to be a melanoma that otherwise would have killed him. So he'd continued to see Frances Thompson, who had a trim figure, red hair and freckles, wore a stylish dress underneath her white coat, and was quite easy to talk to once you realized that you had nothing left to hide.

"What seems to be the problem?" said Frances. "You can undress while you tell me."

"There isn't anything to show you. I just want to ask some questions."

"Yes, but if you come to see me and I don't examine you and something crops up later, you can sue me for negligence—or so my insurance company tells me."

"I'm not a suing sort of person, Frances."

"Henry! You are one of the most famous litigators in the country. Lots of people think you'll be the next Supreme Court Justice. If professional ethics didn't forbid naming patients, I'd brag about having you." She paused and gave him a smile. "Anyway, I like making you undress. It evens out the power relationship between us."

Henry looked at her in amazement. His brain translated her words as a matter-of-fact observation that they could do some very pleasant, entirely human things to each other if they were willing to suspend the proprieties.

"Just kidding," said Frances.

Henry got on with the business of disrobing and Frances studied his file. "What I wanted to talk about," he said, concentrating on his cuff links, "is . . ."

"Is . . . sex," said Frances, interrupting without looking up.

"Why do you say that?"

"First, you made the appointment yourself, according to my receptionist, and second, there clearly isn't an emergency, and third, well, I have hundreds of patients and all of them eventually ask me something about sex—especially the middle-aged men."

"Is there such a thing as testosterone poisoning?" said Henry. Might as well just come out with it.

"No . . . but yes. I know what you mean. Male organisms of a certain age do sometimes sense that their reproductive careers are coming to an end and have a distinct surge of desire. This is particularly true of the successful males that evolution prefers—senior partners of law firms, for example. No, it won't hurt you medically. But let's cut to the chase. Are you already having an affair or just contemplating one."

"Neither," said Henry, which was technically true. "But I suddenly feel like having several."

Frances gave him a nanosecond of that nice smile again. "Well, don't tell Elizabeth," she said.

"Not that it's relevant, but why not? I mean, you knew her pretty well. I've never kept any secrets from her."

"Get on the scale," said Frances. "Right, down a pound from three months ago. Are you getting any exercise? Silly question. Still, you look pretty good." She went on with the usual procedures, including a brisk but thorough examination of Henry's epidermis and "the part that everyone looks forward to"—all without answering Henry's question. "OK, get dressed," she said, and leaned back in her chair.

"Elizabeth and I were friends as children. In the Eighth Grade we were the two smartest girls in the class. Then we went away to different boarding schools and different universities, but I normally saw her at parties during holidays. And if you've been rivals as adolescents you do tend to follow each other's progress through life." She paused. "More to the point, I knew a bit about her family."

Rivals. Henry realized that in sending him to Frances Thompson, Elizabeth had essentially been bragging, displaying her ownership of Henry. And in flirting with him, Frances was making the point that Elizabeth was taking a risk.

"Her father, as you know," said Frances, "was a gifted surgeon and therefore a god. He had permanent testosterone poisoning. He regarded all the nurses in Presbyterian Hospital as 'available,' and a startling number of them were. Elizabeth's mother for some reason simply put up with it. But it had a permanent effect on Elizabeth. She's very like the adult children of alcoholics. She wants to smooth things over. She wants everything to be in order. She wants to be in control. I assume that's why you two never had children . . ."

Henry looked at his lap.

"I'm not asking," said Frances, "and I'm not betraying any confidences, either professionally or personally, because I don't know anything, but I suspect that not having children suited Elizabeth." That smile again. "Nothing puts an end to perfectionism faster than parenthood—as I know from being a single mother."

Henry thought he heard the subtext: if you want some unruly stepchildren, there's room in my bed for a husband. But he was probably hallucinating.

"What became of your husband, Frances?" It was an uncharitable thing to say, but Henry needed to defend himself.

"Unable to grow up," she said fiercely. "Ran off with his personal trainer ten years ago." And then, rather softly: "Their marriage has lasted, though."

Frances waved her arms as if erasing a blackboard, discarding the previous bit of their conversation.

"You asked, Henry, so let me give you the whole picture as I see it professionally. Elizabeth may have despised her father's behavior—his 'weakness' she would have called it—but she also wanted his approval. What else explains that idea of going to nursing school after college. She could have gone to medical school if she'd wanted. Nice of you to propose and bring an end to it after her first year."

"Elizabeth would have made a fine nurse," said Henry, feeling a need to defend his wife. "She has aplomb. She deals really well with reality."

"You don't think doctors do?"

"No criticism intended, Frances."

Dr. Thompson took a deep breath and went on. "I suspect that Elizabeth encouraged your pursuit of her—because I promise you, plenty of boys were after her . . ."

Henry interrupted: "She made it clear she wanted me to keep asking her out."

"As any woman would," said Frances adroitly. "But I expect she married you because you seemed exactly like her father—smart, ambitious, tough, masculine, and with a career she could manage—but without his Zeus-like indiscipline."

"If that was a compliment, thank you," said Henry.

"It was."

"So?"

"Don't have an affair—which I know you're not planning—unless you are willing to hurt Elizabeth rather badly. If testosterone poisoning overwhelms you, do it in another country and lie about it. That will be two hundred fifty dollars, please."

Walking back down Park Avenue to his office, Henry reflected that Dr. Thompson was brave and attractive and perhaps he'd stop going to see her.

Veronica was better on Tuesday. It was hard to imagine she'd been sick. She came into Henry's office and shut the door, which wasn't her normal practice, as no one could see in from the hall. She was agitated to the point of shaking from too much adrenaline. She put Henry in mind of one of those female warriors in Asian mythologies. Veronica would make a ravishing archer, he realized.

"Would you like to sit down?"

"No, today I'll be giving the dictation."

"I'm ready," said Henry, still bemused.

"You are suffering from testosterone poisoning," she said.

Henry paused. "One kiss?"

"It was an excellent kiss," said Veronica, "and fortunately you bestowed it on the one person in the entire firm who won't try to use it against you."

"Isn't that what you're doing now?" said Henry.

"Now, don't turn lawyer on me," said Veronica. "You're my boss. You can tell me what to do. You don't have to win any arguments."

"I await your instructions," said Henry. Veronica was clearly terrified by whatever she was about to do, and her courage made her doubly attractive.

"You and I are going to have an affair," said Veronica.

This seemed like a nice idea in principle, but there were bound to be practical difficulties—and also they shouldn't. Doctor's orders.

"I'm not giving you a choice," said Veronica. "Within thirty days you must take me somewhere beautiful and we will share a bed. Repeat the exercise three times a year."

Henry opened his mouth to speak but Veronica was in full flight—and also he wasn't sure what he wanted to say. So he just listened.

"Things didn't work out for me the way they were supposed to. My mother was supposed to die ten years ago. I was going to become your mistress and then your wife. You were going to become famous. That at least has happened. But my mother refuses to die. Another thing that happened is that I got to know Elizabeth, and instead of supplanting her, I conspired with her to make you successful."

She didn't have to remind him of the successful maneuvers the two of them had urged upon him.

"A successful man in his 50s is in a dangerous way, Henry. His brain thinks he is a conqueror but his body knows it only has so much time. Prudence evaporates. Women understand this. So when Elizabeth saw the lipstick that Millie put on your collar, she called me right away. We had lunch. What could we do? I told her I would deal with Millie—and if that little strumpet comes after you again, I'll pull her hair."

"She came yesterday. She wants to be my 'assistant.'"

"I will fix that. But we also have to settle accounts between the two of us."

"You're a terrorist," said Henry, half delighted.

"Correct," said Veronica. "And I intend to remain so. You must take me abroad and buy me beautiful clothes and fuck me senseless in extravagant surroundings three times a year—for as long as you can."

Henry was speechless. Vulgarity, blackmail, aspersions on his masculinity—all in the service of long-suppressed passion. "Elizabeth?" he said, as if looking for a way out.

"This has nothing to do with Elizabeth." And then, "she must remain ignorant."

Henry sat in silence, taking it all in.

"Lipstick on the collar!" said Veronica. "That Millie knows nothing. She has no shame. She thinks in clichés. She could not make a fuck last more than ten minutes."

"I can," said Henry, quite unexpectedly. What he intended to convey was that his fifty-five-year-old body moved at its own speed, that Veronica should be prepared for that, but it came out more like bragging. Much of life is full of double meanings. "What if I refuse?" said Henry.

"I think you've already agreed," said Veronica. "I can read you pretty well after sixteen years. But in case you waiver, the answer is that I will quit. Your office will become a jumble. No one else will understand my filing system. No one else will get along so well with Elizabeth. And no one will be appointed to the Supreme Court if there are rumors he molested his secretary."

"I don't expect to be nominated for anything," said Henry.

"You don't have to pretend with me," said Veronica.

"Anyway," said Henry, "half the partners here are divorced. Most of them have had affairs."

"But not you, my sweet. Your magical hold on your partners results in part from the fact that you've never succumbed. You're a bastard but you're a virtuous bastard. Which is why Elizabeth and I . . . which is why I worry about testosterone poisoning. And which is why we must be totally discreet."

"How do you fancy Paris?" said Henry.

"Shall I get your coffee now?" said Veronica.

When they got to the beautiful hotel Henry had chosen for them in Paris, and Veronica had with brave eagerness herded Henry into the shower and then into bed, she became unexpectedly tentative. "I've not done this . . . much . . . before," she said.

"Living with your mother gets in the way of romance, I expect," said Henry.

"So does being in love with my boss," she said.

Henry was formulating a response when he realized Veronica was crying. The only answer seemed to be to kiss her. They did that for a while. She turned back into the sensible woman who ran his office so brilliantly. "Could we get this over with?" she said. "We can talk afterwards." They did both.

Henry told Millie "no," but didn't mention it to Elizabeth. With Veronica in the room, he explained to Millie that only someone who was a partner could help him with the "personal issues" a senior partner was sometimes expected to resolve. And by the way—and to get the matter into the rumor mill and laid to rest—arrangements had been made for Veronica's mother so that his secretary could travel with him if he needed a "maneuver element." "I like that phrase, Millie," he added, just to be nice.

He put a weeklong business development trip into his calendar four months hence, but said nothing to Veronica. She made the arrangements without comment. He mentioned it to Elizabeth, who duly noted his prospective absence in the little calendar she carried in her purse.

And then, one Saturday morning, Elizabeth brought croissants home from the bakery. "An innovation," she said.

"I'd rather have muffins," he said.

"They do these well, though, you'd have to agree."

"They do," said Henry, "but this is Westchester County. Croissants belong in France."

"As you wish dear." And then, "Has Veronica benefitted from her holiday, do you think?"

"You talk to her almost every day," said Henry.

"I wanted your opinion."

Henry thought for a moment. "Yes, I think so. And it does her good to know that her mother can manage for a few days without her. Gives her a sense of freedom, I imagine. Her mother's not really bedridden, I gather."

"Yes, I've found Polly to be quite mobile when she wants to be."

"Polly?"

"Her mother's name, dear. Didn't you know it?"

"You looked in on her while Veronica was away?"

"Sometimes when I'm in the city I do. I can easily run an errand for her when I'm doing errands of my own."

"Um," said Henry.

They sat in silence for a bit, as long-married couples can, Henry leaning back against the pillows, Elizabeth sitting on the edge of the bed but turned toward him with the twisting upright posture of a Renaissance nude.

Henry spoke finally: "I have a confession to make."

Elizabeth said nothing.

"I've forgotten your birthday again."

"No you haven't," said Elizabeth. "You've bought me a lovely diamond bracelet." She went to her dresser and brought a box tied up with a ribbon back to the bed.

"Very handsome," said Henry when she had put it on.

"Thank you, Henry," said Elizabeth, and leaning toward him kissed her husband.

Being a famous lawyer with a fine analytical brain, and also a bit of a shit, or at least a normal male, Henry enjoyed comparing Veronica and Elizabeth. It was nice to have a mistress. It was nice to sleep with someone new, which Henry hadn't done in approximately thirty years. And it was nice that Veronica had cried on his shoulder. Tears were evidence of trust.

Elizabeth was still a beautiful woman, if a bit severe. She did not have Veronica's figure. She did not have Frances Thompson's permission-granting smile. Some might with justice suggest that she was a control freak. Henry took an alternative view. He thought his wife was superb.

Henry had considered the matter quite a lot in recent weeks, and it all ran through his mind again as he kissed his wife. It was a two-part kiss, beginning in a semiofficial way—a smooch for a birthday present—but then ripening into something lasting and sincere, at the end of which he had to wipe his eyes.

"You won my heart when I was twenty," said Henry. "And you have it still."

Tutorial

A client had advised on an acquisition that turned out badly. There was litigation. Sandra was a litigator. She had to prepare a young investment banker for his deposition.

"Good morning, Stephen," she said.

"You think so?" he said.

"It was a greeting rather than a value judgment," said Sandra briskly, "but it is pretty nice out. It's hard to beat May in New York."

"But we know what's coming, don't we?"

"Uh . . . June? And then summer?"

"I mean what's going to happen to me."

Sandra waited for him to go on.

"You're going to help me understand which things it would be useful for me to remember clearly and which things, on reflection, I don't recall."

"No, Stephen. I want you to tell me truthfully everything you know, every doubt you had, what you failed to notice at the time that seems obvious now . . ."

"From which you will craft an unimpeachable narrative that will protect my employers."

"From which I will extract evidence useful to both sides, so we know what they could hit us with and what defenses we might offer. And yes, in due course we will need a strategy, assuming we can't get the action dismissed before it comes to trial."

Stephen shifted a bit in his chair, and looked over Sandra's shoulder. They were sitting in her office. She had her back to its glass front wall. This arrangement meant that anyone she interviewed was likely to be distracted when someone walked by. People who are distracted are more likely to give themselves away, and in Sandra's line of work the things people didn't volunteer were often the most important.

The side wall of her office was solid books. Some people thought litigators were cowboys, so she felt she needed to make it clear she was thoughtful. There were novels and histories and biographies scattered among the law books. Sandra wanted people to think there was more to her than being a lawyer—especially because that wasn't really the case. She'd spent a few weekends organizing the shelves when she made partner and got her office. To be fair to herself, she had already owned the books. She read a lot at night.

"Would you like a coffee, or a glass of water?" she asked Stephen.

"Water would be good."

Sandra picked up the phone on the table beside her and called her secretary. She watched Stephen as she did so: blond, not that tall, probably in his late twenties, probably good at one of those Ivy League sports like lacrosse or soccer, that call for stamina and quick reflexes and an enjoyment of bumping into other people in a controlled way, all of which seemed to be qualifications for investment banking.

Being a single woman who didn't go out much—well, to be honest, approximately never—but also being an experienced trial lawyer, she had become proficient at seeing other people, men especially, as material to work with. She depersonalized them: studied them, analyzed them, taught them to perform. Stephen was really just the next one who came along on the conveyor belt of problems the firm gave her to solve. Nothing special about him. She'd extracted clients from bigger messes than he and his employer were in, at least to judge from the brief outline Alice had given her.

It was nice that Alice had started talking to her. She'd understood Alice's caution, especially in the year she was up for partner, but it had emphasized Sandra's aloneness. It had been painful, all those years of buying expensive clothes with no one to talk to about them. Go away, bad memories.

Stephen was an attractive individual, though, she had to admit. Alert, wary, lots of nervous energy, intelligent. He was right, of course, that her job was to protect the investment banking firm he worked for, not him. But their interests were aligned. The only difference was that while Stephen's firm could almost certainly survive any misjudgments he might have made, if the misjudgments were material, his own career would not.

"You are nervous," she said matter-of-factly, "which is why you are being cynical. It does not become you. You are a person of natural honesty. All you need to do is tell me the truth. You aren't being recorded. I won't take notes"—she put her pad and pen aside—"though I cannot pretend I won't remember what you say."

She paused as the glass of water was brought in on a silver tray. There were two glasses, actually, in case Sandra got thirsty—heavy crystal tumblers, along with a matching glass pitcher. A slim waiter in black and gray brought the tray in. Sandra's secretary opened the door for him. He was graceful, anonymous, almost certainly gay. A dozen others would have been interviewed for the job. The firm had a fetish about the quality of everything in their offices. "Clients expect it," Henry had explained to her when she first arrived at the firm. What he meant was that the firm wanted clients to expect it—to assume every bit of work it did would match the quality of its furniture and waiters and the oil paintings of sailing ships on its walls. In Sandra's observation, the strategy worked. Clients paid more for an hour of Sandra's time than they would if she worked somewhere else because the place looked so right. And with the astonishing partnership distribution she received each year, she in turn made sure she herself looked exactly right.

"No interruptions for the next hour please, Lois," she said to her secretary, smoothing the skirt of her suit. It was a yellowy green, of a shade most women wouldn't attempt, and which no man would expect a top lawyer to wear—which is why she wore it. In Sandra's experience as a litigator, "exactly right" always included an element of surprise.

She looked at Stephen again. "Just tell me the complete truth. Without inhibitions."

"You are the most beautiful woman I have ever seen in my life," said Stephen.

Sandra smiled in a controlled way. "That is kind of you to say, but perhaps we should stick to the matter at hand."

"You said, 'without inhibitions,'" said Stephen.

Sandra didn't respond. She didn't know how to.

"The reason I am nervous is that I have a crush on you," said Stephen. "That's only happened to me once before—in the third grade. It happened last week, at that big meeting, where I saw you for the first time—you were wearing sky blue—and they said you would be 'preparing' me. It sounded like you were a chef and I was a turkey who was going to be roasted. I had to stifle a laugh. But at the same time, I kept looking at you and getting butterflies at the prospect of being alone with you.

"The more I looked at you the more gorgeous you became. It was like some good fairy had sprinkled love dust on me. Your figure, the way your body moves inside your clothes, the sound of your voice. The way you react just a little bit slowly. Your perfect face. The color of your skin. What are you, by the way?"

"We don't know what Sandra is," her partner Charles liked to say. She'd overheard him a couple of times and asked Alice about it.

"I'm not sure if he means ethnicity or sexuality," Alice had told her cheerfully. Sandra hadn't taken the bait. She was good at that.

"I'm not sure I can answer that question, Stephen," said Sandra.

Sandra was a Somali. Or to be more accurate, her father was reported to be a Somali, and given what Sandra looked like, he probably was. Sandra was an American, born in Massachusetts, to which the Peace Corps had returned her pregnant mother once the prospect of baby Sandra became obvious. The genetic combination that resulted from her mother's carelessness had made Sandra a honey-colored woman who looked best with short hair, but her history had also made her guarded in personal relationships. To be honest, it seemed to have made personal relationships of any depth extremely difficult.

Tutorial

Sandra had never met her father, and so far as she could figure out, when she turned fifteen and figuring things out became a priority, her mother had never had further contact with the man. He'd taught in the school the Peace Corps had assigned her mother to. Her mother taught English, of course. The man—well, yes, she could probably call him her father—anyway, he taught math. He had wanted to improve his English. He believed that would enable him to become a school principal and earn more money to support his children, about which Sandra's mother never spoke, presumably because she had never met them. Sandra had formed the view that her father's wife and children were back in some village while he taught school in a town. She expected her mother had seduced him, but she had no testimony on the subject.

Sandra was a very intelligent woman, and even at fifteen she had been a realist. She did not idealize her father, or believe that finding him would be the answer to life's problems. She did not judge her mother harshly, even though the woman's strategy for becoming an adult had been deficient. She had presumably been lonely in a minor town in Somalia. Sandra understood about being lonely.

Sandra's mother came from a large and inclusive family, which was useful when she came home with a baby on the way, but it had allowed her mother to grow up less self-reliant than Sandra believed a person ought to be. Sandra's mother had a series of jobs—she got herself qualified as an accountant, or really a bookkeeper—but there were so many sisters and cousins and houses overflowing with dogs and cookies and political opinions and spare rooms that her mother never exactly needed to work, and Sandra never lacked for anything. Anything except privacy, that is. From the moment she was born, her mother's family did everything possible to make Sandra feel welcome, but she never stopped feeling like a guest.

"Sorry," said Stephen. "Can't help myself."

They went back to work as if nothing out of the ordinary had happened, went through some background about the deal and whether it had been a good idea in the first place. In Stephen's view it had been. "I'm the one who thought it up, though, so I'm biased," he told her.

"Have you thought up any other acquisitions in the course of your career?"

"One, but the client wouldn't do it. I'm seen as creative but not necessarily persuasive."

Oh, be persuasive, Sandra said to herself, and quickly pushed the thought aside.

"Of course, I've only been in the business for four years."

Sandra had been a lawyer for sixteen years. "So what was wrong with the idea you did sell to your client?"

"Nothing was wrong with the idea. Plenty wrong with the company's disclosure, which we should have discovered when we did due diligence."

"Which it is alleged you should have discovered." This boy needed guidance, it was clear.

"Right. And the problem, at least for me, is that I did a lot of the due diligence, so I'm the one who failed to recognize the signs of fraud, which was presumably because I was so excited about having a client do a deal I'd thought of..."

"Stop right now," said Sandra. "Others may accuse you of mistakes. Don't accuse yourself. I know you think it makes you look honest and morally blameless, but it will not help in court. Many people test what they are about to say by how comfortable they feel saying it. You feel comfortable taking responsibility. In life, that is a good quality. In litigation it is not."

Stephen was silent for a minute, presumably thinking about that. "May I ask you a question?" he said finally.

"Yes."

"May I touch your breasts?"

"What?" He was mad, of course.

"Not here," said Stephen. "I mean back in your apartment."

Sandra let him go on, explaining to herself that she needed to understand just how this madness worked. Except for his improper suggestions, he seemed so healthy and normal. He matched the paintings of sailing ships so perfectly he could have come out of a catalog.

"You go into your bedroom," said Stephen. "I open a bottle of wine and pour two glasses. You come back in trousers and sandals and nothing above the waist. We sit on the couch. At first I don't touch you. When I do, you gasp and pull away. I tell you that I won't force myself on you. You sit up again. After a few minutes I touch you again. This time you control the urge to escape. You enjoy being touched. I continue for maybe five minutes. Now we have a secret, which is nice."

"If you weren't so sweet about it, I'd get insulted."

"Where's the insult?"

"We are professionals, in an office, doing business. You should be ignoring the fact that I am a woman."

"How could anyone be expected to ignore that?"

"Also I am . . ."

"You are forty-one and I am twenty-eight—I looked you up—which means that it would be biologically possible for you to be my mother. Yada, yada, yada. I know all that. I have a desperate crush on you. That's not my fault. I didn't come to that meeting last week saying to myself, I think today I'll fall in love. I was in love last year. The girl dumped me. It still hurts. I would not have said I was ready to take any emotional risks. Or so I would have told you ten days ago. But here I am embarrassing myself and offering to do anything you want—touching your breasts was just an illustration, though I admit I'd quite like to do it and—well, I think you should take advantage of the situation."

"I don't do domination," she replied, and was immediately horrified at how it sounded.

"No," said Stephen, "I wouldn't have thought you did, though when I close my eyes I see you in a long white coat with a chart in your hands, checking me into the insane asylum. Quote, preparing me for whatever happens to people in insane asylums. I hadn't thought of S&M. It could be a problem—or would have been but it doesn't interest you... fortunately. Having a crush is more of a romantic thing."

"I think you should cool down," said Sandra, and immediately worried that it sounded dismissive. He did seem sincere, even if he was daft.

"Sorry," he said again. "And apologies about the 'yada yada.'"

"In answer to your question, I'm half Somali."

"Cool," said Stephen. "They run marathons. This could take a while."

"Go home," said Sandra. "We'll make a fresh start tomorrow."

I need to get back to the real world, she said to herself. Handsome young men like Stephen don't hit on honey-colored, two-million-dollar-a-year litigators in expensive yellowy-green suits. Or maybe I just don't go to the right bars. Or any bars, actually.

Of course there could never be a fresh start. He had said what he'd said and she hadn't exploded, or at least hadn't refused to deal with him any more. So they had a history—a secret, as he put it. When she got home that evening, there was a big bunch of flowers and a note that said simply, "No Inhibitions?"

As soon as Sandra had gotten the flowers in a vase and thanked the doorman for taking care of them and looked at her mail, she began to giggle. She started to have a serious conversation with herself and decided not to. She opened a bottle of wine that had been in the refrigerator for quite a long time and poured out a glass, which she took into her bedroom. She changed into trousers and sandals and . . . well, just for a minute, nothing above the waist.

Sandra went into her living room and sat on the couch. She got up and walked out onto the balcony. The balconies were designed so you couldn't see onto anyone else's. Her apartment faced the Hudson River. Someone would have to be in New Jersey and have a telescope to see her breasts. Still, it felt daring.

There was this thing going on in the office. Her partner Alice, who now seemed to have administrative duties, had started using the gym. This involved taking her clothes off to put on exercise clothes and then afterwards using a communal shower. The men didn't seem to mind, or couldn't figure out what to do about it, more likely. Alice had tried to get Sandra to follow her example. Sandra had actually peeked in once, but lost her nerve. Anyway, you couldn't hang the sort of suits and blouses Sandra wore on hooks in a locker.

Alice maintained it was restful to be seen naked. Maybe. Depended on the man who got to see you. Sandra hadn't ever undressed for a man—the lights had always been off—but she supposed she could imagine doing so. Charles would be all right. He'd laugh. He'd make her laugh. Making people laugh was one of Charles's gifts. Very useful when people got testy in negotiations. You could get made a partner of any professional services firm in America if you were good enough at making people laugh.

Henry would also be all right to undress for, interestingly, despite the fact that he was nearly a generation older. But some of her partners gave her the creeps even when she was wearing a $5,000 suit. Oscar the Hunchback, for example—her private name for him. He was probably an axe-murderer, or something dire, the way he scurried around being rude and acting important. Well, he probably wasn't a criminal like William the tax partner, whose escape from justice Alice had made them all finance, but you wouldn't want to unpack Oscar's subconscious, that was for sure.

Sandra went back inside and looked at herself in he mirror. She had quite good breasts. Having someone touch them would probably be very pleasant, if you could do that privately and without damaging your clothes. Stephen had volunteered to be that someone.

She considered her face, which she regarded as "OK." It had never occurred to Sandra that she could be considered beautiful. Perhaps she was. She had gone to some lengths never to be vain. She was an interesting color, though.

In college, Sandra had been called "Iced Coffee," a nickname bestowed by a girl who wanted to have a relationship with her. Sandra didn't do relationships, especially that kind, but the name stuck. Stephen reminded Sandra a little of that girl, in that he was awkward and fearless. It made her nostalgic for those first weeks away from home, with new textbooks, new neighbors, the possibility of becoming a new person.

Sandra hadn't been magically transformed that September at Wellesley, but she'd thought about experimenting. You are who you think you are, she told herself. "You don't have to be a lesbian," said the girl who had renamed her. "You just have to accept that I am, and tell me you don't care. I'll do all the work. I'll accept responsibility for whatever happens in the dark."

Sandra decided that she did care. The girl moved on to other amours. Sandra made up for being timid by working extremely hard.

Stephen had mentioned marathons. A client of Sandra's ran in them. He wasn't a fanatic, he'd told a group around the dinner table in a Houston restaurant a couple of months ago. "Anything under four hours and I'm satisfied." The friend he sometimes trained with was a lunatic, though. "His strategy is, at the start, run as hard as you can to get out of the pack. Then, hold that pace for the next twenty-six miles." Everyone had laughed. But that had essentially been Sandra's strategy from freshman year on: run hard and don't slow down.

"This could take a while," Stephen had said. Sandra found herself giggling again. Maybe Alice had a point about the therapeutic benefits of nudity. Better get dressed.

As she put on a slate-colored tee shirt and an unbuttoned navy-blue flannel shirt, Sandra remembered the formal dinner she had to go to next week. Henry had taken her aside recently and said she needed to be more "social." Henry had treated Sandra well over the years. He'd been a litigator himself, before he turned to "client-tending," as he called it, and became senior partner. As much as anyone, he'd taught Sandra how to do her job. And never made a pass at her. She always took his advice. So when a client had invited Sandra—"and guest" the card had said—to the dinner, she'd said "yes" right away. But she hadn't remembered to indicate she'd be on her own. She tended to assume people knew her situation, but there was no way this client would have known. "Guest" meant "husband or lover if you have one; please advise." So what if she showed up with Stephen?

Stephen wasn't exactly unsuitable. He worked at a prestigious firm, same as she did. He wasn't an employee. He was her client, in fact, if you ignored the legal niceties. He'd gone to Yale. He had good manners. He could be quite amusing. He looked fabulous, to be honest. The only problem was he was twelve years old. Not really, but there was something transgressive about the idea. There'd be serious people at the table, now that she thought about it. Might even be a judge. Could she get away with it? Could Iced Coffee pull it off? Could Stephen?

I'm having a mid-life crisis, she told herself.

"So we begin again," she said at ten the next morning, when the graceful waiter had brought in another silver tray, this time with a coffee service. She aimed for the tone a psychotherapist might adopt with a patient who'd had a mini-crisis in the previous session. What thoughts the psychotherapist might have had overnight were not relevant.

Twenty-eight years old and definitely a man. Stephen had a glow about him that morning. He must have had a good run. After which, a shower.

Stephen in the shower was not what she wanted to be thinking about. He started to say something but she interrupted. It was important to be the one in control—as

Henry had always told her. "In exchange for my forgetting everything about yesterday," she said, "...including the flowers...I need a favor."

Stephen was poker-faced.

"I need a date." She handed him the invitation. "It's next Tuesday. I've realized my hostess assumes I'm a couple. I don't want to be rude. I am advised she is the sort of woman who plans these things carefully. If I come alone it will destroy her seating plan." Sandra paused. "I assume you own a dinner jacket."

Stephen studied the invitation. "I'll pick you up at seven," he said.

Pretty cool, said Sandra to herself.

At the event, Stephen was a success. The "lion" at the table, the chief executive of a major public company, knew that Stephen had been an All-American lacrosse player, and seemed to think that was important. Stephen listened to the wives seated on either side of him as if they were important. There were two pretty girls at the table but no other young men. The hostess gave Sandra a look that said, "perfect." There was some swapping of seats before dessert and Sandra wound up next to the deputy editor of Vogue. She admired Sandra's color sense but told her she could wear her hair longer. "I can't control it then," said Sandra. "I know someone who can," said the woman, and suggested lunch.

Sandra began laughing as soon as they got into the car. She hadn't had much wine, but she felt ridiculously relaxed. "How did we get away with that?" she said.

"At a certain level," said Stephen, "people assume you are royalty just because you're there."

"You appear to be lacrosse royalty," said Sandra.

"Oh, that," said Stephen. He was way more sophisticated than Sandra had assumed. "But what about you?"

Sandra gave him a blank look.

"I watched people looking at you. You're unusually beautiful, as I've told you, and you are also a very accomplished lawyer at a famous firm. You could be a celebrity if you wanted to."

"How awful."

"Think about it," said Stephen.

"Henry doesn't like us getting our names in the paper," she said.

When they got to her building, she didn't invite him upstairs for a nightcap and he didn't ask. She kissed him on the cheek. As she got ready for bed she reflected that the power relationship between them was now completely reversed.

The next day Stephen carefully put the power relationship back where it belonged. "Thank you for an interesting evening," he said, and then left the topic alone. He sat up in his chair and was particularly attentive to her instructions.

They had gotten to the difficult part: why had it not occurred to him there might be fraud?

"Because our firm doesn't have crooked clients?" It was a question: is this the right sort of answer, teacher?

"No," said Sandra. "While that is true, it is not an ideal answer. Remember, the acquiree was not your client. You do not have to defend them. In doing due diligence you made no assumptions. You asked yourself whether there could be fraud, and there was no evidence of it."

"Well, I did ask the auditors."

"As you should have. And presumably you asked yourself if it was reasonable for the company to be earning as good a margin on sales as it was."

"Yes, of course I did. It was their margins that first got me interested in them as a possible acquisition for our client."

"And I assume you asked yourself why, with such good margins, the company's shares traded at such a modest level."

"I actually asked their CFO. I had to make it a joke. It was sort of a rude question. I asked him over lunch. His answer was to make a joke himself."

"The fact that you asked is all that is relevant."

"You are looking out for me, aren't you? I thought you were only concerned about my employer."

"If you get squished like a bug," said Sandra, "your employer will get splattered." She'd used the line before. It relaxed people, she'd found.

Stephen smiled. Sandra reflected that it was the smile of a young man who had no experience of being squished. He was like one of those atoms that went from one quantum state to another with no perceptible effort: wise and innocent by turns, one moment forty, twelve the next. "So am I 'prepared'?" he said.

"We'll need another hour or two next week, right before the deposition, but you'll do fine," she said.

Stephen looked away. "You kissed me last night," he said.

"Seemed reasonable," said Sandra. "You'd been very good at dinner."

"Be careful," said Stephen. "I have love dust all over me. It would be dangerous to get any on yourself."

"Stain my suit?" Today it was light gray linen, with pink piping.

"Break your heart," said Stephen.

"I'm not worried." She had to say that.

"I'm way too young for you."

"Which is why I'm not worried."

"So invite me to your apartment for dinner tonight and we'll see how you do."

Do what? And how did he get there so deftly? "You assume I can cook," said Sandra, stalling.

"I'll bring take-out. I assume you have wine."

"I don't, actually."

"I'll do everything," said Stephen, reminding Sandra of the girl who'd named her "Iced Coffee."

"Eight o'clock," said Sandra, knowing she was being foolish, knowing she was lost.

In for a penny, in for a pound, Sandra said to herself as she changed clothes. Trousers, sandals and nothing above the waist.

"Oh, you are brave," said Stephen matter-of-factly when she opened the door. He must have come directly from the office, stopping at a take-out place on the way, because he still had on his suit, making her feel that little bit more uncovered.

It was rather nice being uncovered, once you took the plunge.

Stephen threw his suit jacket on a chair, unloaded the shopping bag, ranging the aluminum containers with their cardboard tops along her kitchen counter. Would they get around to opening them? Stephen looked in several cupboards and found two glasses, gave the top of the wine bottle a twist and poured some out.

Sandra watched him in silence. She liked the way he made himself at home in her kitchen. It occurred to her that he probably knew how to cook. "Next time I'll make dinner," he said, reading her mind. Next time?

They went into the living room and sat on the couch. It was dark outside. He didn't touch her.

"You said you'd touch my breasts," said Sandra finally.

"I recall," said Stephen. But he didn't move.

Sandra took a drink of her wine.

"How much do you know about your body?" said Stephen.

"I'm practically a virgin."

"How much do you know about your heart?"

"Same."

"Bad experience?"

"Indifferent. Embarrassed afterwards."

"We see this," said Stephen.

Now he was the doctor in the long white coat. One of Sandra's cousins was a doctor. She used that phrase from time to time. It meant, essentially, "Do not feel like the lone ranger." It was comforting, in its way.

Stephen set down his wine glass. Sandra didn't think he'd had any of it yet. "Would you like to finish undressing?" he said.

"In front of you?"

"Well, if you're determined to make yourself vulnerable..."

Sandra took off her sandals, stood up and took off the rest.

"Sit down, and tell me what you like."

"I don't know what I like."

"Whisper in my ear, if you're embarrassed."

"I don't know what to say, but yes, I am definitely embarrassed. I shouldn't be doing this."

"Do you like being embarrassed?"

"No. But yes, in a way."

"Do you want to be punished?"

"No no no no no."

"You are beautiful."

"Thank you." She continued to stand in front of him.

"Tell me what you do want. Sit down and tell me. Looking me in the eye if you can, whispering in my ear if you need to."

Sandra sat down. They were close to each other but not touching. She looked at him but whispered: "Contact, sensation, comfort, intimacy, affection."

"You did get some of that dust on you, didn't you?"

"Please," she said plaintively.

Stephen moved closer and put his arms around Sandra. She eased her body toward his. For some reason what she noticed was the feel of his silk necktie. Odd that he hadn't taken it off. Maybe it was a way of leaving a space between them. For some reason that seemed thoughtful of him, absurd as the idea was, given her state of complete undress. He kissed her on the cheek. "That's for last night," he said. Then he kissed her softly on the mouth. "That's for looking out for me in this foolish litigation," he said.

"Not foolish," she said, her voice muffled by being pressed against his shoulder, "... dangerous." She pulled away enough to speak more clearly. "Litigation is going into a bear pit. If the bear is angry or hungry, bad luck."

"For the purposes of tonight," said Stephen, "the bear is asleep and the litigation is foolish." He twisted further away so he could look at her better. "But what is never foolish is pleasure." He touched her breasts, as he'd promised, just brushing one of her nipples. She gasped, as he'd promised she would. "But we have to find out what works best."

"That was good," said Sandra.

"We want to do better than 'good,'" said Stephen. "So we need to conduct a few experiments. Everyone is wired a little differently. Some women like their nipples to be barely touched, as I just did to you. Some want them handled firmly." He took one and then the other between his thumb and forefinger and applied a bit of pressure.

"Umm," said Sandra.

"Some women like their breasts to be kissed and licked." He demonstrated and she felt herself hardening. "They like their nipples to be slippery."

"I like that," said Sandra.

"Hold that thought," said Stephen. He took hold of her by the shoulders and licked first one nipple and then the other. He let go of her shoulders and began attending to the one he wasn't kissing with his thumb and forefinger again. "Hard and soft," he said between kisses. "Soft and hard. Two sensations merging into one."

"You're in the merger business, aren't you?" said Sandra. That sounded dopey but she didn't care.

"I have been in the merger business since I was fourteen," said Stephen, bragging a little.

"Any particularly... memorable transactions?" said Sandra. She was struggling to be ironic, more detached.

"Tonight will be memorable."

"We aren't conceited, are we?"

Stephen didn't answer. He put his arms around Sandra again and ran his fingertips very softly on the back of her neck and the part of her back between her shoulder blades.

"Oh my goodness," said Sandra. "It feels like fireflies look. Every touch is like a gleam of light."

"A very good description," said Stephen. "A lot of tension lives there. You're letting it escape. Not everyone can do that."

"I have special talents?" said Sandra, feeling absurdly pleased.

"I never doubted it," said Stephen. "Now, lie back against the pillows. Your couch is perfect, by the way. Big loose pillows, soft material, room for maneuver. You cannot imagine what ridiculous couches I have been required to operate on. I mean you'd think the girl didn't want my attentions. Sorry. Bad manners to mention other women. Put your hands behind your head and be gorgeous. I need to find out whether you are also ticklish."

"Oh, God," said Sandra.

Stephen immediately stopped touching her thighs. "Bad memories?"

"When I was eight. My cousins held me down. I wet the bed. They got in terrible trouble."

"How about you?" said Stephen.

"Well, I assumed I'd done something bad, of course, but I was never punished. Still waiting to be, I guess."

Stephen began to touch bits of Sandra's belly and then her ribs. She made herself allow it. "You wanted them to do it again, didn't you?"

"No," said Sandra. "Yes, of course."

"At some level, everyone wants to let go," said Stephen. He dug his fingers into her ribs. "Like that?"

"Oh dear. Yes. Don't."

"Shall I get a towel for you to sit on?"

"I don't want to let go that way."

He gave her a wicked smile. But he didn't tickle her any more.

"I do believe I'm starting to relax," said Sandra. "Would you like some more wine?" She needed a moment to collect herself.

"Thank you," he said, giving her space again.

When Sandra returned with their wine glasses, Stephen had stripped.

"Oh," she said. "That's friendly."

"I told you I had a crush on you."

"You're pink and I'm honey-colored," she said, sitting down next to him so that their bodies did touch. "Here's your wine."

"Your nipples are dark brown," said Stephen.

"My nipples like you," said Sandra.

"Parts of me very definitely like you," said Stephen.

"Not all of you?" said Sandra. Why was she so fearful? She had her hand on his shoulder, and suddenly wished she didn't.

"The nature of a crush," said Stephen, "is that attraction gets way out ahead of understanding or acquaintance or what's appropriate."

"So parts of you are having second thoughts?" said Sandra, taking her hand away and sitting up a bit. She had never gotten close enough to a man to be rejected.

"No," said Stephen. "My desire for you is all-consuming."

That was better—possibly. "But the fire may burn out by morning?"

"I told you this would be dangerous," he said.

"I'm not a fool, Stephen."

"Nor frigid, which is what you most wanted to find out, I think."

"Thank you for that," she said briskly. "I especially liked the fireflies."

Stephen pondered that for a moment. "So, I should leave?"

"Oh, I think we'd both be disappointed with ourselves if we let that happen," said Sandra, remembering how to take control—of a conversation if not of her emotions. She was Henry Franklin's protégé, after all.

A wave of incongruous softness swept over her. "And I know I have more to learn," she said. Oh, God, do I ever, she added to herself.

"You do show aptitude," said Stephen.

"So may I suggest that we agree to a three-month affair?" said Sandra. "By which time . . ."

"Option to extend?"

"By which time you should be ready for a younger woman."

"They're overrated," said Stephen gallantly.

"So, shall we get on with it?" said Sandra.

"Can we go into your bedroom?"

"You prefer horizontal?" said Sandra.

"Yes," said Stephen. "And I want to populate your bedroom with memories."

The Angel Host

To understand the statement that God manifested himself to Thomas as punctuation, you would need first to have encountered enough contracts to know that many of them, or at least large sections of them, are single, run-on sentences in which powers or remedies or conditions precedent are separated by semicolons, which give up their familiar function of joining sentences that constitute a single thought and essentially become super-commas; you need secondly to know that for an experienced lawyer, reviewing a contract drafted by someone else is a meditative as much as an analytical activity, in which remote contingencies become obvious the way love becomes obvious; and finally that Thomas was applying just this sort of languorous attentiveness to a complicated and probably fraudulent will when it came to him that these omnipresent semicolons could be understood as angels: a head, and attached to the shoulder, a wing.

No sooner had this faintly embarrassing thought occurred to Thomas—if pressed on the subject, he would have described himself as an agnostic—than Leonard, the firm's messenger, appeared with his mail cart. He was wearing a baseball cap, on which the word "asshole" had been embroidered.

Thomas got to watch this vision of corrupted innocence for a good thirty seconds because Leonard had something wrong with his legs that made him walk slowly, and because Thomas's office, which in common with every other office in the firm had a glass front wall, was at the end of a very long internal corridor. Thomas had an office in this unprestigious location because there had been something wrong with his ambition. Or so he told himself.

He'd been a fifth-year associate when they asked him to "fill in" for Mr. Winslow, who did trusts and estates, while that gentleman went on a long holiday, and when he returned Thomas was asked to keep on helping him out—"to the extent you don't have other work, of course,"—and Thomas turned out to be good at trusts and estates. Magically, the flow of corporate work that used to occupy him began to thin out, until one day three years later they came to Thomas's office to say that old Winslow was going to retire and they'd like to make Thomas a half-partner.

They didn't put it that way. They offered him "a partnership," which was gracious. But Thomas knew that when he read the partnership agreement he would find that his share would be perhaps half his contemporaries' share. Then again, he also knew that most of his contemporaries were being passed over and would have to leave. So maybe being a half-partner was just fine.

Thomas had known what was happening from the start. An intelligent corporate law firm has to have a trust and estates function, if only to do the wills of client chief executives, who mustn't be allowed to spend as much time as will-making can involve in the offices of a rival firm. You don't charge chief executives as much as the time spent on their personal affairs would justify if they were companies rather than people, so you can't have an expensive partner doing the work. On the other hand, the person who helps them decide how to distribute their wealth (or not) to the children of several marriages has to be "a partner" and look like one, and importantly, not screw up. Such people do not always present themselves in the jungle of a major law firm at the exact moment that "old Winslow" reaches retirement age. Thomas had an excellent brain and the abnormal capacity for work that his firm required of everyone. In his first few years as an associate, when self-abnegation was the requisite survival skill, he had thought he might some day be a real partner. But the men who ran the place had noticed his good manners and sensed his weakness. He'd been asked to "fill in" to see if he would accept lesser status. Being deficient in ambition, Thomas acquiesced.

Under ordinary circumstances it took three glasses of scotch whiskey to make him regret doing so. He'd learned to put the bottle away after the second. And the money, even at half-partner level, was pretty good. The past year, in fact, it had been very good.

Which only left the problem of loneliness. Thomas had sort of postponed the matter of finding a life partner until he either made partner himself or had a less demanding job. Then when he did make partner—half-partner—he was sufficiently chagrined that he didn't have the self-confidence to pursue women. How could he pretend to be a partner and then turn out not to be a real one?

Now he was forty and a bit, and it became more and more awkward. He hadn't imagined things working out this way. His mother had always talked about the social advantages of being an "extra man," but no one seemed to invite him to the dinner parties his mother had talked about, where he would meet suitable candidates for marriage. No one, to be honest, probably knew he existed.

The sight of Leonard's humiliation woke Thomas's demons. "Where did you get that cap?" he asked softly as the part of his brain that doubted the existence of God reminded him that the word "angel" meant messenger.

"Boys in mailroom give it to me."

"Do you know what it says?"

"Bad word," said Leonard, and blushed, as perhaps an angel would when required to contemplate human physicality. There was no requirement, as Thomas understood the matter, that an angel be handsome or intelligent, only pure.

"Why do you wear it, then?" Thomas asked.

"If I don't, they take my lunch." Leonard stood patiently, waiting for Thomas to speak. He looked down at Thomas's desk, in the corner of which was a technical work from the firm's library regarding taxation in divorce settlements. "You want me to take that back?"

"Yes, please," said Thomas. "And please bring me the second volume. The librarian will find it for you."

"Miss Harriet," said Leonard carefully.

"Is that her name?" said Thomas. He had noticed her, actually, but never spoken to her, which he bitterly reflected could be the story of his life. He picked up the book, revealing, underneath it, a paperback copy of one of Henry James's novels.

"That one too?" said Leonard. He picked it up and looked at the cover, which had a reproduction of a striking John Singer Sargent painting.

"No thank you, Leonard. That one's mine. I read it on the subway."

"Hard book," said Leonard, flipping the pages. "No other pictures."

"Pictures in words, Leonard."

"Too hard for Leonard," said the messenger, handing the book to Thomas. He turned and left.

Thomas waited for Leonard to be around the corner and out of sight before he went to the mailroom. He took the stairs two at a time. "Why?" he asked the boys.

"What does it matter? Leonard is an idiot."

"Yeah," said another, "he probably can't even read."

"Of course he can read," said Thomas. "He delivers the mail, doesn't he?"

"I suppose."

"You realize what you've done could get several of you fired? We fired a secretary last month for using obscenities in emails she sent from her PC. This is worse. What if a client sees it?"

"We only gave him the hat this morning." There was a chorus of agreement, as if that made a difference.

"Here's what you have to do," said Thomas. "Go find Leonard. Take the cap and throw it away. And tell him it was a joke." Thomas paused as inspiration hit him. "Tell him you did it because you all *like* him."

One of the boys in the mailroom started to say that Thomas's idea was crazy, that Leonard would never believe it. Thomas looked at him severely and he shut up.

"Everyone likes to believe he has friends," said Thomas.

"We do like him," said another of the mailroom crew. "He's just a little goofy."

"Let me know when you've done what I said and I'll start forgetting your names," said Thomas.

"Betcha don't even know our names," said the one who'd questioned Thomas's plan.

"No, but I can find out." Pause. "So what is it?"

"Angelo," he said, after a second's hesitation.

"Screw you," said another of the crew. "I'm Angelo. He's Jerry."

None of the other mailroom workers rushed to identify themselves. Thomas decided not to press the point. "Nice to meet you both," he said. "I'm embarrassed that I don't know all your names. I am Thomas Hastings."

"We know that," said Jerry. "You're important. You're a partner, for Christ's sake."

"Everyone is important to God," said Thomas. Astonished by his own words, he would have added "in a manner of speaking" or some such qualifier but at that precise moment, Leonard returned to the mailroom, and everyone turned to look at him.

Real Angelo made the first move. "Yo, Leonard. We gotta get rid of that cap. It might embarrass the ladies."

"Yeah," said Jerry. "It was a joke ... cause we *like* you ... like, we thought you'd just wear it in here."

"Let's get rid of it," said Angelo. He took it off of Leonard's head and threw it in a trash barrel.

"Recycle?" said Leonard dubiously, for they had thrown the baseball cap into a container marked "Paper only." He looked over at Thomas.

"It's all right, Leonard," said Thomas. "It's all *fibrous* material."

Going home that night, Thomas asked himself what had made him say that, why he had used what his grandfather would have called a "highfalutin" word. Trying to demonstrate my superiority, he decided. Trying to recover my poise. For indeed his confrontation with the boys in the mailroom had left him breathless.

Cooking his lamb chops and boiling some frozen peas, Thomas decided that being angry hadn't felt all that bad. So he tried not drinking any more of the whiskey he'd poured before he took his coat off. This was doable. And it made it possible to read Henry James for an hour before going to bed.

Pictures in words. Pictures in his head. Now that he knew the librarian's name, it was difficult not to think about her. Slender, with blue eyes and a sly smile sometimes.

Next morning Leonard left Thomas the second volume of the wrong work. It wasn't about tax and divorce. It was about mediation. Thomas stared at the title on the spine, and his mind began to play hopscotch the way it had with the semicolons. The word "media" jumped out at him. Was there a connection? Not really. Media was newspapers and television. Mediation didn't involve reporting on a trial. It was about avoiding a trial. Mediation meant finding the middle in a dispute, getting the participants to agree on the point of balance, where what each got or gave up was fair. Or felt fair to the parties.

But he wondered if there might be a buried connection. I'll have to meditate on that, he said to himself. And then he laughed, because he realized that the only difference between "mediation" and "meditation" was a "t." Which could be read as a cross. Thomas thought about his semicolons. I am getting daft, he said to himself. God is hunting you down, said a voice in his head.

Or perhaps what Thomas was meant to do, in response to whatever message Leonard had brought him, was to meditate on mediation. Thomas didn't do divorces but he tidied up afterwards, so he knew that family disputes were inherently ghastly. People who had once loved each other had fishing lines in their hands with the hooks imbedded in each other's faces, and if they all struggled as they were entitled to do at law, the only result would be blood and disfigurement. This was so obvious that Thomas had never really thought about it before.

So why did so many people go to court? There was money involved, of course, but litigation is like burning hundred dollar bills—eight or ten of them an hour if you had a first-class team advising you. The answer was probably that sending in the lawyers was like conservative Republicans talking about sending in the Marines. It made people feel strong at a moment of maximum vulnerability. Whereas mediation sounded soft and social workerish. What I need to do, Thomas said to himself, for the disputatious rich people of New York, is offer mediation but dress it up as something tough. Do it at a commercial firm like ours, which is known to be tough but would never stoop to family law.

There is money in this idea too, Thomas said to himself. If we become known as the firm that can get you through a personal crisis without the pain and exposure of a trial, there should be even more chief executives of other firms' clients who start spending time in our offices. They would find the surroundings familiar . . . offering business development opportunities to Thomas's real partners . . . who might in due course let him be a real partner too. Thomas knew that capturing another firm's client that way could happen because he'd facilitated it a few times.

Facilitation, if you thought about it, was a form of mediation. The chief executives in question, whom Thomas had come to know by doing and undoing their wills, generally wound up wanting *Thomas's* advice. They didn't want to be introduced to one of his partners. The problems they most wanted to talk about were interpersonal problems—like how to handle a headstrong director, or how to persuade a colleague of thirty years that it was time to retire, how to enable said colleague to tell himself that it was his own decision. But if they, or to be accurate the companies they ran, were to be "captured," the firm had to be solving legal problems. And that required getting them comfortable with the partners best equipped to do so. And getting said partners to do their best work, even if their egos made it hard for them to "audition." Which sometimes required—to be brutal about it—self-abasement.

Alice-who-runs-the-place—Thomas's private name for her—had come to see him a few months ago. "You've done it again," she said. "Your Mr. Brown has just been on the phone to Henry."

"Am I in trouble?"

"Right," she said sarcastically. "The man who runs America's fifth-largest corporation likes the work you've done on his will and he wonders if the firm can help him with another delicate matter."

"That new regulatory agency whose name I can never remember."

"You might have told me."

"He didn't go into it. He just mentioned it several times. He said it reminded him of dealing with his daughter. He has to leave her a fraction of his estate even if she treats him like . . . well, badly."

"OK," said Alice-who-runs-the-place, cutting Thomas off. "Now you get to see what I do for a living."

"You manage the firm, sort of," said Thomas.

"There's a lot of 'sort of' to the job," said Alice with a laugh. "Here's the deal. The person who can be of the most help to the corporation your client runs is our distinguished and insufferable partner Oscar."

"Edward Brown won't like Oscar," said Thomas.

"None of us like Oscar. That's why I give him a big office with his own conference table—so he can't usurp a conference room someone else has reserved just to be a shit. That's why I let him go to so many conferences—to get him out of the office. But he is the best there is at the particular bit of administrative law that is troubling your client, and not, incidentally, many of the largest corporations on the planet . . ."

"It also has to do with his general counsel, whose judgment seems to be eroding . . ."

"You can explain that to Oscar. He will pretend not to listen to you, but he needs to know it. More broadly . . ." she paused. "You are a nice man, Thomas. Many of our partners are not."

Your partners, Thomas said to himself. This made him think about Charles, but he brushed the thought away.

"Let me cut to the chase," said Alice. "You will have to let Oscar be in charge."

"It's his field of expertise," said Thomas.

"Yes, but Mr. Brown wants you involved. He told Henry that quite specifically. He likes your judgment. He's a very smart businessman so we should probably pay attention to that, but not this minute. Your client wants you in the room. You will have to do that without getting in Oscar's way. You will have to let him treat you like an associate, pick things up when he throws them on the floor, keep your Mr. Brown from strangling him, and tell him afterwards that he was brilliant, witty, masterful and has the biggest dick you have ever seen, which will be particularly galling, Thomas—and I can tell you this because I've played this part myself—it will be particularly galling because although I cannot speak for his other endowments, Oscar *is* brilliant."

"So I have to be the girl," Thomas had said, surprising himself with the bitterness of the remark.

Alice-who-runs-the-place said nothing for a moment, and Thomas blushed. "You'll have to be the adult," she said finally, "which I know you can."

This had proved to be true. Oscar had devised a wonderful strategy that got the desired ruling from the regulator, and crowed about it—Alice's words—"like a sixteen-year-old who's gotten his first blow job." The man who ran America's fifth-largest corporation had kept his temper, though he often needed half an hour in Thomas's office to decompress. Henry had taken the general counsel out to lunch one particularly difficult week. More business had come in.

Alice had asked Thomas, a month after the successful conclusion of the matter, whether he'd by any chance like a bigger office. "My clients tell me private matters," he'd replied without thinking. "I think they find it easier here, where no one walks past and looks in." His secretary even worked out of sight.

And in any event, Thomas told himself that night, a half-partner would look foolish in one of the big offices.

Thomas knew his mediation idea had to be impractical—it would mean setting up a new line of business for the firm—but he liked having it. One act of spontaneous courage—outrage really, for who could fear the boys in the mailroom—anyway, protecting Leonard seemed to have

77

changed Thomas. It was no longer possible to see himself as the sort of man who would *never* do that sort of thing. Run upstairs and confront the boys in the mailroom, that is. Or get the firm to do domestic mediation, for that matter.

So with a burst of energy he took the book that Leonard had left in his in-tray and hurried downstairs to exchange it, not for the book he'd wanted, but for the *first* volume of the treatise on mediation.

Happily, his sensible self was unable to undermine his confidence before he reached the firm's library, where he discovered Harriet, the librarian he had noticed but never spoken to, holding the second volume of the tax treatise that Leonard hadn't brought him. "I think this is what you're after," she said.

"How do you know that?"

"You sent Leonard to get it," she said.

"Well, he brought me this—on mediation—and I'm actually quite interested in the subject but I want to start with the first volume."

"Do you still want to know about taxation in divorce?"

"I wouldn't say I want to know, but I fear I am required to know."

Harriet laughed, but quietly, which Thomas liked.

"How did Leonard happen to bring me the wrong book? Though I must say I am very glad he did, because it has given me some interesting ideas."

"He brought it to you because I gave it to him."

"Why did you do that?"

"So that you would have to bring it back to exchange it." Harriet paused and then added, "So I could meet you." She hurried on. "You normally never come yourself." Her body was trembling a bit; Thomas wished he could hug her. "I figured you would know that Leonard has to do his mail run now, so it would be at least two hours before you'd be able to have him do the exchange, and I was hoping you would be impatient."

"So you could meet me?"

For an answer, Harriet held up another book: the Henry James novel with the Sargent reproduction on the cover. "We're both reading it," she said.

"How do you know that?"

"Leonard told me. He saw my copy."

"Oh."

"And I want you to take me out to lunch so we can talk about it. If that's not too forward of me. Not many Henry James readers in my circle of friends."

"Oh," said Thomas, not knowing what to say or how to say it. "OK. That would be nice." And then, "I might bounce off you an idea I've just had."

"That would be nice, too," said Harriet.

"I suppose you're responsible for the idea," said Thomas, "since it was getting the wrong book that sparked the idea."

"Doesn't that mean it *wasn't* the wrong book?" said Harriet.

"You have a point," said Thomas. And a good brain, he said to himself. And you think complexly, like Henry James.

Lunch *was* nice. They were both self-conscious. They were both lonely. She was thirty-five, which felt old, she told him. I'm a make-believe partner, he told her. No, you're not, she said. He decided he didn't have to tell her about having to flatter Oscar, even though that would prove his point.

She understood his idea—liked it—but they agreed maybe not to talk about work, or not just then. "I don't want to talk about divorce on our first date," said Harriet.

First date, Thomas said to himself.

They agreed to have dinner the following weekend. On the way back to the office they went to a bookstore to choose the next novel they'd read. They decided to avoid Henry James for a while. "Too roundabout," said Thomas.

They did have dinner. She talked about the Ohio town she came from, and her determination never to go back to it, pleasant as it was. He talked about coming from a faintly distinguished Boston family, a father who died when Thomas was twelve, a mother who expected him to be "successful like your father." They discussed the similar routines they followed on Saturday mornings: exercise, dry-cleaning, groceries, maybe a movie for later.

"And Sundays," he asked her, "do you go to church?"

"Sometimes."

"So you believe in God."

"On good days I do," she said.

"Do you have a lot of good days?"

"Not really," she said. "How about you?"

"Same," he said.

They talked about mediation. Harriet said it was a good idea. "You are quite passionate about it, aren't you?"

"The fishhooks," said Thomas. "I don't know where they came from."

"Your ambition," said Harriet. "I think there is someone wise and angry struggling to break out of your half-partner prison."

"You think so?" said Thomas. He wanted to tell her about dealing with Oscar, how angry the man made him with his rudeness and self-importance. But that had been months ago, and it was embarrassing, really. He wanted to tell her about the chief executives who confided in him, but that would be bragging.

"Don't you feel like breaking out?" said Harriet.

"I haven't felt much of anything for a good many years," said Thomas, knowing he was lying.

"Yes, you have," said Harriet. "You were angry about the obscenity Leonard was made to wear. You went to his aid."

"Maybe he came to mine," said Thomas. "Same as you have." And then, "Why did you?"

"Send Leonard with the wrong book?"

"Choose me."

"OK. I confess. I wanted to meet you before I knew we were reading the same book. I'd seen you in the elevator. You looked like someone I could talk to," said Harriet.

"Has that turned out to be true?"

"You shouldn't have to ask," said Harriet.

"Bad habit," said Thomas. "One acquires bad habits, living alone."

"I know," said Harriet.

"I do not see you as someone with bad habits," said Thomas.

"Oh, nothing lurid." For a moment she smiled beautifully. "I ask too much of myself, probably, and too little of the universe." She paused and then added, "Same as you."

Thomas started to say something and then couldn't. In the ensuing silence, Harriet reached across the table and put her hand on his arm.

"We're wasting our time," said Thomas finally.

"I agree," said Harriet.

Getting undressed was embarrassing. The whole endeavor was awkward. But they persevered. Pleasure found them.

Afterwards, lying in each other's arms in the single bed in Harriet's tiny apartment, they looked each other in the face, daring to let their emotions show.

And then, without fanfare, they were one. Invisible wings beat over them, sheltering them from all confusion.

"This is unexpected," said Harriet, putting her head on Thomas's shoulder as he lay on his back looking up. "I mean, I did set out to meet you. But all I was hoping for was conversation. I didn't count on happiness."

"I thought love was longing," said Thomas. "But I was wrong. Love is courage."

One of the boys from the mailroom was hanging around the door of his office when he arrived on Monday. For a stupid moment he pretended to think it was an angel. Thomas had had to work all of Sunday, to finish a trust agreement, so he'd come in a little late. Except for the fact that he hadn't called Harriet, he was in a terrific mood.

"It's Jerry, isn't it?" he said as he took off his overcoat and hung it on the back of his door.

He and Harriet agreed they wouldn't see each other until Monday evening, in theory because of the trust agreement. But they were probably both a little scared, Thomas told himself, needed to gather their wits after such a cloudburst of joy. Probably a good idea, though by six o'clock on Sunday it hadn't felt like one.

"No, Mr. Hastings, I'm Angelo."

"Are you sure?" said Thomas. He was definitely in a good mood.

"You gotta talk to Leonard, Mr. Hastings."

"Why's that?" Thomas put his briefcase on the chair beside the desk and removed the newspaper. There was an item he wanted to show Harriet. He had no experience having a girlfriend. There was this phrase, "I'll call you in the morning," lurking in his brain that was either an injunction or a bad joke. He would have to stop by the library as soon as possible.

"Hard to understand Leonard sometimes, but it seems to be about the chick in the library who got fired this morning."

Thomas froze. "I'll come up to the mailroom a little later," he said. He needed information. He needed oxygen. Why had Harriet been fired? Thomas didn't even have her phone number, their . . . courtship, if that was the word, had been so brief. The terribly important chief executive was coming in in twenty minutes.

"You OK, Mr. Hastings?" said real Angelo, who for some reason hadn't left.

"No, actually," said Thomas. "I have to speak to her. The girl who was fired. And call me 'Thomas.' You don't, by any chance, know why she was fired? No, of course you wouldn't."

"Cost-cutting is the word, Mr. Hastings. If it's OK, I'll keep calling you that. Jerry got the can too. Kinda odd they hung onto Leonard, though I guess he is a hard worker."

"Leonard will never be fired," said Thomas. "He's been at the firm for twenty-five years. He is special."

Thomas had a blinding vision of Harriet, who had been at the firm for maybe six months, sitting on the edge of the bed in her tiny apartment, thinking about what the two of them had done there on Saturday night. "Wasting our time," he had said. She would be putting a different construction on that now.

"I need to find her," said Thomas. He knew approximately where her apartment was—it was part of a broken-up brownstone—but he couldn't have said what the number was, or which block off of Second Avenue, to be honest. He'd been in a trance Saturday evening, walking with her from the restaurant. He'd probably recognize the building if he went and looked for it, but he couldn't stand up that chief executive.

"The librarian chick?" said Angelo. "She a friend of yours?"

Long years of discretion intervened. "No, but, well, she's been so nice to Leonard. Maybe he'll want to send her a card. But I don't know where to have Leonard send it."

"No sweat, Mr. Hastings. We have all the addresses of the people who got the chop this morning. We have to box up their stuff and send it to them. Not that there's much in her case. Just a paperback novel with a pretty picture on the cover. She left it on her desk. Leonard said it was hers."

Thomas looked at his watch. "Angelo, can you sneak out for an hour? I'll pay for your time."

"Wouldn't want to do that just now, Mr. Hastings, what with people getting let go for no good reason. Jerry'd been at the firm as long as me, you know. He was a good worker, even if he had a bit of a mouth."

"I will square it if anyone complains," said Thomas. "I need you to take a letter to the librarian chick, as you call her. Her name is Harriet Loomis. By hand. To the address you have for her, which should be on the Upper East Side. And wait for a reply."

"She won't know who I am. She'll probably call the police."

Thomas acknowledged to himself that Angelo probably came from a world where strangers who knocked on doors were asking for trouble. "Take Leonard with you," he said.

"I suppose I can say I took him outside for a walk around the block because he was upset."

"Brilliant," said Thomas. "Wait. Let me write the letter. I can do it by hand."

It took all of Thomas's professional discipline to attend to the chief executive who had thought about it over the weekend and wanted to make a dozen changes in the trust to be created under his will. He imagined Leonard and Angelo in the taxi he had told them to take, with Leonard holding onto the roses he had told them to buy with the $200 he'd given Angelo, and then trying to persuade Harriet to buzz them into the building, or at least to come down and look through the glass door to see that it really was Leonard. He imagined Leonard remembering the card he was taking Harriet but leaving Thomas's letter in the taxi. He imagined Harriet seeing the return address on the envelope and tearing it up unopened. He apologized to the chief executive for losing the thread. He made copious notes, willing Angelo to give him some sort of signal of success down the long hall.

The client finally left. Thomas stuck his head into the mailroom. Angelo came out into the hall. "We found the girl. Leonard gave her the flowers. She gave him a kiss on the cheek. I gave her the letter. She said she'd read it later. I think she'd been crying."

"You didn't tell her the letter was from me?"

"You didn't tell me to do that," said Angelo.

"No, I suppose I didn't."

Angelo took a fistful of money out of his pocket and handed it to Thomas. "You don't need to pay me nothing, Mr. Hastings. I gotta go back to work." He started to go back into the mailroom and then turned to speak to Thomas again. "Seemed like a nice girl," he said. "Why don't you talk to the woman who runs the place? See if you can get her job back. Leonard would like that. You said he had pull."

Thomas went to Alice's office. "So who do *you* want me to unfire?" she said. "Really, I have to assume no one reads anything I send them. I let all of you know who we were going to cut in case there were any issues. And you, Thomas, don't even come to Second Friday. You probably didn't even know we were considering cuts."

"No, I don't come," said Thomas, referring to the monthly partners' meeting. "I don't feel I have any say in how the firm operates, so why pretend? And it's Harriet Loomis in the library."

"Do you read the memos I send you?"

"She's the one I want you to reinstate," said Thomas. "And, no, I don't. Am I in trouble?"

Alice got a funny look, and contemplated Thomas for several seconds. "No," she said finally. "And I should probably thank you for being so little trouble rather than getting crabby. What's the deal with Harriet the librarian?"

"I'm, um, she's . . ."

"You're seeing her."

"Only recently," said Thomas. "Saturday, in fact. And lunch last week. We're reading the same book."

"Thomas, you are beginning to sound like Leonard."

"One could be accused of worse things," said Thomas, regaining a bit of his poise.

"He is rather sweet, isn't he?" said Alice.

"I think he's heroic, actually," said Thomas. "The world must be a frightening place for him."

"I imagine he takes exactly the same path to work every day," said Alice. "That way he avoids encountering anything unfamiliar. Some members of my family are in hazardous professions. They say routine is essential." She paused and seemed to be thinking about that. "Thomas, you didn't by any chance fail to read the memo Henry and I sent you on the 15th of December last year?"

"I don't remember. How would I remember that? But I tend to throw away the admin stuff. You and Henry do a good job. I have no complaints."

"Well, you clearly didn't read it," said Alice, "because it informed you that your percentage share of the partnership was being substantially increased. You're doing a really good job, Thomas. And you never make trouble."

"Oh," said Thomas. "Thank you. I should thank Henry too, shouldn't I? But going back to Harriet . . ."

"Just marry her," said Alice. "It will save everyone a lot of trouble. It will make you both happy, I expect. You're reading the same book, for Christ's sake."

"How do you know that?" said Thomas.

"I know everything," said Alice.

Thomas went back to his office, having accomplished nothing, really. Harriet was sitting in one of the wing-backed chairs. "Angelo let me in," she said. "I called the mailroom. I got your letter, and what I have to say"—she took a deep breath—"is that I don't want my job back. I just want you."

"I didn't know anything about this," said Thomas. "I never read the memos. I was terrified I had lost you. I didn't even know where you lived, the address I mean. I didn't know what to say in my letter. I didn't know if you'd believe anything I said."

"I was pretty angry," she said. "Hurt and angry, but I thought better of it. I decided you were sincere."

"Thank God," said Thomas.

"The semicolons did it," she said, with that partial smile he so liked.

"Did I tell you about my semicolons? I didn't think I had."

"Late Saturday night, or more accurately, Sunday morning. Right before we fell asleep."

"I remember now."

"Do you remember what you said in your letter?"

"Not really, to be honest. I was in a panic."

Harriet smiled again. "Terrible mistake, semicolon; will get you your job back, semicolon; desperate to see you, semicolon; I love you, comma, Thomas Hastings."

"Pretty pathetic," said Thomas, "signing my full name. Brave of you to come here." He suddenly thought about Leonard, armed with roses, venturing into unknown territory. "Can we get married right away?"

"Yes, please," said Harriet, and began to tremble.

This time Thomas felt it would be all right to give her a hug.

Improvisation

Oscar went to a conference and met a lady judge. He was on a speaking panel. She came up to him after the dinner. "I like self-confident men," was her pick-up line.

"Let's go upstairs," was his response. He wasn't all that confident, actually, but what else was he supposed to say? When cornered, he often said the first thing that came into his mind.

She must have been fifty, which was his age, but if he hadn't known she was a judge he would have guessed early forties. Smooth skin, lustrous dark brown hair, good figure, good posture.

"Why do you hunch forward?" she said.

"Bad habit." Oscar had a lot of bad habits, in his private, personal opinion. He would stare into his shaving mirror in the morning and lecture himself about them. You are nothing but brains and bluff, young man, he would tell himself, as if he were his dead mother lecturing a younger Oscar. You are rude to your colleagues because you are afraid. Lucky they don't realize how easy it would be to show you up. Then of course he'd go to work and be rude some more, because it was the only strategy he had.

"I want to see what you look like when you stand up straight," said Miriam. Oscar considered a crude response but thought better of it. "Yes, I know, I know," she said, having evidently read his mind.

They went to the elevator. Oscar had never been to a judge's hotel room. He supposed it wasn't a breach of ethics. He had no matter before her, and was unlikely to. He practiced in a narrow field. She was a Federal judge in a city he had never even been to. He couldn't remember which, actually, but it definitely wasn't New York or Los Angeles. He knew about her from the program. She'd spoken the day before, though he hadn't gone to that session. Her name was Miriam something.

They went to his room. She made him tell her the number and give her the key card. She put the key card in the lock. She made him take off his jacket and stand up straight, and walked around him like a judge at the Westminster Kennel Club Show, which Oscar had seen once on television. Oscar watched a lot of television in hotel rooms. At his firm's request, he went to a lot of conferences. He was famous in his narrow field, which brought in a fair amount of business.

"Throw your chest out a bit and look haughty," said Miriam.

Oscar complied immediately. When he wasn't thinking about it, especially when he was sitting at his desk intensely focused on solving a problem in his narrow but intensely lucrative field, he did hunch over, as the lady said, but when he remembered, he strode around the firm like a field marshal. He was good at haughty, good at contemptuous. It was a substitute for confident, which he had discovered in grade school, where he got near-perfect grades and was hopeless at softball. He could actually take a full swing at a slow pitch, whirl around without hitting it and fall over in the dust around home plate. Contempt for sports was the only defense. It worked quite well if you didn't mind getting beaten up occasionally.

"Now say something rude," said Miriam.

"You aren't Jewish, are you?" said Oscar without thinking. She had to be, but asking her seemed like a way of being rude. Or maybe he was trying to find a basis for a relationship. Oscar's maternal grandmother had been Jewish, though he never talked about it.

"Not bad," said Miriam, as if enjoying a joke. "Now let's get acquainted." She started to unbutton her blouse.

Oscar caught a glimpse of blue on her skin, and gasped. "You have a tattoo."

"Quite a good one," she said.

"Oh, please," said Oscar. "I mustn't see it."

She stopped. "Mustn't?"

"I have a horror of tattoos on women. I avoid those magazines."

"Why?" she said, honestly surprised.

"The violation . . . I think."

"Hmm," she said, standing with one hand on her hip and the other at her throat holding her blouse closed, contemplating Oscar. "From what I've read, horror almost always has sexual content. I suspect that at some level the prospect of violation . . . interests you?"

"I don't even want to analyze it."

"All right," said the lady judge. "You can have a blindfold." She hitched up her skirt and unfastened a nylon stocking. Oscar looked away, but the corner of his eye caught sight of good legs and no ink. "Turn around," she said. "Versatile things, stockings," she said matter-of-factly, as she improvised his blindfold.

After that there was the sound of clothes dropping to the floor and then the sensation of having his belt undone. Oscar moved to assist in the process but she stopped him. "I'll do it all," she said. "It will be hard to keep your balance when you can't see."

She stepped back, having finished with him. "Don't move," she said. She walked around and around him, touching him gently in unexpected ways. "I am heightening your senses," said Miriam.

"How do you know all this... technique?" said Oscar. "You aren't married."

"You don't know that."

"I suppose I don't."

"But I'm not, as it happens, and neither are you."

"You don't know that," said Oscar.

"Of course I know you're not married. I see everything. I'm a judge. I make my living watching people lie."

"I never thought of judges this way."

"Naked, you mean."

"Oh, that, yes," said Oscar. "It's a good way not to be frightened of them."

"Are you frightened a lot? I'm finishing getting undressed, by the way, so you can be frightened of your blindfold slipping."

"I mustn't tell you how many things I am afraid of. Men are supposed to be brave."

"And some are," said Miriam. "You look fabulous when you stand up straight, by the way."

"Naked and blindfolded, you mean?"

"I mean just the way you fit into your skin."

IMPROVISATION

"I don't feel comfortable in my own skin."

"Of course you don't. I saw that right away. It's part of why I was attracted to you. You radiate energy. Your brain is unruly. I watched the way you answered questions on that panel. You were constantly in doubt how far to go into the detail with each answer, what novel theories to propose. You didn't want the audience to think you were showing off but you couldn't help yourself. You had to show off. You probably did it in the first grade, when you could read before the others but couldn't tie your shoelaces. It was dazzling. You are such a gorgeous mixture of fear and ego, I had to meet you." Miriam paused and stroked Oscar's cheek—very gently, just the once. "Being with someone who is uncomfortable in his own skin can be very sexy."

"I suppose we're about to find that out," said Oscar.

She pulled back the covers and they lay parallel on the bed without getting under them. "You may approach," she said. Oscar reached out awkwardly. "Start with my ears," she said. "Slowly."

Oscar's grandmother had been like that: soft and commanding at the same time.

After a bit, the lady judge directed Oscar's hands to her shoulders and her breasts and around to her back.

"What you would see, if I undid your blindfold..."

"Please don't," said Oscar quickly.

"I'll be considerate," she said. "But you must let me tell you that my entire torso is covered with an espaliered rose bush. There are sixteen blossoms. My nipples are rose buds. A thorn has punctured the skin on one of my shoulder blades and there is a drop of blood on my bottom where it curves out."

Oscar worked on his composure. "Where are the roots?"

"Use your imagination."

"I'm trying not to. But why did you do this?"

"I come from a very traditional family. My father refused to send me to university. He said my role was to be a wife and mother. So I made myself unfit."

Oscar ran his hand down her side, but he couldn't feel the thorns.

"Jews don't approve of tattooing," she continued.

Oscar knew that but he didn't say so. "So he sent you to university after all?"

"He disowned me. Made it all a lot easier. I moved away, got a job—two jobs, actually—and went to school at night."

She paused, and for the better part of a minute they listened to each other's breathing.

"You can learn a lot in the dark," she said finally.

In the morning, of course, she was gone. She had her own room. She'd untied his blindfold while he was still asleep. He found her at breakfast.

"Did I dream all that?" he said.

"Dream what?" she said.

Miriam had to leave mid-morning, had to return to the city that wasn't New York or Los Angeles. There were so many people around that it was impossible to have a conversation.

"How can I see you again?" he said.

"Can you cope with this?" she said, taking a ballpoint pen from her purse.

"Cope with what?" said Oscar.

She wrote a telephone number on the back of his hand. He didn't recognize the area code. When he looked up she was gone.

He waited a week to call her, out of self-respect. The number turned out to be her home so first try he got the

IMPROVISATION

answering machine. "I'm out," it said. "And the cat won't answer the phone. Or if she does, she never tells me who called. So leave your name and number, and if I don't know you, tell me briefly who you are, which will increase the odds of my calling you back. Sorry to be rude. Click."

"I thought you liked rude," said Oscar when they finally connected.

"I do, but most people don't. Why didn't you leave a message?"

"I wasn't feeling clever enough," said Oscar.

"Boston," said Miriam.

"What?"

"Cambridge, actually. I want to go to the Harvard bookstore. It's a three-minute walk from the Charles Hotel."

"It's called the Coop."

"You would know that, wouldn't you?"

"It stands for 'cooperative.'"

"Even I know that," said Miriam.

"So why don't you just call it the 'Coop'? Are you concerned that people will think you are pretending to have gone to Harvard?"

"Bingo." Pause. "You were a pretty good lover, by the way."

Oscar didn't see how she could possibly think that. "So are you," he said.

"Wrong," said Miriam. "I am a magician."

"Weekend after next?" said Oscar, who was beginning to see how the game was played.

"I think you should wait a little longer than that. Fifteenth of next month. And think about tattoos." Click.

Oscar couldn't decide whether he was elated to have such an inventive lover or annoyed at being so easily manipulated. If Miriam was a magician, which in some respects he had to agree she was, presumably she could enchant anyone she wanted, and she'd chosen him. On the other hand, she was better at the game they were playing and Oscar disliked contests he was unlikely to win.

Another week into the month she was making him wait, it occurred to Oscar that Miriam was likely to insist he look at her tattoo, even if only for a minute. He had to be able to do that. Presumably that was the hint she had given him. So he went to a newsstand and bought one of those awful magazines. Or in fact two of them.

Just having the magazines in his apartment was unsettling. The newsstand vendor had put them in a paper bag and Oscar left them there. He put the package in a dresser drawer. He moved his socks around to cover it, as if it needed to be weighted down or it would fly out of the drawer at night and shout "Boo!" at him.

Oscar sat in his living room and thought about roses. When ballerinas are given a bunch of them during the ovation, all the thorns have been cut off, which if you think about it neuters the roses. Getting a tattoo involves letting a needle go a little way into you over and over again. What if at the end of a performance a tattooist came on stage and they held the ballerina down as he did a rose on the inside of her arm. That would only happen if the performance had been extraordinary—maybe once or twice in a dancer's whole career. Maybe never. The audience would gasp when the tattooist came on stage in jeans and a two-day beard because they were about to witness something rare and exciting. The ballerina would turn pale. She had desired and feared this moment all her life. How much would it hurt? Ballet is a life of pain but this was different. The needle. Could she run away?

IMPROVISATION

Whoosh, said Oscar to himself. Where did all that come from?

In the event, he forgot about the magazines, the fifteenth arrived, he went to the Charles Hotel in Cambridge, which was full of hopeful parents bringing their brilliant children to Mecca, and she didn't take her clothes off. She made him undress as soon as he arrived on Friday night, and drew on him with a felt-tipped marker pen: stars all over his chest and belly.

"Will this come off?" he said.

"Over time," she said.

"How can I go to the gym?"

"With aplomb," she said.

"My partners wouldn't understand."

"You have partners other than me?" she said in mock outrage.

"Law partners," he said.

"I suppose that makes me your outlaw partner," she said.

"Partners in crime," he said.

"No, sweetheart. I'm a criminal but you're an innocent."

For some reason this statement inflamed Oscar, a reaction that was immediately evident.

"I think you may be ready," said Miriam, "in another month."

"Oh God," said Oscar.

"Yes, I think I've found out how to please you. What buttons to push." She touched one star after another with her index finger. "I do like the way you fit into your skin," she said. "Now you get dressed and we will go downstairs to dinner."

Most of what she did that weekend was teach him to accept uncertainty. She stretched out dinner. She required him to be passive. She had a more professional blindfold. He said he'd preferred her improvisation. "This one won't come off in the night," she said. "I want you to be disoriented when you wake up."

He was. He wasn't sure where he was. "I'm ordering breakfast," she said.

"We didn't make love," he said.

"This isn't about love," she said. "I am giving you the most intense sexual experience you have ever had in your life."

"Why?"

"Because I can."

It was true, as she had told him in the middle of the night, that his desire to be touched, which she did very softly, at irregular intervals, was taking over his brain. "When can I take this off?"

"I have nothing on," she said. She came up next to the bed and pressed her body against his back to prove it.

"I thought the waiter just came in with breakfast."

"He did."

"And his reaction was?"

"Good-looking middle-aged lady in a bathrobe that's too big for her, but what is she doing to the dude with the stars on his chest?"

Oscar had to laugh.

"You put on a hotel robe?"

"Of course I put on a robe. Now come eat breakfast." She held his hand and led him to a chair at the room service table.

"I don't get a robe?"

"I want to admire my handiwork."

"It's cold."

"I like a man with goose bumps."

"How am I supposed to eat when I can't see the food?"

"Focus on the texture."

Oscar felt around cautiously and found a muffin, which he unwrapped and nibbled at, finding mushy blueberries. Locating the orange juice was more hazardous but he accomplished that as well. It hadn't been strained.

"This is a metaphor for human relationships," said Miriam. "Most of us have no idea what we are doing. We are hungry, so we eat whatever we find. The trick is to know what you want, really, and then of course to get it."

"Harder when you can't see," said Oscar.

"We're all blind," said Miriam. "We all pretend. If I ever stop bossing you around you will see how vulnerable I am. You ordered scrambled eggs, I think. Do you still want them?"

Vulnerable? "Yes, I do. And I'm ravenous."

"Ravenous is a good quality in a man. When I was nineteen I hooked up with a truck driver. I was living in Jersey City at the time, where he delivered things that were manufactured in the middle of the country somewhere. He lived in East St. Louis, which is not a nice town, he told me. When he'd delivered his load he'd come up and see me in my fourth floor walk-up. I'd dribble honey on myself and he'd lick it off."

"Why in the world?"

"He liked honey. He was hungry after driving sixteen hours."

"Wasn't it sticky? Didn't he find it gross? Didn't you?"

"The line between gross and sensual is a matter of fine judgment. My girlfriend Judy loved it when she saw a big truck parked in front of my building. She'd say to herself, 'Miriam's getting sticky,' and get quite excited."

"Your friend Judy told you this."

"Girls are shameless."

"Really?" said Oscar.

"Not with men," said Miriam. "You have to pretend with men, as I've told you. My other girlfriend, Rosie—we shared the apartment and went to night school together—she said she could never eat honey again."

"You told her?"

"Of course. I needed her to stay out for a few hours. She claimed to be horrified, but you know what? Whenever she saw that big truck parked in front of our building, she somehow managed to think of something she'd forgotten and had to pop into the apartment to get it. Anyway, I'm going to put your scrambled eggs exactly where you'd expect and you can eat them without silverware."

"You *are* making this up, aren't you?"

"Why should I lie?"

Miriam led him back to the bed. There was the sensation of Miriam getting onto the bed beside him, then the sound of a spoon being scraped on a plate and the plate being set on the bedside table.

"Get them while they're still warm," said Miriam.

"This is gross," said Oscar.

"OK, I'll go take a shower," said Miriam. She started to sit up.

"Wait," said Oscar.

"See," said Miriam.

After breakfast—or it was brunch, really—they went to the Harvard Coop. Miriam bought sixteen books. Oscar bought three. "Where I live, there are no decent bookstores any more," she said.

"Where do you live, by the way," said Oscar.

"The scrambled eggs were too much, weren't they?"

"No, that was fine," he said.

"We should go somewhere formal for dinner."

"To balance the adventure with the scrambled eggs."

"You're catching on."

"I was thinking conventional intercourse would be a good way of achieving balance—aesthetically, that is." Oscar was quite pleased with that sentence. Miriam made sex less abnormal.

"What you have to decide," said Miriam, as they waited for the traffic light, "is which is more intense: the pleasure of fucking me or the pleasure of being made to wait."

"I think there needs to be a balance."

"It's always a matter of judgment," said Miriam, "but I think you need to wait. And maybe I do too. This afternoon, we'll read our new books."

"I will find that difficult."

"Go to the gym, then. Or visit the Episcopalian monastery down the road. Cowley fathers. Very intellectual crowd."

"I'm already an intellectual," said Oscar with slight exasperation. "Look at the fucking books I bought."

"They are not *fucking* books. They are collections of political and philosophical essays. I think they look quite interesting."

"Where *do* you come from?"

"If you didn't look up the area code you don't really want to know."

Oscar thought about that. They were back in the hotel room. "Perhaps I should just go back to New York," he said.

"Please don't," said Miriam in an unexpectedly plaintive tone. "We've come all this way." She took a deep breath. "What you should do, my sweet, is go talk to the concierge and make us a reservation at the starchiest restaurant in Boston. Then you should exercise—violently, if you can manage it. Then you should take a nap. You are showing all the signs of being sleep deprived. After dinner I will blindfold you again and we will snuggle in bed. We might leave it at that. I am certain the eggs were a mistake."

"Did you really live in Jersey City?"

"That isn't the half of it. Now go talk to the concierge."

It came to Oscar, who was indeed an intellectual, as he was waiting for the concierge to finish telling a family of four how to get to Old North Church, that what he found most erotic was things he didn't know, things he couldn't see. What was happening on the other side of a bedroom door? What did a willingness to be tattooed say about a person's openness to other experiences? What was Miriam about to do to a blindfolded Oscar? What was Miriam really thinking? She did seem to like him.

"Have you thought about tattoos?" she asked over the oysters.

He told her about the magazines still prisoner in his dresser drawer.

"You have to spend time with them. How can you expect me to do what you want if you won't do what I want?"

"You want me to prepare myself for your espaliered rose bush?"

"That would be nice of you. There's nothing I can do about it, you know."

"OK," said Oscar, though he wasn't sure what he meant by that.

"You may assume," said Miriam, "that a girl who foolishly allowed the best tattooist in New Jersey—it's illegal in New York, as you probably know—who allowed Tony the Needle to work his magic on her will have a *number* of things she needs to hide from an inquiring world."

IMPROVISATION

"Worse than Jersey City," said Oscar.

"Bingo," said Miriam. "If you can overcome your fear of my tattoos, perhaps you can accept the things about me I will *never* tell you."

"Ah."

"And if you are willing to endure an agony of waiting, which I inflict on you with loving care, perhaps you will be able to get past the hurts I know I will inflict on you unintentionally."

"So this isn't just a game?"

"No," said Miriam. "I have to know I can trust you with my heart."

They concentrated on their oysters for a bit, and then they talked about the books they had bought, about the one she had started to read, the one he planned to read first when he got to it, how wise she had been to make him take a nap, how nice it had been to fall asleep as she sat across the room reading.

"I'll bet you are rude to your law partners," she said. "And it's partly that you're sleep deprived. You should take power naps."

"Our offices all have glass front walls." He hadn't told her about being rude.

"You could get a big chair and put its back to the glass. And tell your secretary not to let anyone in. You can't be doing yourself any favors being rude, no matter how eminent you become."

"Umm," said Oscar.

He wasn't rude to Alice. They'd seen each other naked in the gym. It made rudeness seem foolish, somehow. And anyway, she was nice to him, solved problems for him, got him a bigger office.

He wasn't rude to Henry either, though that was because Henry could throw him out of the firm if he chose to, which was an awful thought because being a partner of the firm was the foundation of Oscar's carefully erected self-esteem. Oscar didn't like Henry one little bit, but he didn't let that influence his behavior. Fact was, he was careful to not even look at Henry in the shower room. Henry reminded Oscar of the bullies in grade school. To be honest about it, Henry just plain frightened Oscar—which was why he never complained about his partnership distribution, even though it should probably be larger, given the business he brought in.

"I'm not rude," said Oscar.

"I'm a judge," said Miriam. "Remember?"

"Umm," said Oscar.

After dinner everything happened exactly as she had promised—the blindfold, unconstrained kissing, tickling each other's ears, nothing beyond that—but with the added detail that she wanted to be touching as they fell asleep. "Just a hand," she'd said. "Even a foot."

He'd rolled toward her and put his arm around her shoulder. She was smaller than she seemed. "Lion-hearted Miriam," he'd said to himself. Or maybe he'd said it to her. Couldn't remember. She was breathing steadily already. They slept for more than nine hours.

"Cincinnati?" she said as they parted at the airport. "Four weekends from now?"

"Whatever you desire," he said, feeling strangely chivalrous.

The magazines stayed in their drawer for the first few nights. Oscar needed to let his libido calm down. His libido was not cooperative. He went and got one of the magazines. It wasn't quite as horrific as they had become in his imagination. He assumed the other magazine was worse. The monster is always around the corner, he said to himself. That was possibly an insight.

The other magazine *was* worse. The photographs were more natural. The girls seemed relaxed about their violation.

Oscar was not relaxed. How would he do with the rose bush? Would it be easier to contemplate than Valkyries with swords on a woman's thighs? Or would the beauty of roses and the quiet menace of their thorns be harder to confront?

Miriam called. "How are you doing, sweetie?" It hadn't occurred to him that they were allowed to talk between visits.

"I've looked at the magazines," he said.

"What other punishments have you imposed upon yourself?" she asked.

"One of my partners is marrying the librarian. Or *a* librarian. We had two. This one got fired so he's marrying her. I was in the middle of explaining to myself that he was an idiot when I started to get quite sentimental about the whole thing."

"Umm. What was the punishment—and more importantly what was the crime?"

"I don't know, but it affected me. I thought I should tell you."

"Thank you for telling me."

For a long minute neither of them spoke. "How's your cat?" he said finally.

"Skeptical," said Miriam.

"About what?"

"The nature of reality."

"Let me know if she has an intellectual breakthrough."

"Are you reading those essays you bought in Cambridge?"

"I can't seem to concentrate."

"Which is your favorite tattoo?"

"The one you haven't let me see."

"Haven't *made* you see," she corrected. Click.

Cincinnati Friday, as he'd taken to calling it, finally arrived. He had gotten very tired of the magazines. He'd thrown them out, in fact. Down the garbage chute to where they would be burned. Burning seemed like a good ending for them. They were totems, receptacles of magic, though sad and diminished from overuse. The only honorable end was ashes.

It occurred to Oscar on the flight to Cincinnati that he himself was a receptacle of magic. Or beneficiary. This lady judge he'd come to know had woven a spell. He wanted to see her. He was willing to admit to himself that he wanted to see her, which for Oscar was quite an advance. He hadn't asked a woman out for almost ten years when she picked him up at that conference. He'd told himself he was too busy, but the honest answer was fear of rejection. He wondered if Miriam would kiss him when he arrived.

The prospect of arrival allowed Oscar's brain finally to remind him that he had no idea what hotel to go to. He'd have to call her. He had her mobile number now. She'd used it to call him and he'd retrieved the number.

She met him when he came through the door that said, "No Return to Air Side." He took a deep breath when he saw her. "Thank you for meeting me," he said. She didn't kiss him. "I realized you hadn't told me what hotel to go to, and by the way, why are we in Cincinnati?"

"It's a rich and cultured community, built on the banks of a mighty river. Calls itself the 'Queen City.' Also, I live here."

"Why?"

"Moved here when my father threw me out. Never left."

"Why'd you choose Cincinnati?"

"You'll laugh."

"Try me," he said. They got into her car.

"When I was trying to decide what I'd do after college, I read the travel section of the *New York Times* a lot. I read an article about Cincinnati, from which I learned that Proctor & Gamble has its headquarters here because in the nineteenth century it was a good place to make soap because there was a lot of lard because it was a hog market, and I liked that factoid, and decided a hog market that made soap was a good place for a Jewish girl to wash off her past."

"Did it work?"

"Well, I'm a judge. But you can never wash off your past."

"How'd you get to be a judge?"

"Went to law school. Here in Cincinnati. Needed a job. Didn't think I'd fit in in a law firm so I went to work in the U.S. Attorney's office. Did some good work."

Oscar was watching Cincinnati go by and was mostly saying "mmm," which must have gotten on Miriam's nerves.

"You do realize I'm quite a famous judge, don't you?"

"Are you?"

She mentioned a long-running trial whose name he did recall.

"You tried it? Yes, I remember. The judge was a woman."

"I'm that woman. I was on television about twenty times. There were lots of protests and demonstrations. At one point they decided I had to have a policeman outside my apartment building. My decision was appealed, and affirmed, and then taken to the Supreme Court and affirmed again. You didn't go to my panel, did you?"

"I'm sorry but I didn't. I didn't know you then. We met the next day, remember? I don't go to many of the presentations at those conferences. I have nothing to learn. My field is narrow. They send me to conferences so people will listen to me, so I can be famous, so we will get more business. But you know all that." There was some bitterness in his voice. "You are a judge. You are an expert at human folly. Are we going to your apartment? And why in the world did you listen to my panel."

"Your field is growing in importance. As a judge I might need to know about it. And, yes, we're going to my apartment. I thought you should see it, try it out."

"Is there still a policeman?"

"Not any more. The Supreme Court decision was five years ago. The people who were angry with me don't seem to be angry any more."

"I'm sorry I didn't know who you are."

"Nothing to apologize for. I liked being anonymous. Gave me more freedom."

There was only one bedroom. She told him to put his suitcase in it and come back to the living area. She had a lot of paintings. The cat was a tortoise-shell. He was very anxious. Oscar, that is. The cat was cool.

"Sit down," she said. "I would give you a drink but it deadens the senses, and I like awakening yours."

Oscar didn't know what to say. He knew she was going to undress pretty soon and he wasn't sure he'd handle that well.

"What is it?" she said.

"I've been thinking," he said. "As instructed."

"Thank you," said Miriam.

"The monster around the corner."

"Yes."

"That's what I fear. What I can't see. Tattoos represent that."

"What you can't see? That doesn't make sense. It is seeing them that seems to trouble you."

"The monster around the corner," Oscar repeated. "It's a manner of speaking. It's a metaphor. I feel like a four-year-old." He stretched to let off some nervousness. "The corner of a woman is below the fuzzy bit. Tattoos call it to mind."

"I knew the scrambled eggs were a mistake."

"Not at all. I was blindfolded, remember. And I was able to concentrate on *texture*, as you suggested, which helped me escape my logical, rational, deeply unhelpful brain. And I began to find the rhythm that gave you pleasure. For all of which I am grateful, because—and despite the nice things you have said to me—I am not sure I have ever given much pleasure to anyone before, in bed or elsewhere. So the tattoos are my friends, even if they terrify me. I didn't mean to say all that right away."

"You sit right there," said Miriam. She went into the bedroom for a couple of minutes. "Close your eyes," she called out. Oscar obeyed. "Now open them."

She had no tattoos, front or back. She turned around slowly to show him. Her body was lovelier than he had imagined it. He'd read somewhere that age is kinder to bodies than to faces, but he hadn't collected a lot of evidence.

"You never lived in Jersey City, did you?" said Oscar.

"Metaphor," said Miriam.

"And your father never threw you out."

"Is it OK that I am not the embodiment of what you fear?" she said.

"I guess so. You took me into an enchanted forest, I'll say that."

She came over to him and started to undo his necktie, a task with which he proved unable to help her. "Elves and dragons," he said.

"It's all right," she said. "You are stepping from fantasy into reality. That is always a frightening passage. Fantasy we can control. Reality is more intractable. Now sit down and take your shoes off. You can lie on the bed with your clothes on if you want, but I don't want to get marks on the spread."

"I can undress myself," said Oscar. "I've just always been blindfolded before."

"Would you like to be blindfolded again? I can be what you imagine rather than what I am, at least for a while."

"I like looking at you."

He finished undressing and they got under the covers. He kissed her in a fumbling fashion, with his eyes open. "That's very sweet," she said, "but you are terrified. Let's go back to make-believe for a while. It's safer than real emotion."

Oscar would have disputed several of these assertions but he recognized that everything she said was true.

"Would you like to draw on me?" she said.

"I would," said Oscar, shocking himself.

Miriam opened the drawer of her bedside table and took out a collection of marker pens.

"You were ready for this?" said Oscar.

"Blue, I think," said Miriam, putting the others back in the drawer. "That was the color of the underwear I had on the night we met."

"Which my subconscious extrapolated into tattoos," said Oscar.

"Which are symbolic of feminine reality," said Miriam, "That's my euphemism. Yours is 'the bit below the fuzzy bit.' Which at some level horrifies you."

"Why?" said Oscar

"Men are afraid of women. We have powerful magic. Doesn't matter. It didn't get in the way of your performance the first night. Or with the scrambled eggs."

"Or prevent me from desiring you for the past two months," said Oscar.

"Roll over, sweetie," said Miriam. "I'll go first and get you in the mood." She began to make marks on his back. "Broad shoulders," she said. "As I've told you before, you have a fabulous body."

"Now that I've seen all of you, I can return the compliment. What are you drawing?"

"I'm writing," actually. "On a scroll. Which goes right across your broad shoulders. You may have to stay out of the gym until is fades completely. Unless of course you've lost your inhibitions about sex. You didn't go, did you, with the stars."

"To the gym, no. I wasn't prepared for the questions it would provoke. I didn't have a clever enough answer."

"I suppose your firm's gym would be a jungle of clever answers."

"I will have to tell you about it, but not just now," said Oscar.

"Now come look in the mirror." She led him into the bathroom. "Look over your shoulder."

"gnihtyalp dna evals s'mairiM ma I," said the mirror, but with the letters reversed.

"I forgot about that," she said.

Oscar decoded the message slowly: "'I am . . . Miriam's . . . slave and . . . plaything.' Oh, you are an evil woman."

"At your service," she said.

"My turn," said Oscar. "No, on your belly. Your front I will deal with in another fashion."

"Yes please."

Oscar labored away for several minutes.

"You can't tell me you are trying to write backwards," said Miriam. "It can't be done, or not without making mistakes."

"When I was in the seventh grade," said Oscar, "I got a perfect score in geography. Every test, all year, including free-hand maps. The teacher said she hadn't believed that could be done. But I did it."

"What was your secret?"

"A large and empty brain," said Oscar. "I absorbed so many useless facts when I was eleven that some of what I learned is still stuck in there: the capitals of all the states that aren't the cities you expect, like Salem, Oregon and Lansing, Michigan and Augusta, Maine."

"Weren't those always compromises between the two biggest towns?"

"Some were, like Columbus here in Ohio. But I didn't do enough history to know all the answers."

Miriam sighed. "One can never know all the answers," she said.

"You seem to know a lot," said Oscar.

Miriam ignored that. "Do any of the states have invented cities—like Washington or Brasilia or Canberra?"

"Don't think so. Oklahoma City maybe." He continued to concentrate on writing backwards.

"Invented cities are a mistake," said Miriam. "They separate the bureaucrats from reality. Now, London, that's a proper capital—with finance and the arts and outrageous newspapers and lawyers who are more than lobbyists . . ."

"Stop moving."

They both were silent for a few minutes.

Improvisation

"So as a believer in reality," said Oscar, "how did you decide to tell me you had a tattoo?"

"I didn't decide. I just did. Love is an improvisation."

"We're going to have love as well as sex?" She'd told him that already, actually.

"If it wouldn't be too much trouble," said Miriam.

Oscar pretended to be concentrating on his work. "Are you as lonely as I am?" he said finally.

"More, I'll bet."

"But you picked me up rather than anyone else?"

"I've never done anything remotely like that before. I'm famous, remember. And a judge. I have to be enormously careful."

"You said you liked confident men, but I'm not, you know."

"That's why I said what I said."

"My lady of riddles." He kissed her shoulder. "Everything you say makes sense, actually."

"I make it up as I go along—subject to certain ethical limits, of course."

"Of course," he said. "Now come see what I have written."

"I'm afraid," said Miriam.

She hopped off the bed, marched into her bathroom alone and shut the door. Oscar sat in the bed feeling very naked. She was in there quite a while, which filled him with anxiety. He thought about the long sentence he had written on Miriam's back: "Oscar is my devoted knight and shields me from all harm."

The door of the bathroom opened and she came to him. "I have a lot of dragons for you to slay," she said. "Monsters I haven't even hinted at." Her voice caught. "Sorry, I can't seem to hold it together all of a sudden. We need to spend about ten years getting to know each other. So I hope you like my cat." She wiped her eyes. "I wanted to stop crying before I came out," she said, "but I can't seem to."

"Maybe we should get back under the covers," said Oscar.

"Good plan," said Miriam.

Millie's Career

When Millie got a call from Henry's secretary, telling her to come to the senior partner's office right away, she decided she'd better take the stairs. Always burn off a little adrenalin, she'd been taught by her father—a career Army officer who'd won the Distinguished Service Cross, which is quite an impressive medal, but retired as a lieutenant colonel, which was only OK. Both outcomes resulted from features of his personality he'd passed on to his non-conforming daughter. You can't get a DSC without being a little bit crazy, he liked to say to Millie's mother when he'd transgressed, and you can't get past "telephone colonel" without kissing ass.

This was an old joke. If you were a lieutenant colonel you were called, and were permitted to call yourself, colonel, which sometimes got you a bit more deference from someone who couldn't *see* your rank. Millie's father had been known to *identify* himself as a "telephone colonel." It was his way of saying that he was above such games.

Millie had kissed Henry once, and not metaphorically— sort of on a dare she'd made with herself but also because she found him quite attractive. Underneath the senior partner's perfect manners and pantomime incompetence at the copying machine, there was something hard and honest that the daughter of an infantry officer could only admire. Profoundly stupid behavior on her part, though, even if there'd been a kind of excuse.

After that episode she'd kept her head down and learned to be a pretty good lawyer, staying at a firm where she would never be a partner because it was "a good outfit," as her father would have put it. She figured she'd let God take care of her career, which had also been her father's approach. Now God had summoned her and while common sense told her she was going to get "the message"—we like you, Millie but it's time to find another home—there was something on the horizon of her consciousness that said otherwise. Seeing Henry in the hall the previous day, maybe. He hadn't adopted that look boys got when they needed to break up with you even though you were "terrific" and "fun to be with" and the other bullshit with which they casually ruined your weekend.

Millie was out of breath when she got to Henry's office, which she did not trouble to disguise. Veronica waved her in right away. Henry's was the only office in the firm that didn't have a glass front wall. Alice turned out to be there, which increased Millie's apprehension. Alice was "managing partner," which meant Henry's problem-solver. They appeared to be discussing a problem, but it didn't seem to be Millie, which was encouraging.

"Sorry, Millie," said Henry. "Please sit down."

Alice looked agitated, as if Millie's arrival had interrupted her, so Millie offered to wait outside, but Henry motioned her to a chair and Alice kept on with whatever they had been talking about before Millie's arrival.

"Henry, you have to get involved," she said. "I cannot do this on my own. You are our senior partner. Their senior partner is involved."

"*Protocol* requires it?" said Henry. Whatever the two of them were discussing, Henry seemed to want to keep his distance.

Alice turned to Millie as if appealing for her support. "Do you know Joe Phillips?" she said.

Millie did but only vaguely. There were a lot of associates. You couldn't know them all. And Joe was married. His wife worked for one of those flashy, politically connected firms that did criminal defense work and represented some celebrities. Their senior partner had received a lot of notice for a case he'd run when he was in the District Attorney's office, and then he'd been deputy mayor, and now there was a rumor he might run for Lieutenant Governor. You'd see his picture in the paper or his face on TV every so often. Good-looking guy. Unmarried. Probably an asshole. Why would someone want to live in Albany unless he was an egomaniac. Millie had never met Joe's wife.

All these thoughts took approximately three-quarters of a second. "Situational awareness," Millie's father called it.

"I think I'd recognize him," said Millie, "but I can't say we know each other."

"He's a very nice young man," said Henry.

"He's in jail," said Alice.

Millie wasn't sure how to respond.

"He's charged with murdering his wife," said Henry. "Alice was just filling me in."

Alice told the backstory, evidently for the second time, pacing up and down on Henry's carpet.

It continued to be unclear why Millie needed to be there. She had been told by more sophisticated contemporaries that the trick in such situations was to act like you *belonged* in the room. If you could do that well enough, people would conclude that you did belong there. Which was half the battle. The other half was getting them to accept your point of view. But getting them to accept your presence came first, was subtler, and required a form of self-belief that Millie had been taught by her father to regard as pretense.

It seemed that Joe and his wife had an understanding that unless there was a crisis at work they would both be home by eight o'clock, and have dinner together "like normal people," as Joe evidently put it. Alice had gone to see him in jail.

"Most nights, though," said Alice, "there seemed to be a reason Mrs. Joe, whose name is Abigail, or *was* Abigail, couldn't leave the office on time, so Joe was the one who stopped off to buy the take-out, or as it happened on the night in question, some groceries. Joe seems to have been very patient about this but he was getting angry about it— anger he didn't acknowledge to himself, I would guess, which as I'm sure you know, Millie, is dangerous stuff. The 'crisis' making Abigail late too often seemed a bit trivial."

"Her senior partner often needed to speak to her at the end of the day," said Henry, with a look that suggested this was not the way senior partners ought to behave.

"Michelangelo Forrest," said Alice.

"I thought his name was Mike," interrupted Millie.

"It is when he runs for office," said Henry. "Alice calls him 'Michelangelo' because she likes him."

"I call him that to keep him at a distance," said Alice. "But to continue, on the night in question, poor Joe decides to suppress his anger by cooking dinner, so he is in the kitchen pounding pieces of veal with a wooden mallet in order to make schnitzel. Abigail arrives about eight-thirty, wanting to tell Joe some City Hall gossip Michelangelo has told her, so she comes into the kitchen, pours herself a glass of wine without offering to do the same for Joe, sits down on the ledge at the base of the kitchen's large casement windows and goes into a monologue populated with people Joe has never heard of without bothering to say, sorry I'm late, aren't you sweet to be cooking, I'll make it up to you, would you like to fuck me before dinner, or any of the things a woman who has tried a man's patience ought to be smart enough to say, and Joe loses his cool. He has an overwhelming need to make her stop talking, or so he said. He's got this heavy wooden mallet in his hand so he takes a swing past her shoulder to smash one of the windows . . ."

"Not an ideal way of making his point," said Henry.

"But understandable," replied Millie. Her father had been a case study in unacknowledged anger. How had Alice known that? Or did she assume Millie herself was angry? Maybe she was. She wore some pretty aggressive clothes sometimes—high boots, short skirts, a sundress one Friday in July.

"Unfortunately," Alice continued, "Abigail thinks he's aiming for her—presumably she was a little bit guilty about being late so often—tries to get out of the way, falls back against this big open-out window, which is already half-open because that's how they ventilate their tiny New York apartment kitchen, and dies on impact in the courtyard eight stories below, still holding onto the wine glass."

For a moment, none of them spoke, and then Alice continued, not the story exactly, but the debate she had evidently been having with Henry before Millie came in.

"So, you see," said Alice.

"Tell me again, Alice, why is Mike Forrest involved?"

"He was sleeping with Joe's wife."

"How do we know that?" said Henry.

"I know the man," said Alice. "I went out with him once. 'Once' as in only once. He does not like to waste time on courting rituals, as he calls them. He would not have been asking Abigail to see him at six o'clock every other evening because he needed briefings."

"So, go on," said Henry.

"Well, here we get to the part where Joe was a bit stupid."

Anger can do that, Millie reminded herself. She'd lost a few friends over the years, over issues of principle that if she was honest were really just a matter of hurt feelings.

"When Joe sees what he's done," Alice continued, "he doesn't call either you or me or his brother in Boston or even the police. He opens Abigail's purse, which is still sitting on the floor under the window, takes out her mobile phone and calls Mr. Forrest the famous prosecutor, whose number is on Abigail's speed dial, and tells him he's murdered his wife, which of course he hasn't, and he needs help."

"He never touched her," said Henry, "either with his hand or with the mallet?"

"No."

"Guilt is very bad for a person's judgment," said Henry.

"So Mike tells Joe to go sit in the living room," said Alice, "and not touch anything, which Joe obediently does. After he's had half an hour to brood on what has happened, Mike shows up with a couple of policemen and has Joe arrested, explaining it all to the officers, which Joe confirms with a tearful confession right there in the living room."

"And he lets Joe spend the night in jail?" asks Henry.

"And calls me in the morning," says Alice, "all full of helpfulness and concern."

"So he wants to defend our Joe," says Henry. "Why?"

"For the publicity," says Alice. "Everything will come out. A famous prosecutor undertakes the defense of the man who's killed his mistress. Imagine the headlines."

"But the mistress was Joe's wife," said Henry.

Millie spoke, somewhat to her surprise: "That will just make Joe look guiltier."

"Won't . . . Michelangelo be embarrassed?" said Henry.

"No shame," said Alice. "And the really ugly part is, from a fame and fortune perspective, it won't matter to Mike Forrest whether he wins the case or loses."

For perhaps ten seconds none of them spoke. "So we are in the presence of evil," said Henry.

"Thank you," said Alice.

"So . . . why am I here?" said Millie.

"Reconnaissance," said Henry. "Sit down, Alice. You're making Millie nervous."

Millie considered contradicting him but thought better of it. She'd been getting marginally less impulsive in the past year. She hoped that represented maturity rather than defeat. "None but the brave deserve the fair," had been her father's motto. Deserve perhaps, achieve perhaps not—which was her mother's view.

"Your Michelangelo called me last week," said Henry, addressing Alice.

"He's not my anything," said Alice.

"Bad joke," said Henry. "Apologies. In any case he called me and asked if we were 'shedding' any associates."

"So that's why I'm here," said Millie.

"Yes and no," said Henry.

"Tell me about the 'no,'" said Millie.

"Let's do the 'yes' part first," said Henry in a not unkindly tone. Alice sat on the sofa saying nothing, evidently lost in her own thoughts. It was as if Henry and Millie were alone.

"'We're getting a bit of corporate work,' Mike said," Henry went on. "'Some of the individuals we represent own private companies. And of course there are a few'—these are his words—'there are a few corporate clients whose chief executives are star-fuckers'—you'll pardon me for using his language, Millie, but it gives you a better feel for the situation—'people who come to us because of our entertainment practice. Anyway, I won't pretend we can generate good corporate lawyers—or anywhere near as well trained as yours are. So if there are any of those nice young men who won't be making partner, I'd be happy to interview them. Bit of style would be useful, but what I'm after mostly is good brains and good training. So a brilliant workaholic nerd would be OK.'"

There was a pause. Alice looked up, demonstrating that she had been listening after all.

"Not that we think . . ." Henry continued.

"No one," said Alice firmly, "would confuse Millie with a nerd."

There was another pause, during which Millie's brain did its annoying trick of getting to the punch line before the joke was half-finished. "You want me to fuck him," said Millie.

"Not exactly," said Henry.

"You had Veronica call me upstairs because it was time to fire me and while I was on the way you thought of a different way to have me screwed."

"No," said Henry. "There's no reason you have to leave for a couple of years . . ."

"Or ever," interjected Alice.

"I'm just trying to be realistic," said Millie softly, her reservoir of unacknowledged anger having been temporarily drained.

"So am I," said Henry, also softly. "You may remember that we passed in the hall a few days ago."

"You smiled," said Millie.

"I had just spoken to Mr. Michelangelo Forrest and was thinking about his statement that he would prefer an associate with style. I thought he might like you. Very few of our associates get to stay. I try to think about what comes next, at least for those I have come to know. I didn't know until this morning about Mr. Forrest's involvement with Joe and Abigail Phillips. I would not now feel right about sending you to him permanently, but Alice has suggested to me that by going for an interview you might learn something that would be helpful to Joe."

"We can make it a lunch," said Alice quickly. "Just get him talking. See what you can learn. See what your instincts tell you."

"If it doesn't frighten you to meet him," said Henry slowly, "it will probably prove useful to have done so. He is mildly famous. Clients will ask you if you know him. They ask that sort of question." Henry looked to Alice for confirmation but she was looking out the window.

"More importantly," Henry continued, "Mike Forrest is a very good example of a different kind of lawyer. He has a different style than you will have become familiar with, working here. He is not to my taste, nor evidently to Alice's, but his firm is very successful, he is only in his mid-forties and he will be around for a long time. As you get a little more senior you will find it helps to know your adversaries. We haven't asked you to handle a matter on your own very often yet, but..."

"Listen," said Millie, suddenly feeling the need to take command, "I know what this will be like. I know how to do this. I grew up in towns full of soldiers. I know how to flirt. I know when to leave a bar. I can't seem to hang onto a man but I definitely know how their brains work.

"Mike Forrest will think the firm has sent him an early Christmas present. The fact that Henry has sent me will be much more important than me. He called and asked Henry for someone from the discard pile. I take it he hadn't done that before. Even a man with his sense of self-importance would have thought about it before he made that call. He will regard me as a message that Henry believes the two firms can work together on a broader basis. We do things they cannot do and vice versa. They accumulate clients a few of whom we might like to serve, though we'd never know how to pursue their business. Our reputation and their growth rate."

Henry started to protest but Millie wouldn't let him. "I'm not describing reality, Henry. I'm describing the visions he will see when I show up." Pause. "He will take it as evidence—I do apologize for saying this—as evidence that Henry is the sort of man he himself is, that a pretty girl who describes herself as Henry's... 'acolyte' has been offered to him. He will see it as a bonding gesture, like an investment banker lending a client his Ferrari. And because that gesture will have dispelled whatever niggling anxiety calling Henry had left him with, he will be gratifyingly horny."

Millie stopped.

"Are you a Ferrari, Millie?" asked Henry.

"I wouldn't have thought so," said Millie, "but I can do a plausible imitation for an afternoon."

No one said anything for a moment. What they were up to was really quite inappropriate. "Let's move," said Millie. Another of her father's phrases.

Henry reached for his phone but Alice intervened. "I'll call him," said Alice. "I can be chilly with him. We'll leave him with that niggling anxiety Millie spoke of. And we'll make Millie a surprise . . . as she suggests."

Veronica came in with Mr. Forrest's telephone number. Alice dialed it from the phone on the table beside the sofa. "Alice O'Malley. No, I'm not angry at you. It's up to Joe who represents him. Look, I'm a bit pressed. Different subject. Henry said you were looking for a corporate associate. I have an idea—I need to compare notes with Henry, of course—but you've got to buy him a good lunch. Tomorrow at the Four Seasons would be fine. Twelve forty-five. I'll have him ask for your table. Yes, right, maybe a drink next week." She hung up.

"Nice," said Millie.

Alice smiled and then got serious again. "Listen, I should warn you. You've probably seen pictures of him, but in person he is even more attractive."

So is the devil man, Millie said to herself. Her grandmother used to say that. And regarding Alice, there was definitely some bonding going on.

"Situational awareness" came to Millie's aid again when she arrived at the Four Seasons. "It's your most important asset on the battlefield," Millie's father had taught her. "Especially in the jungle."

Millie figured the Four Seasons at lunchtime *was* a jungle. There were people she recognized and people pretending not to notice people they obviously knew, waiters being very attentive to certain customers and inexplicably inattentive to others. Underneath the ankle-deep leaf litter of ambition and damaged reputations, there were probably dust mites snubbing each other.

Millie knew—because it was the sort of thing a person knew—that the first room you came into, the Grill Room, was the prestigious place to have lunch. Michelangelo Forrest was in the larger second room. She knew as soon as she saw him exactly what he needed. He needed to be important. Watch over me, grandmother.

"How much time do we have?" she said as soon as she sat down, preventing him from speaking. "Because I need your advice and I don't want to waste time on banter. Oh, and Alice said sorry for switching associates on you but Henry thought I was what you wanted."

"I have all afternoon," said Michelangelo Forrest.

Millie let that pass. "As I'm sure you will quickly realize," she went on, "I am in the wrong firm. I am ambitious in a place that frowns on it. I call Henry 'Henry,' when associates are supposed to address him as Mr. Franklin. I am condemned to reading contracts when what I am good at is reading clues, condemned to writing dull documents when what I am good at is talking . . ."

"So I see."

"And listening," said Millie slowly. And then, "You are an entrepreneur within our ghastly profession, Mr. Forrest. Teach me how you do that."

"Call me Mike."

"Whether or not you want to hire me, I need a mentor." Millie looked down at her napkin for a moment, and then directly at Mike Forrest. He blushed. "I'm sure you have a lot to teach me," said Millie. "Perhaps you'll start by telling me what to order. I'm entirely in your hands."

"How much time do *you* have?"

"All afternoon," said Millie. "Or perhaps only until five. There's a very sweet boy at the office who's taking me out for drinks after work."

"Who's the boy?" said Alice when Millie reported to her the next morning.

"I made him up," said Millie. "I wasn't sure how much of Mike Forrest I wanted to sign up for."

Alice didn't say anything.

"I stood the boy up, if that's your question," said Millie.

"Don't tell Henry," said Alice.

"Different generation?" It occurred to Millie as she spoke that Alice was protecting Henry from knowledge he already had. He projected rectitude, and both of them were conspiring to help him do so.

"Different generation," said Alice and paused. "So how did your reconnaissance go?"

"I asked him about police work. Was it anything like TV? *Interrogations*, for example. I told him my father had done some of that, or had people under him who did, but he'd never wanted to talk about it."

"I can imagine," said Alice.

"Oh, I made that up too. My father just *shot* the bad guys. But Mr. Forrest fancies himself as a prince of the dark side, so I gave him a little catnip.

"Anyway, what he said was that most normal people are scared shitless when they get arrested, and quite a few are so programmed to respect authority that they confess to whatever you suggest—that is, if the interrogator is authoritative enough. He liked that word, 'interrogator.'"

"So what did you get out of him?" said Alice.

"Well, just by coincidence he had an example I might be familiar with."

"Our Joe."

"Indeed. Married to one of his best associates. Joe hadn't probably meant to kill her, but he's confused and feels guilty about losing his temper. In shock, really. So when Mr. Forrest explained to him that he'd pushed his maddening and unfaithful wife out the window, Joe didn't contradict him. So Mr. Forrest explained to him, it will go better if you confess. Judges like that. So Joe signed a statement and is now in custody, as the *Daily News* yesterday informed us all."

"Did Mike say he believed Joe is innocent?"

"Not in so many words, but the story was about his ability to influence Joe and it wouldn't have made the same point if Joe was actually guilty."

"I suppose a good defense attorney could make that obvious in court, always assuming we can get Joe to hire a different defense attorney."

"This matter won't get to court," said Millie.

"Because?"

"Because Mr. Forrest got Joe to confess without anyone reading him his Miranda rights."

"Mike told you that?"

"He did. While he watched me undress. He's just fucking with Joe because he can."

"And—though this is not a consideration for us—as a way of embarrassing our firm, with which he quite stupidly believes himself to be in competition." Alice looked out the window. "What a shit."

"I think Henry said it better," said Millie.

Alice looked blank.

"Pure evil," said Millie.

"So what do we do?" said Alice.

"Oh, that's easy," said Millie, who having no means of burning off excess adrenalin was beginning to shake. "I recorded the conversation. I had a recorder in my purse. Put it under the bed." Millie took a cassette out of her pocket and handed it to Alice. "There's probably enough there to get Mr. Forrest disbarred."

"But how can we use it without damaging your reputation?"

"Different generation," said Millie, letting out a big breath.

There will have to be a moment, her father had told her, after a soldier hops on a live grenade to save his buddies— there will be a moment before it explodes for a person to wonder why he's done what he's done.

Alice put the cassette in the middle of her desk, walked around to where Millie was standing and gave her a hug. "How can we repay you? How can I?"

"Teach me to be a grown-up," said Millie.

Three weeks after the charges against Joe were dropped— with a vague statement from the authorities about a "misunderstanding"—Millie woke up thinking about Michelangelo Forrest. This was not supposed to happen.

Millie's role had never been disclosed. She had carefully extracted from Alice a promise not to tell Joe Phillips what had been done for him, not to tell anyone anything, in fact. She had taken to calling Henry "Mr. Franklin"—as if she had never kissed him and they didn't share a secret. She had "put the matter out of her mind," as her grandmother had so often advised her to do when she'd had a disappointment.

She had further extracted from Alice an admission that no, Millie did not dress like someone who was likely to be a partner of a major New York firm, and they had gone shopping together, to buy Millie a new wardrobe. They had taken a day off to do this, and had a late lunch with a second glass of wine, which entailed some sharing of personal background but—and Millie was proud of this—no discussion of Mike Forrest. Millie had even thrown away the underwear Mike Forrest had enjoyed watching her remove.

So she'd thought she was out of the woods.

But she wasn't. She acknowledged that as soon as she finished waking up and her memories came into focus. He was intelligent. He made her laugh. He had, as Alice had warned her, a restless, dominant cat-like quality that could be mesmerizing. But the thing was, she had seen something in Mike Forrest's face that no one was supposed to see. He was vulnerable—afraid of something. And that had touched her.

Millie attempted to be analytical about this. She knew quite a lot about soldiers. Soldiers had many things they were afraid of, including landmines and sadistic sergeants and the possibility of cowardice. Soldiers employed well-understood strategies for coping with their fear, including beer, bravado and humor. Mike Forrest's strategy was to be a shit—which didn't necessarily mean he *was* a shit. That depended on how badly he'd been *damaged*, to use one of her father's words. But what was he was afraid of?

Situational awareness, said her father's voice in her head. What had she seen in that nanosecond when Mike Forrest lost hold of his defenses? And when had she seen it? They'd been lying in bed after he'd "interviewed" her. He was a skillful interviewer and he knew it. Millie had made sure he knew she appreciated his skill. "I think we should go to Vegas," he'd said. "You won't understand our entertainment practice unless you've seen the place. People wallowing in money." That was presumably a job offer. Or it was supposed to sound like one—a version of "I'll call you in the morning."

"Figuratively wallowing, I trust," she'd said, ignoring the putative job offer. There might have been an edge to her voice. She may have been copying the "superior" tone her grandmother could put on for effect—which was a family joke, even if it unsettled Mike Forrest. Millie didn't like gambling. She'd seen what compulsive gambling could do to a family of four trying to survive on a sergeant's salary.

"Yes, of course," Mike Forrest had said quickly. That's when she'd seen the shimmer of uncertainty cross his face.

What Michelangelo Forrest feared was rejection. That's why he'd adopted the role he had, as shamelessly exploitive, dismissive of other people's feelings. That's how he'd experienced the edge in her voice. I am not the sort of person who goes to Las Vegas, he had heard her saying, even if I am willing occasionally to go to bed with someone who does.

Alice was right. Mike Forrest would have given a lot to be a partner of the firm Millie currently worked for—and which, for that nanosecond, she embodied. He had aspirations. He wanted to be accepted into a club that existed in his head—whose membership, Millie's grandmother would have pointed out, consisted of people who didn't *need* to be grasping because their great-grandfathers had been successful bandits. Mike Forrest would have benefitted from knowing Millie's grandmother, but unfortunately the lady was dead.

Nanosecond? Mike Forrest had said something about "moving a lot" as a child. What she'd seen was a little boy in the playground of a new school, wondering who the bullies would turn out to be, wondering what humiliations would be required. Millie knew a bit about that world. She understood what it might have done to Mike Forrest. She reached for the phone.

He had written his mobile number on the back of his business card and given it to her before she'd left his apartment. "Call when you're ready," he'd said. She'd thrown out the card but remembered the number.

"Mike Forrest," he said. It was six thirty on a Sunday morning.

"Can you talk?" said Millie.

"Sometimes I talk too much." He'd recognized her voice.

"Do you want to fuck me again?" she said. No superior tone.

"Do you want to video it this time?"

"I had to do it."

"I suppose you did. I suppose it was Henry's idea."

Millie didn't respond.

"Have they fired you yet?"

"It's a classy firm, Mike. They'll wait another six months."

"So you'll be needing a job?"

"I need another interview."

Millie persuaded Mike Forrest to come to her apartment this time. "I'll cook you a steak," she said. "I'll make you a martini."

In the event, though, she was a different girl. She put on a nice dress—and the wire-rimmed glasses Alice had made her buy as part of her "new look." She made him sit in her living room and gave him a glass of cider. She was proud of her apartment. It was in an older building in an unfashionable neighborhood. She had a fireplace. It wasn't cold enough for a fire, but the thought was nice. They sat on matching chairs on either side of the fireplace. Millie knew from her grandmother what a proper sitting room looked like. She'd inherited just enough money from her to have one.

"So look," she said, not looking at him, by which she meant, "let's start again."

Alice had said Mike didn't go in for "courting rituals," but Millie wondered. "Were you an Army brat?" she asked without further preliminaries.

Mike Forrest laughed. "My father wouldn't have been much good as a soldier."

"Alcoholic?"

"Compulsive gambler. Kept getting into debt."

"So you moved a lot?" said Millie. And to herself: so that's why you go to Vegas—to prove to yourself you're not your father.

"We often moved at short notice. You?"

"My father was a soldier. Pretty good one, actually."

"So you moved a lot, too?" said Mike Forrest.

"Not as often as you, it sounds like."

"You stayed long enough to have friends."

"Yeah," said Millie. "I was pretty good at making friends. 'Gregarious,' the teachers tended to call me."

"Meaning trouble."

"Not always. I had a strong family."

"Wish I could say the same."

"So how'd you get to college?"

"Italian mother. Died when I was fourteen. She had an uncle who was owed a favor."

"The uncle was a . . . businessman?"

"No, the uncle was a priest. There are plenty of good ones. I got sent to a Catholic boarding school. They straightened me out, convinced me I had a brain."

"*You'd* been trouble."

"Lotta fights, once I started to get my height."

"And before that?"

"I was a very unhappy little boy." He paused. "I got picked on a lot."

"Beaten up?"

"Sometimes. Some towns. Mostly just teased—about my name among other things, about my father, once word got around." Mike Forrest paused again. "Lotta anger in here." He touched his chest. "Makes it hard for me to trust people. Can't believe I'm saying all this to you. You of all people."

"I was just saving poor Joe. " Millie got up from her chair, came over to his, and began to loosen his tie.

"So what are you doing now?"

"Saving you," said Millie.

She led him into her bedroom, which was full of ghosts, as the bedrooms of single women tend to be.

Mike Forrest paused in the doorway. "I imagine you've made a lot of friends in here too," he said. Millie couldn't decide if he sounded angry or wistful.

"I've made a lot of men happy," she said, "but they always leave in the end."

"I'm good at leaving," said Mike Forrest.

"Let's live in the present," said Millie. And later, when they'd slipped under the sheets, "I want you, but let's be slow and deliberate about it. I'll stay on my side of the bed. You stay on yours."

He complied.

"Now, tell me about the worst thing that ever happened to you . . . as a little boy . . . in a new town . . . on a dusty playground . . . when going home had no appeal."

"I have trouble opening up," he said. But after a minute he began to talk. He spoke very quietly. They were children hiding in a closet or under the house or in the tall grass at the edge of town, and sharing secrets. Millie didn't interrupt, but as the secrets became more painful, she reached out and touched his cheek, on which there seemed to be moisture, which she pretended not to notice.

"I am not a good man," said Mike Forrest.

"I understand," said Millie. "My own behavior has often left a lot to be desired."

"I like to crush my opponents."

"So do I."

"But you are nice to the boys you sleep with. I can tell that."

"What about what I did to you . . . last time?" she asked.

"That was just . . . lawyer stuff," he said. Absolution. "Not that I won't have to repay you eventually."

"So how do you treat the other women you sleep with?"

"Badly. Afterwards. Don't call. Get one . . . interested in me, and then get my picture in the paper with someone else. Intentional hurtfulness."

"You don't think you could break the habit?"

Mike Forrest closed his eyes. "I can't believe I'm telling you this."

Millie was, as far as she could figure it out, a Presbyterian, but the US Army is nothing if not ecumenical. "Hail, Mary, Mother of God . . ." she recited.

"Pray for us sinners," Mike Forrest said slowly, "now and at the hour of our death."

"Amen," said Millie. "Now come over here and be forgiven."

"I may not call," said Michelangelo Forrest. "If you fall in love with me I probably won't even offer you a job."

"It would be better not to work in the same firm," said Millie.

"That is, if you fall in love with me."

"There probably isn't a lot of 'if' about it," said Millie, knowing she was being reckless.

"There is no recorded instance of my being nice to a woman for more than a month."

"But *you've* never been in love before."

"You think I'm in love with you?" said Michelangelo Forrest, as if in shock. "Just because I've told you things I've never told anyone else? Don't assume I'm telling the truth. And by the way, your firm is not about to fire you. Henry's put you on two deals with important clients."

"How do you know that?"

"My friends have friends. It's my job to know what the enemy is up to. And by the way, you just admitted I'm right."

"Terrible man," said Millie, and began kissing him. And by the way, she said to herself, you just admitted being interested in my future.

The problem, which presented itself to Millie as soon as Mike left and which did not go away, was what to say to Alice, who had rejected Michelangelo Forrest. Or to Henry, who had threatened him with disbarment. Alice was now a—whatever she was—friend? mentor? Anyway someone Millie shouldn't lie to. And Henry was introducing her to important clients.

The answer, of course, was to say nothing to Alice or to Henry, which wouldn't be a lie, even if it felt like one. But what was she herself doing, going out with a man she had described as "pure evil." They'd had two more dates within the week.

He *was* evil. Or he used to be. Now he was sending her flowers. And the fact that he used to send people to prison made the flowers disturbingly sexy. I do not have to be here, each bouquet would whisper as she unwrapped it. I am here because the dangerous man who bought me cares about you.

Also he called in the morning, which he had claimed he never did.

They were seeing each other two or three times a week, mostly in restaurants but often enough in her bedroom, where she wore the wire-rim glasses Alice had insisted on but nothing else. "You have to find kinky things they like," she'd said after the second glass of wine, leaning into the presumption that Millie's love life was deficient. "Or anyway, you need to surprise them from time to time. Nude with glasses would be a good look for you. Makes you look thoughtful. Boys like girls to be thoughtful about their pleasure." Millie had wondered whether this lecture was for Millie or for Alice herself, but if a partner gives an associate advice, the associate is crazy not to pay attention—so she'd done as she was told, and sure enough, Mike liked it.

Because Mike was famous, or at least recognizable, they went to obscure, non-trendy restaurants. When they found one they liked, they stuck to it. "How is Mrs. Forrest tonight?" the proprietor would ask, and both of them would just smile.

"Did you tell him we were married?" said Millie.

"No. I just treat you politely, so he makes that assumption."

It wasn't that their liaison *needed* to be a secret. They just found they wanted it that way. Perhaps caring about a woman wasn't consistent with the image he needed to project. Perhaps Millie assumed he would eventually dump her, and wanted it to happen in private.

Mike turned out to be extremely well read—another aspect of his personality he tended to conceal. After the Roman Catholic boarding school that had straightened him out he'd gone to a decent college—not Ivy League, you understand, which intensified his hunger for social acceptance, but good enough to give him a first-class education. He'd worked extremely hard. He'd studied history and politics, same as Millie had, each of them doing so on the assumption it would be a good background for law school. But over the summers he'd also consumed dozens of famous novels, which he could talk about with considerable insight.

Sex and conversation, Mike said, were the reasons to get married. They had plenty of both. Perhaps he was telling her why he didn't need to propose. Anyway, Millie didn't particularly want to get married. Too many explanations would be required.

They took to lying in bed naked. They skipped normal meals. Millie would go into the kitchen and toast a couple of English muffins, bringing them back buttered and spread with raspberry jam.

"What do you think of my breasts?" she asked, sitting cross-legged on the bed with the plate on her lap.

"I wholeheartedly approve of them," said Mike.

"Not too small?"

"They suit you," he said.

Becoming comfortable with each other naked took no particular effort. They just were. It helped that he was handsome. It helped that he told her she was beautiful.

"Shall we order pizza and shock the delivery boy," said Millie.

"No one gets this view but me," said Mike.

"I guess that's right," said Millie. "That's got to be right."

Thirty or forty was how many people he'd sent to prison. She'd asked. He didn't remember the exact number. Or so he said. He also said that a successful prosecutor needed to be able to dissemble, so perhaps he did know but wanted to appear casual about it. Wanted to seem not to care, not to have kept count. An interesting thing about prosecution, he said, was that you had to show the defense your evidence, but you could keep your strategy to yourself. Like a novelist in a way, he said.

Millie heard this, and realized that Mike was telling her not to trust him. She wondered if he was aware he was doing that.

Millie found she was quite... interested in this criminal justice stuff. She liked it when Mike talked about that phase of his career. She hoped she didn't have some sort of unhealthy obsession. Police work, Mike had told her, involved maintaining one's composure in the face of all that was nasty and irrational about the world.

It was turning out that there were some grubby aspects to corporate practice too. One of the important clients Henry had introduced Millie to was... she would have said "shady" if the company weren't so well spoken of. Anyway, they weren't breaking any laws that she could point to, but there was an undertone of moral deficiency about their chief executive, which one could work around but had to keep in view, like a dog that might bite you if you didn't stare it down. Millie had gone so far as to hint at this with Henry when he asked her how the deal was going. "No," said Henry. "I wouldn't propose him for my club."

"You wouldn't propose me either," said Millie.

"It's a men's club," said Henry.

"I could cut my hair off," said Millie. "I could cross-dress. Would that make a difference, Mr. Franklin."

"May I be 'Henry' again please, Millie."

"If that's what you'd like," said Millie sweetly.

"You realize he likes it when you tease him?" Alice had told her.

Millie had figured that out. She'd come to realize that her tomboy iconoclasm gave her power. She was a walking permission slip. People wanted to tell her their secrets. "Make sure you don't lose that," Mike had told her.

"Why do we keep them as a client, then, Henry?"

"Everyone is entitled to representation. We have represented them for eighty-five years. Their dubious chief executive will retire in three."

"So . . . ?"

"Be careful, Millie. I think you know how to do that."

"I appreciate your confidence, Mr. Franklin."

Mike and Henry were more alike than she'd realized. Both very smart, on guard, comfortable with ambiguity, honest with themselves. And they both liked Millie.

Millie had no idea, she realized, whether Henry had put her on a couple of important deals to test her or to ease his conscience. When it came time to fire her he could tell himself he'd given her a chance, that he'd repaid her for that piece of "reconnaissance" in aid of Joe Phillips, in defense of the firm's reputation.

Nor had she any idea whether Mike was setting her up—arranging to break her heart to repay her for that same maneuver.

If it was any comfort, she suspected he didn't know either. He had been suppressing his emotions since he was a small boy. Do not let anyone see that you are afraid, that you hurt, that you care. Do things to demonstrate indifference. Hurt people you are in danger of becoming attached to. Never confess. Never confess. Never confess.

"Do you think I should be a cop?" she asked him, lying on her side and staring at his handsome profile. It was an unpremeditated question. Honesty often seemed to be easier after intercourse.

"I thought you wanted to be a partner of that pompous firm you work at."

"Well I do, of course. I work hard enough. But it's a bit . . . sheltered."

"The Samuel Johnson problem."

"Yes?" His erudition breaking cover.

"Every man thinks poorly of himself for not having been a soldier," he quoted.

"Yeah. Or being 'airborne' in the Army. You should have jumped out of an airplane a few times, just on general principles. If you hadn't, why hadn't you? Why be in the Army at all, my father used to say, if you aren't going to have the complete experience? Why be a lawyer and avoid the rough bits?"

"So secretly recording Michelangelo Forrest wasn't enough?"

"It was an improvisation," said Millie.

"Meaning I shouldn't take it personally?"

"That's what *you* said. "Lawyer stuff," you called it. And we've been through all this, sweetheart. When I put the recorder in my purse that morning I had never met you. What you should take personally is that now I do know you, I want to spend so much time with you."

"You're sure you're not just in it for the sex?"

"Oh, that's definitely an enhancement." Having said this Millie ran her fingers down the side of his face.

Letting her touch his face, he had told her, was a sign of trust. Millie believed that trust and sex were partners. "You turn me on by trusting me," she'd said.

The next day he said to her that he had a client he wanted her to meet. "He needs a new will," said Mike.

"We have someone who does that," said Millie.

"I know," said Mike. "But be sure the right people know the man is *your* client."

"Um," said Millie.

One weekend Millie got up out of bed, leaving Mike talking to her—"Go on, darling," she said—and instead of English muffins came back to bed with a pink hair ribbon. "I want to tie your hands," she said.

Mike put his arms out in front of him with the wrists touching. "See how agreeable I am," he said.

"Behind your back," said Millie. "More vulnerable."

Mike rolled over with just a suggestion of reluctance. Millie bound him and rolled him over again so he was lying on his hands.

"Uncomfortable?" she asked.

"Only slightly," he replied.

"Only slightly would be about right." She got up, pulled the bed covers and pillows off the bed, which made it a place of execution, put back on the white linen shirt she had taken off an hour before, which made her very much the person in charge. Millie looked at herself in the mirror. The shirt was a size too large, which was how she liked them. It covered her, just, but when she moved it was evident that the shirt was all she had on. She knew Mike liked her in that shirt.

Mike had stopped talking and was watching her.

"You're wondering what comes next," said Millie. "So am I. You're wondering why you let me do this. I thought you might."

Silence extended itself as presumably they both thought about that.

Millie put on her wire-rimmed glasses and sat down on the bed, next to Mike but not touching him. "You were saying?"

"I've forgotten."

"Jane Austen. George Eliot. Someone's theory about women being naturally empathetic and therefore better novelists. Go on. I'm very empathetic." She touched his ear with her fingertips, eliciting goose bumps on his neck and chest. "Conversation is disclosure. I listen sympathetically." She touched the inside of his thigh and he gasped. "I pay *strict* attention to what you say."

"What is this about, Millie?"

"You're the one to say, Mike. You're the one who let his hands be tied."

"Are you going to hurt me?" he said. He was watching her intently. There was some small boy in him now.

"No," said Millie. "You know that. Or you almost know that. I *could* hurt you. Part of you definitely knows that. But I'm never going to hurt you—physically or emotionally or professionally. You just have to practice believing that."

"I feel a bit foolish," said Mike.

"I'm not surprised," said Millie. "You'd certainly look foolish to anyone who walked in. Big handsome man, getting aroused, I notice, pretty much a captive, pretty much at the mercy of his girlfriend's imagination. But don't worry. No one will ever know about this game except the two of us. I could take pictures of you and post them online. You would be famous for new reasons before breakfast. You know I won't do that. Or to be precise, you *almost* know I won't do it. And you like that sliver of risk . . ."

"But go on about the lady novelists."

"I don't think I can."

"Oh, but I love listening to you. I love the sound of your voice. I love your unexpected knowledge, which you keep hidden most of the time. So tell me about Jane Austen. List her novels in the order she wrote them and tell me the names of the principal characters. And while you do that I will try to distract you."

"*Sense and Sensibility,*" he said. "I can't do this."

"Of course you can. You have immense powers of concentration—which I am helping you to keep strong."

"The family was named 'Dashwood.' The heroine . . ."

"Do you think I would make a good heroine?" said Millie, interrupting. "I'm intrepid. I'm resourceful." She touched him again in an "intimate place," as a police report might have put it.

"You're brutal," said Mike.

"One has to take hold of life," said Millie, touching him again, with predictable results.

"Is that why you want to be a policewoman?"

"I'm beginning to think I'd rather be a prison guard," said Millie. "Or a very strict governess."

"Is that your fantasy?" said Mike.

"I suppose it is," she said, a bit surprised.

"Am I being helpful?"

"Very cooperative," said Millie. "Though under the circumstances, that's not too surprising."

They both laughed.

Millie got up and retrieved the bed covers. She threw them over Mike and got under the covers with him. "Time to warm you up," she said, rubbing her hands over various bits of him, all of which were chilly. Then she kissed him for a while. When she'd finished with him she untied him.

"That was astonishing," he said.

"It's all about trust," she said.

"Did you get Roger his new will?" said Mike, as if this somehow followed.

"I did," said Millie.

"And he has other problems," said Mike.

"I wasn't going to tell you about them."

"Of course not. Privileged information. That's why I couldn't tell *you*. It had to be Roger's decision to do so—which I take it he has now done."

"Long lunch last week."

"And he needs a long-established firm to represent him in this delicate matter," said Mike. "I am known to be his friend. I am, therefore, not the lawyer—and we are not the right firm—to persuade the majority of his board to back him in a conflict with his most distinguished director."

"That's what he said." Millie paused. "I assume you also know he needs to be extracted from a very unsatisfactory marriage."

"I told him he can't afford the publicity just now."

"We may have a way to help him with that. Get it done without going to court. But I told him that has to come later."

"So what comes now?" said Mike.

"Probably can't discuss it further," said Millie. "You represent the company. I represent him. Or rather, we do. I introduced him to Henry the day before yesterday."

"Smart girl," said Mike Forrest.

"Would you consider kissing her breasts?" said Millie, unbuttoning her oversized white linen shirt.

There was still, of course, the issue of Joe and Abigail Phillips, which neither of them raised. Why did you have an affair with her? Millie imagined herself asking.

Because she was willing, Mike would say. I was promiscuous before I met you.

But you aren't any longer?

Can't you tell?

Yes, I can tell.

Why did you get Joe to confess? she would ask him.

Because I could. Would that be his answer? Because I knew I was responsible and wanted to shift the blame. That might be the answer.

Millie knew that she would know at once whether Mike had answered her honestly. So she didn't ask. And she reckoned he didn't raise the topic because he knew that anything he volunteered would be suspect. So the matter lay there, like an unexploded bomb in the hall, as he taught her guile and she taught him trust.

And then one Sunday afternoon, when they arrived at her apartment worn out and thirsty from walking all over the city because it was one of those late September days when New York is perfect, Mike told her to undress and tied her to a kitchen chair—hands behind her, piece of twine woven through the upright struts in the back.

"Can you get loose?" he said.

She pulled on her restraints without success.

"No," said Millie. "May I have a glass of water, please?"

Mike took a tumbler out of the cupboard, filled it from the faucet and then set it on the counter without giving it to her. He pulled the other chair close to hers and sat down on it backward, facing Millie like a cop in a movie.

"I'm *thirsty*," she said.

"Why did I kill Abigail Phillips?" he asked.

"She was getting on your nerves," said Millie.

"Wrong," said Mike.

"She was making you feel guilty."

"Wrong."

"She was taking advantage of you," said Millie.

"Getting warmer," he said, gently touching her left cheek.

"She was exploiting your need to be a shit."

"Bingo. How did I kill her?"

"You gave her a glass of wine and a head full of gossip, and... sent her back to her long-suffering husband *un*-fucked, telling her she looked too perfect to touch and anyway you were taking her to Vegas the following week, even though you didn't plan to, knowing she would be completely not there for poor Joe, whom you had never met but imagined must be a nerd to be working for a white-shoe firm like ours."

Mike blushed. "How do you know all that?"

"I know how you operate. I know what turns you on. You seduced me, remember? You made me undress and practically demand sex before you would even loosen your necktie in your own apartment."

"No, my sweet, it was you who seduced me, just as you are doing now by making yourself vulnerable."

Just for a moment Millie wondered whether Mike would turn out to be a lunatic and was about to strangle her.

"Did I *ever* have sex with Abigail Phillips?"

Millie paused. "Probably not."

"Was I thinking about it?"

"Of course. You liked the fact that she would have. You liked sending her back to her nerdish husband just a little bit late."

Mike paused. "Have I ever slept with one of my... employees?"

"Perhaps not. You care about having the power to do it more than about the thing itself."

"Why did I . . . interview you in such an unusual way, then?"

Millie paused. "I appealed to you . . . differently from other women."

"Why have I not dumped you when it's been more than six months?"

"You've . . . become . . . fond of me."

"And so to shorten this interrogation, I will confess that I got poor Joe, as you call him, to say he'd pushed his long-legged wife out the window because I was spooked, because I could see that I was responsible for her death in a way, and I wanted to shift the blame. I wanted to skip town the way my father used to, which I am not proud of and confess to you with considerable reluctance. And then I figured out how to unscramble the situation, which I would have done the following week had you and Henry not intervened. We all do stupid things sometimes, Millie."

Millie's head was spinning. "May I have a glass of water please?"

"Not until you tell me I am a very bad man."

"You are a very bad man."

"Which was worse, not sleeping with Abigail or getting Joe to confess?"

"Not sleeping with Abigail was a form of cruelty. The bit with Joe was just a mistake. But you shouldn't have let him spend the night in jail."

"He shouldn't have let his wife tempt me."

"What an absurd thing to say."

"I am an absurd person. You've known that all along. You see right through me. I wake up every morning amazed that our romance persists."

"Me too, actually."

"I have broken too many hearts, bruised too many egos and, by the way, stepped on the fingers of too many colleagues struggling up the same ladder. Young, trusting women bring out the worst in me. Abigail Phillips was way too attractive to be allowed to work for someone like me."

"More attractive than me?"

"Different section of the orchestra."

"So what instrument am I? No, don't answer that."

"You are the instrument of my redemption," said Mike. He untied Millie's hands and gave her the glass of water. "So do I have to apologize to poor Joe?"

"Possibly," said Millie. "If you want to marry me. I will have to consult with Henry."

"Do that," said Mike.

They stood in the kitchen hugging. Eventually she took him into her bedroom, where they made love among the ghosts.

Henry said essentially three things: (1) poor Joe was moving to a very good firm in Minneapolis and probably hadn't acknowledged to himself that his wife had had some sort of relationship with Mike Forrest; (2) many good lawyers are deeply flawed people; and (3) none of us have a lot of choice about where our heart leads.

"So I shouldn't ask Mike to talk to Joe?"

"No."

"And you'll come if there's a wedding?"

"Yes."

"But you said he was pure evil," said Millie.

"I said what he was doing at that moment was evil," said Henry. "Much of human behavior is evil. That's why there are laws."

"And therefore?"

"Mike has been on the side of the angels for important parts of his career. We at this stodgy firm have occasionally helped unprincipled executives elude the consequences of their own bad judgment. Bad behavior even."

"Roger," said Millie.

"Not a bad man," said Henry. "Just incautious. I am confident we can help him. You've already told me how we should approach the matter."

"I suppose I did."

"And when we are done, we will hand Roger and his quite interesting company back to Mike Forrest."

Millie was relieved that she was not expected to steal the business from Mike. She wouldn't be able to do that. "The long game," she said, quoting something Henry had said to her some months earlier, in connection with another matter.

"Precisely," said Henry. "Roger will need to take his company public, in part because he needs several million dollars for the very quiet financial settlement you can now put Thomas to work on."

"Yes," said Millie, "and because he liked the establishment feel of this place, he will want our help with that. Mike will understand that. And his firm doesn't do much securities work."

"We are never in a hurry because we do not need to be in a hurry," said Henry. "Mike Forrest is and does—which is not to be despised."

"I'm glad you don't despise him," said Millie, sitting on Henry's couch, wearing the exactly perfect suit Alice had helped her find. It was "a suit for formal occasions," they had agreed, and that's what this was. Millie was asking for Henry's blessing.

"Mike Forrest wears his ruthlessness on his sleeve," said Henry. "You and I, Millie, conceal our weapons. So who is the more honorable?"

Millie had no answer for that. There was quite a long silence.

"Are you going to quit and have babies?" said Henry finally.

"Should I?" said Millie.

"I wouldn't have thought so," said Henry.

"What *should* I do?"

"Take your time. If marrying Mike Forrest is right for both of you, it will only feel more so a year from now."

"Thank you, Henry," said Millie. She stood up and walked across his office to the chair he was sitting in. And for the second time in eight years, she kissed him on the cheek.

Enhancements

"I have a surprise for you," she said.

"I like surprises," said John.

"Good," she said, keeping her eyes on the road as she drove away from the airport.

There was a longish silence, which they pretended was so she could concentrate on the driving. He ached to touch her. She doubtless knew that. Not getting what they wanted was part of their game.

"Nice of you to pick me up," he said. This was his first visit to her hometown, which was also home to a corporate client he occasionally worked for and with whom he would have a meeting the next day.

"Think of it as a kidnapping," she said.

He could tell she was waiting for him to ask her what she had planned, so he didn't.

"I've booked you in with a dominatrix," she said finally.

"You're kidding."

"Her name is Sally. She seems to know her business."

"You tried her out?"

"No. I just talked to her, looked her in the eye. Interviewed three other girls, in fact—or mistresses of pain, as they seemed to want to be called."

"And you decided on Sally?"

"Right."

Enhancements

"A 'mistress of pain' would be a lover of pain," he said.

"More of an administrator."

"Like an HR department," he said.

She laughed but didn't respond.

"How long?"

"One hour minimum, but she can go on longer if you like. She doesn't have anyone else scheduled."

"Business is down?"

"She says she's not *brisk* enough—or maybe she means brusque. Doesn't take charge the way most clients want her to, and of course most business for these girls is repeat business. It's like being a hairdresser, she says. How many 'heads' do you have? She gives the impression of not being completely into it. But she seemed the best choice."

"Because . . . ?" He still assumed this was an elaborate joke.

"You decide," she said briskly. "And here we are." She pulled into a quiet street a few blocks short of his hotel and parked. Trees blocked most of the light from the streetlamp up ahead. It would have been a good place for spies to meet, John said to himself, if this were a movie. He felt like he was watching a movie.

Her name was Barbara. They'd met at a conference. For the past year, they'd been coming as close to having an affair as it is possible for two healthy people to do without actually getting into bed. John supposed that was the point: chastity as an extreme sport. He'd done some fairly aggressive skiing. He knew the lure of risk.

He was a young partner of a famous law firm in New York. She worked for one of the big accounting firms, in their "risk practice" ironically, and her career was evidently going well. She described her job as "helping clients envision things that will never happen—since they generally do."

"Not that different from writing novels, I would suppose," John had said when they first met, which she'd liked because it seemed to indicate he took her profession as seriously as she did, and recognized that it had a creative aspect. She claimed once to have set off a firecracker in a client's boardroom. "'Now that I have your full attention'—that sort of routine" was how she'd described it.

Barbara was married—happily, she said. She and her husband and so far no kids lived in this city, which she described as "small enough to know everyone important, but large enough to have an opera company and a decent museum, so it's not completely unsophisticated." She'd been asked to join a charity board—not the opera or the museum, you understand, which required you to be a serious donor, but a "good" one.

Barbara's husband was a salesman of "big machines that crush stuff," as she put it, which meant that he traveled a lot. "World class engineering, but you'd never have heard of them." John figured Barbara got bored when her husband was away, as she'd said he would be that night. He could tell when that happened by the character of the text messages he got. Or perhaps it was that she was bored with her husband, but could only do something about it when he was away.

John was married too, loved his wife, didn't see enough of his three young daughters, lived in a surround of guilt for that omission. "It's like the noise a radio makes when it's on but not tuned in to any particular station," he'd explained to Barbara.

When they'd met each other in the gym in the basement of the hotel where the fatal conference was, they'd started flirting immediately. Barbara liked to say it was instinctive. John didn't think that was quite the right word but he knew what she meant, which was that there was an undeniable physical attraction. He'd been on the stationary bicycle, and she'd been doing crunches on a mat that was pretty much directly in his line of sight. She stood up, stretched, which raised the bottom of her tee shirt to show off her abs, and mounted the adjacent bicycle. Without any acknowledgment of what they were up to they began to compete. He increased his speed. So did she. The bell went off that said he'd done the time he'd entered into the machine. He reset it. Both of them dripped sweat.

"You planning to do this all day?" she said finally.

"Up to you," he said.

"Well, I don't want to miss the first session," she said, and then coyly added, "I think I'm giving it."

"Are you interesting?" said John.

"Come and see," said Barbara.

You mean, now that we're both soaking wet, he'd said to himself, why don't we go to your room and get into a shower together and finish the job? Can't do that. Mustn't do that.

Happily, the conference broke up that afternoon, but they'd exchanged cards. So there were some guilty lunches at good restaurants when she visited her firm's headquarters in New York, a run in Central Park and lunch from a hot dog vendor one memorable spring day, increasingly frequent late-night phone calls between their offices—and now he'd come to her city the night before his meeting when he probably could have caught an early morning plane.

Neither of them had said anything about doing anything except having dinner, but there was the undeniable fact that she was single that night, that he would have a hotel room, and had no colleagues traveling with him.

your lover at all. And now I'm your victim, he added, which seems to be a way of being your lover, even if it frightens you.

"No, don't sit down yet," said Sally. "I want you to undress him. You just stand still, darling. We'll do all the work. You haven't done this before, have you, Barbara?"

Barbara made no audible response. John could sense her hands shaking as she unbuttoned his shirt. He didn't seem to be trembling himself.

Sally continued her monologue: "Some of our clients like to be humiliated, but I don't agree with that. If you want foot-licking, I'll have to get you a different girl. I say anyone who comes here to be hurt is a hero. They should be treated with respect, and as much gentleness as the situation permits."

"Could I have a drink of water?" said John, surprising himself.

"No, darling. That would not be consistent with our mission here. There is a lot of thirst in being frightened, and a bit of frightened in being thirsty. We want to make the most of it. And it would be best if you don't speak."

John was suddenly very thirsty, so maybe he was frightened after all.

Barbara seemed to be kneeling in front of him, untying and removing his shoes. Under ordinary circumstances, he would have quite liked having her do that. A little subordination would do her good, he'd sometimes told her. Or told himself; the dialogue they had with each other was part of an ongoing interior conversation. It was hard to keep them separate sometimes. She was so proud of her body, her fitness, her professional accomplishments. If they ever lived together, perhaps he'd make her taking off his shoes and socks a regular "duty."

inside, where a trim young woman in a short black skirt and a tuxedo jacket asked their names. She turned to Barbara. "You'll be watching, I believe," she said. Barbara nodded. "You blindfold him, then." She took a long piece of black silk out of a drawer and handed it to her.

Barbara had to help him down the stairs. The blindfold had foam rubber pads sewn into it, which forced him to close his eyes. Nothing was visible at the edges. No light came through. There were a lot of stairs.

Thinking about it later, John decided he must have gone into a sort of trance. The whole way into town he was intensely conscious that they were skiing close to the edge, that at any moment he could reach out and touch her arm or her cheek. Her announcement that they were about to do something intimate and forbidden was so much of a piece with the thrill of just being alone in a car together that he didn't seem to take in the prospect of that something being painful. Or maybe it was that the prospect of pain intensified the intimacy. Any sane person would have said, "Stop. Wait. I'm not agreeing to this." But he just let himself be led down the stairs.

Sally spoke, presumably to Barbara. "Are you going to let him talk, or shall I tape his mouth shut?"

"Let him breath," said Barbara. After a second she added, "Please."

"And how long did you have in mind?"

"As long as it takes," said Barbara. She sounded like someone intent on sounding confident. John had become an expert, over the past year, at reading her moods, sensing how things affected her without having to be told. I'd be a wonderful lover, he'd said to himself more than once, if I were your lover at all. And now I'm your victim, he added, which seems to be a way of being your lover, even if it frightens you.

"No, don't sit down yet," said Sally. "I want you to undress him. You just stand still, darling. We'll do all the work. You haven't done this before, have you, Barbara?"

Barbara made no audible response. John could sense her hands shaking as she unbuttoned his shirt. He didn't seem to be trembling himself.

Sally continued her monologue: "Some of our clients like to be humiliated, but I don't agree with that. If you want foot-licking, I'll have to get you a different girl. I say anyone who comes here to be hurt is a hero. They should be treated with respect, and as much gentleness as the situation permits."

"Could I have a drink of water?" said John, surprising himself.

"No, darling. That would not be consistent with our mission here. There is a lot of thirst in being frightened, and a bit of frightened in being thirsty. We want to make the most of it. And it would be best if you don't speak."

John was suddenly very thirsty, so maybe he was frightened after all.

Barbara seemed to be kneeling in front of him, untying and removing his shoes. Under ordinary circumstances, he would have quite liked having her do that. A little subordination would do her good, he'd sometimes told her. Or told himself; the dialogue they had with each other was part of an ongoing interior conversation. It was hard to keep them separate sometimes. She was so proud of her body, her fitness, her professional accomplishments. If they ever lived together, perhaps he'd make her taking off his shoes and socks a regular "duty."

And what would she require of him? There'd need to be some sort of reciprocity. They'd made that a rule from the start, understood it without ever discussing it.

He'd wondered about specifying some wifely duties for Felicity, when they were first married, but she'd shown no aptitude. When he asked whether she liked the sense of being held down, when they were in bed, she'd just laughed. Would she like to restrain John in some way? She was dismissive. "Isn't intercourse enough?" she asked him. That was the hygienic word she used for it. "I enjoy it. You appear to enjoy it. We do it regularly." All this was true, but, well, why did she have so little imagination? As children filled up the house, sex became something John only did to relieve pressure—and so that Felicity, who probably recorded orgasms in her Filofax in a secret code, wouldn't ask him if he'd lost interest.

Sally was putting something soft on his wrists. Soft and firm. His arms were being lifted over his head. There seemed to be a machine doing it. There was a faint whirring sound somewhere in the room.

The machine began to lift him off his feet. This was not wholly uncomfortable, though John recognized right away that it could get old. "I'm just going to let you swing a little," said Sally, giving him a gentle push on the chest. "It enhances the experience. Helps you to absorb the fact that you have no control."

"I accept that," said John. He was way more relaxed about the situation than he should be. His mind seemed to be playing a trick of standing outside the situation and watching him.

"Good for you, sweetheart," said Sally. "Now stretch your feet out and see if you can reach the floor with your toes."

"I can't," he said.

"Well the floor is only a few inches away, but you don't know that. So for our purposes you are in very deep water. Or if you prefer another metaphor, the ground has opened under you. You are lost," said Sally. Umm, said John to himself.

For a while there was silence and then there was a bit of tugging and the sound of sewing scissors cutting through his underpants, which Barbara had primly left on him. "Don't worry, darling. Castration costs extra, and your friend here is frugal."

More silence. John swung back and forth from a ceiling that was definitely far above, gradually becoming motionless. "Now I think we can begin," said Sally. "No, it's for you." She seemed to be addressing Barbara. "You didn't think you'd just get to watch, did you?"

Barbara seemed to be incapable of speech.

"Stand over here. I recommend the cane for a beginner."

John had run three marathons. He'd dislocated a shoulder playing soccer in college. He had endurance. He knew about pain. He'd certainly fantasized about this sort of thing. But it hurt like hell.

He could hear Barbara breathing. Then she hit him again.

"Take your time," said Sally. "Let him recover and be unprepared for the next blow."

John's body was suddenly on fire. Correction, a pitcher of ice water had been poured over him. It didn't hurt but he started to tremble.

"Monks have a saying," said Sally, as if it followed from the ice water, "that your cell will teach you everything. Little rooms—one to a monk, assuming they are good monks—with a bed, a chair and a place to kneel. No heating, I expect. They spend years reading and praying and meditating.

Solitude instructs them. Have you heard that saying, darling? Are you familiar with that concept?"

"Yes," said John. He'd taken a European history survey course. He assumed he knew about monks. The thought flickered in his brain that he knew about solitude because of his marriage, but he quickly extinguished it. That particular solitude hadn't taught him anything.

"You see, darling," Sally continued, "this situation your girlfriend has put you in is just like a cell. You are alone, even if others are close at hand. Your friend cannot help you. All she knows how to do, for our purposes, is hurt you. And I'm prepared to let her do that longer than you can stand it."

Was she talking about Barbara or Felicity? Barbara, of course. This was all make-believe. And that couldn't be true—that he couldn't put an end to the session when he chose to.

Sally must have made a signal to Barbara because the cane cut into him again, though perhaps reluctantly. Ouch, he said to himself. More than ouch. This was *not* sexually exciting, which was presumably good news.

Sally gave him another gentle push on the chest and he began to swing. He thought that meant he was safe for a moment, which must have been her objective because almost immediately the cane struck him again. And then again. No reluctance there. John wondered how close he was to screaming that he could not take it. He assumed it would make no difference to Sally if he did. Maybe the point was to scream and discover that it made no difference.

"You see," said Sally, "part of the experience is its unpredictability. That was the point of the ice water, in case you hadn't figured it out. Down here, as we call it, is exactly like life, but intensified. Sometimes those monks are visited by actual devils, but it takes twenty years. Eventually, if they are persistent and resilient monks, they see God. I myself have no command of spirits. I missed that course in college. But if *you* have any demons this may just bring them out."

Barbara spoke: "I'm . . . I'm not sure . . ."

"I wasn't speaking to you, young lady. Your only role here is to give your friend a baptism. Now, come over here and put your hand on his bottom, and see what lovely welts you've raised."

Barbara had never, to John's certain recollection, touched him before. They'd made an unspoken fetish of it from their first lunch in New York. That was why sitting next to her as she drove in from the airport was so intoxicating. Even as she'd blindfolded and undressed him that evening, there had been no skin contact. And now there was. It was a warm hand.

John was suddenly in a sort of meditation. This stranger with warm hands thought he talked about S&M because it attracted him. He talked about it because *the idea* excited him and because it seemed to him that it excited her. Which he liked. Actual pain shouldn't have been necessary. It was teasing they were supposed to be engaged in. So why had she brought him here? Had she sensed that underneath it all he had an urge that was more than curiosity, that he had a need? Did he? He wouldn't have said he did, but he hadn't refused to be led downstairs.

Or perhaps she had some sort of need.

Thwack.

Yes, unprepared.

"I thought we'd switch to a leather belt," said Sally. It works better on the back and chest. Can you tell the difference, darling? You've been very good about not crying out, by the way. Your girlfriend should be impressed."

Enhancements

Hold on, said part of John's brain, Barbara sounded like *she* was crying. Or sniffling.

"Again," said Sally. "The belt takes a little practice."

Thwack.

"Now his chest."

Thwack.

"Do you think she's got the technique, darling?"

John's cell began to close in around him. There was pain everywhere. What did a monk do if he was claustrophobic? Focus on the pain. Don't panic. "It hurts very much," said John.

"Do you want me to keep hurting you?" said Barbara, her voice sounding strained. Why would she ask such a question?

"It mustn't be my choice," said John. And what a strange answer—as if the game had established rules. They'd always made up their own rules: desire but no touching. Intimacy blended with the ache of separation. Forbiddenness—if that was a word—as a source of both pleasure and sadness. Sadness as an enhancement, actually.

"Stop a moment," said Sally. "Say that again."

"It depends on what the objective is," said John. "Speaking for myself, I think I've learned all I need to."

"You're done," said Sally. "Down you come."

There was the whirring sound and his feet touched the floor, but he didn't seem to be able to stand on them. Barbara had her arms around him, holding him up, but it didn't work and they were both on the floor. She was crying, touching his face, trying to free his wrists and remove the blindfold. Everything came out in a rush.

"It wasn't supposed to be this way," she said between sobs. "*She* was supposed to whip you, not me. I was supposed to save you. I was supposed to take you home. I don't even have a husband. You were going to realize that when you saw my apartment. No men's clothes in the closets. You'd ask me why I pretended to be married and I'd say I wear a ring when I travel on business so guys won't hit on me, and when we met in the gym and we were so attracted to each other—you have to admit we were—I figured if you thought I was married I wouldn't scare you away, that we could flirt without any danger to your marriage to what's her name and your three daughters you don't see enough of, and maybe just maybe attraction would morph into love."

"It can do that," said Sally. John and Barbara turned to look at her, as if surprised to find her there. "You see a lot in this business," she said. "I'll go get you some new boxer shorts."

Sally left. John remained cross-legged on the floor, with Barbara kneeling beside him. He looked around at the room. No windows. No pictures. What might be a duty roster taped to the wall at the foot of the stairs. Polished concrete floor. Ropes hung from pulleys attached to the ceiling. The machine that made the whirring sound was in the corner. There were a couple of comfortable chairs, and an expensive-looking sound system, twinkling in readiness.

"She said we could have music," said Barbara, turned to follow John's gaze.

"I don't think I need to do this again," said John. "I'm not sure we needed to do it in the first place."

"No," said Barbara.

"Listen, I don't think . . ."

"That's all right, I . . ."

"What I mean to say is I can't explain what I just experienced."

"Pain?"

"No, after that. Along side that. Clarity. A vision of how things work."

"Does that vision include me?" said Barbara, ever a brave girl, dreading the answer.

"No," said John, as if she'd asked him something trivial, like whether he'd brought the mail in yet. Barbara felt as though her chest was about to collapse. "But, you know," he continued, "I should thank you for bringing me here. Everything is simpler. The games we were playing were so unnecessary."

Sally came in with the boxer shorts. "I think you're a medium," she said to John.

"I think he's a mystic," said Barbara, getting to her feet.

"They come along," said Sally.

"He seems to think he's had a vision of God."

"Probably has."

"So what am I supposed to do?" said Barbara.

"Get him dressed, take him to his hotel, run him a bath, do *not* get in with him, kiss him on the cheek as you leave, and don't call him."

Barbara felt disoriented. Perhaps she hadn't thought this whole thing through. This was supposed to have been an intensification, but it seemed to be a derailment.

"And *my* vision of God?" she said suddenly to Sally, while John was putting his clothes back on. "Where do I sign up for that? What do I do about my loneliness, and my fucking fake wedding ring?"

"I can't call up spirits, remember. Just wait to see what happens."

Having no alternative, Barbara did as she'd been told, kissed John on the cheek and left, trained extra hard each morning—there was an accommodating hill near her apartment—drank too much most evenings, and stared fixedly at her cell phone. Sally had told her not to call John but she hadn't told *him* he couldn't call Barbara.

He didn't. Days passed.

One night Barbara had the idea of googling John. It was a way of being in contact without his knowing it—like stroking the head of a sleeping child. There wasn't much information. Partners of famous law firms weren't supposed to get publicity. They were supposed to be like the stage hands in Noh dramas who dressed in black and were defined as invisible—same as people of the opposite sex in a Japanese bath. Barbara had a sudden vision of naked lawyers getting in and out of New York taxis, walking down Park Avenue, taking notes at board meetings. John had looked very good without any clothes on.

Barbara googled herself. Because she spoke at a lot of conferences, there were actually more items about her than about John, even though he clearly ranked higher in any objective hierarchy of professional status. Which led to the question, what did Barbara aspire to? Becoming a partner of her accounting-and-consulting firm, of course. There were so many it was embarrassing not to be one yet. To have a national professional reputation was a better aim, to be described by journalists as "the well-known risk expert . . ."

Or did she want to be a factor in the social life of her medium-sized midwestern city, to in fact be on the board of the opera or the museum? That would be hard to achieve without a husband. If she turned forty still single she'd be leftovers. People would say she "tried too hard." That was clearly what she'd stupidly done with John. Or part of what she'd stupidly done.

Enhancements

Tried too hard. Barbara remembered being in the eighth grade at Theodore Roosevelt Junior High School. She'd set herself the objective of getting "all A's," which she had accomplished, but which hadn't been as satisfying as she'd assumed it would be. Barbara had been the oldest of six closely spaced children. "My parents liked sex," she'd sometimes say to get a laugh. But growing up with three sisters and two brothers had involved a lot of not getting all the attention she craved. Her mother's reaction to her grades had essentially been, "So?" Her father had added, in an aside, "No point, really. We can't send her to college."

Barbara had thwarted her parents' instinct to crush her by continuing to get A's, getting a scholarship to a decent liberal arts college, getting a good job with a good firm . . .

But what had she done to provoke that instinct? Did they interpret her ambition as some sort of rebuke?

About the time she'd gotten her first perfect report card, she'd overheard a teacher using the term "over-achiever." She'd asked her mother what it meant. "Someone who isn't as smart as she thinks she is," said her mother. Barbara still hurt when she remembered that moment—standing in the kitchen with the red and white linoleum floor, her mother answering over her shoulder as she fried pork chops, hoping it was a joke, not being able to see her mother's face but knowing it wasn't a joke.

Why had she chosen to work so close to her hometown—in a city that wasn't big enough to support its own risk practice, that was spiritually a large version of her hometown—rather than going to Chicago or New York? She'd told herself it was because her salary would go farther in a small city, that she'd wanted to help her younger siblings, etc. But she didn't actually see that much of her sisters and brothers.

They didn't actually *like* her, if she was honest about it. She'd overheard three of them last Christmas, talking about the objectively generous presents she'd given them. They thought their over-achieving sister was "a show-off."

Perhaps she lived where she did because she was unwilling to give up on getting her parents' approval. Or unwilling to stop *not* getting it? Perhaps she, rather than John, was the masochist, and needed constant reminders of her parents' indifference. Clearly it was the pain of that indifference that had driven her to be a mild success.

After about two weeks of these unhelpful reflections, the Holy Spirit presented itself to Barbara in the form of an idea, or actually a series of ideas. She assumed it was the Holy Spirit, even if she didn't believe in it except as part of the general arrangement that Episcopalians who don't go to church accept as theoretically possible. And never mind if what got called the Holy Spirit was probably better described as one's subconscious burping up an insight.

Barbara would have preferred an actual angel, but she told herself that was being greedy. If an idea can just happen in your brain, it doesn't need to be delivered by a person with wings.

It occurred to Barbara that the anguished flirtation she had conducted with John was essentially a reenactment of the frustration of not getting her parents' approval. And she had arranged to have him punished because she was angry with him for not providing sex. She'd experienced the absence of sex as rejection.

But—and this was the important part—she'd collaborated with him in arranging that experience of rejection. She'd called him as often as he called her. She was the one who'd invented a husband. She was the one who'd said, "We'll never touch each other." The "ground rules" as she called them, masqueraded as protective boundaries, but they were instruments of torture for Barbara as much as the cane and the belt and the machine that made a whirring sound had been for John.

When she exercised, Barbara liked to push herself. She believed in "leaning into the pain." She embraced the desperate breathing that running up that bastard of a hill required of her. But this had been different. It wasn't pain in pursuit of fitness. It was pain to sneer in the face of pain.

Having John whipped, a man she was pretty completely hooked on, was a form of self-abuse. She'd been trying to hurt *herself*. And she had. He was gone. She was the one crying at the end.

Why do I assume, she said to herself, that I can *arrange* anything? I've been setting and achieving goals since I was thirteen, and I'm miserable. Perhaps I need to be more passive, more accepting.

As some book she'd bought in an airport had explained it, you don't go *find* God. You open yourself. He is there all along, a presence on your doorstep. This triggered a memory of some intentionally forgotten horror movie. God as a monster. Even to a non-observant Episcopalian, this seemed briefly blasphemous until she reminded herself that the Jews, who knew Him first, considered God to be so scary they wouldn't even say His name.

John wasn't God, of course. She was just thinking by analogy. "Not calling John, hoping he will call me but not really expecting him to—that's the position I want to be in, the frame of mind, the frame of soul, if there is such a thing. And I promise you, that's not masochism but spiritual discipline."

Barbara explained this to the space in her kitchen where the angel wasn't, the angel who hadn't been required to deliver the ideas that increasingly possessed her. "You probably don't drink," she said out loud, addressing the place the angel would have been if one had been leaning against her kitchen counter. "So I won't either. Not tonight, at least."

The angel said nothing, as might be expected of someone who wasn't there. But after ten years of living alone, Barbara was quite good at that sort of conversation.

The thought presented itself that those midnight conversations with John had also been conversations with someone who wasn't there. And the girl he was talking to wasn't there either. She wasn't Barbara. They'd invented each other—same as she'd invented appreciative younger sisters—out of their own desires.

The angel's silence reminded Barbara that hoping John would call was tantamount to hoping John's marriage would break down. "I assume I'm not supposed to hope for that," she said. "Or perhaps I'm supposed to be honest with myself about that"—Barbara paused—"honest with your boss about it." Pause. "We're not having any wine, right?"

Silence.

"What was it that interesting person, Sally, said about monks in their cells? 'Your cell will teach you everything.' This is my cell. I suppose the life any person makes for themselves is their cell. Pretty shitty cell, even if there's a lot about me on Google."

Silence.

"I cannot honestly say that I do not want John's marriage to fail. The fact that I didn't even know his wife's name until I googled him and found the wedding announcement from the *Times*, I have to admit that seems a hopeful sign. He never referred to her by name. 'Felicity.' Rich girl. Her father seemed to have been a partner of John's firm."

Silence.

Barbara went looking for her Bible, which had been given to her by an aunt who was also her godmother. The aunt was a Methodist. Barbara had been baptized as a Methodist. She'd become an Episcopalian in college. Her sisters thought that was a form of social climbing. Now that she didn't go to church she was prepared to admit that it probably was. She flipped through the Gospels in search of insight. She figured a person could do that without turning into a creationist.

The main advice on offer was, as she put it to herself, to "lighten up on the possessions." She started with her Cuisinart. The secondhand store took it. "It frightened me," she explained, "the violence it was capable of, and all on show inside the plastic housing." Also, it was emblematic of the pretense that she was a good cook. Or could be if she had the time. Barbara was hoping to lighten up on pretense. She put away the Bible.

Barbara went through her closets and found a lot of clothes to give away—clothes she'd bought a decade earlier, trying to be older, or as recently as the year before last, trying to look younger. She depleted her cornucopia of self-help books. "It's not that I don't need advice," she told the angel, "but those books are so noisy."

As an absence of things began to fill her apartment, Barbara found it natural to spend more time with her thoughts. Why had she taken John to a dominatrix? That is, in addition to her other theories? "To break through" was the thought that came immediately to mind, and the angel who wasn't there didn't argue with her. "We were *playing* with each other, dancing on a crust of eroticism that covered a lava pit of emotions. That's what I felt like, I think. And John must have experienced our relationship the same way—as a construct, as camouflage, a way of hiding from his feelings, something that had to be cleared away. Why else, one might ask, did he let me blindfold him, and all the rest?"

Silence.

"I know what you're going to say—except of course that I seem to do all the talking—which is that John's reasons for allowing me to hurt him may have been entirely different from *my* motivation. I mustn't assume that what happens to me, what happens inside my head, is what happens to the whole world. I don't necessarily know anything about John, really."

John had told her a story one night. Maybe it was a fantasy, but he'd pretended it was true. True stories were more exciting. It was about a group house he had been in one summer. Three men and three women, none romantically involved. The house had once been a small hotel or something. Big kitchen. They all had their own bedrooms—like monks. All six of them were graduate students or in law school. They all had summer jobs or academic projects with important deadlines, but devoted a lot of their free time to fitness.

The house was close to a beach. The only shower was in the backyard, so you could wash off the sand. Nudity was inevitable. They were all fit, so there was no aesthetic hesitation, just social convention. "If you're not sleeping with a woman," said John, "and you're both doing thirty miles a day on a bike or ten running, plus some floor exercises and work with free weights, and one of you is under the warm water letting tired muscles relax, it seems pretty reasonable to invite the other person in, there being two shower heads."

Enhancements

Then, one evening in about the third week, one of the girls starts walking around in a sarong but topless—the initial explanation being that her sports bra has rubbed her shoulder raw—and the others follow her example "out of solidarity," so after a couple of bottles of wine at dinner the girls say, "How about it, guys?" so the three men strip off, which is hard to do without getting aroused, and the girls act all interested and admiring, as if they hadn't been bumping into each other in the shower, as if they'd never seen a guy before, like they're specimens in a tropical greenhouse, and then one of the girls says, "We're none of us getting laid, right?" Nods all round. "So, let's see how long we can go without it. I mean, were not teenagers any more. We can control ourselves, right? First pair to crack gets spanked, agreed?" They all agree. "And no masturbation." Agreed. They've had a lot of wine, remember.

They do pretty well for a week in their separate bedrooms, so over lunch on Sunday one of the girls says, "Let's make this more interesting. Let's start sharing beds, but without touching." And the girls agree to draw the men's names out of a hat each night to see how they pair up. "I like this experiment," one of the guys says. "It's not an experiment," says one of the girls. "It's a contest. We know how it comes out. We just don't know which of you guys can hold out the longest." So John says, "Five hundred dollars says I can." Before the other two guys can respond, one of the girls says she'll take the bet, provided she can pair up with him every night "to be sure you're not cheating."

So, did he win the bet? "I lost," said John. "Slowly, excruciatingly, explosively, the week the summer holiday ended. Best sex I've ever had."

What had she done? "Nothing. I'd get in bed each night and turn on my side so I wasn't facing her. She'd get in behind me and talk. She didn't touch me but she was close enough that I could feel her body warmth. 'I'm going to make this easier for you,' she said. 'If you last, you get the five-hundred dollars, but I won't take anything if you lose. I just want to see how desperate you become.' Then after a week or two she began to touch my back, very lightly, with her fingertips. 'The rule is that you can't touch me, but nothing says I can't touch you—except in some obvious places.' That I could handle."

Then after another week she asked me to lie so we were facing. "You should always look your tormenter in the eye," she said. So I rolled over. She just smiled. I began to tremble, literally. "It will only get worse," she said. "And you don't need to confess, you know. This is between the two of us. The others don't have to know."

"I give up," I said finally. "So, you've lost?" she said. "Utterly," I said. "Excellent," she said. "But there's just one thing," she said. "Yes?" I said. "You'll have to wait a couple of days," she said. "You're indisposed?" I said. "No," she said. "Plumbing's not an issue. I'd just like to enjoy your desperation for while longer."

And he agreed? "For about half an hour."

Had he kept seeing the girl when the summer ended? "No. She went back to South Africa."

"Girls in fantasies tend to disappear," Barbara had said. "The girl James Bond sleeps with always gets killed."

"Why do men pay women for sex?" said John.

"So they'll leave afterward," said Barbara. She'd never liked that joke.

"'Saskia' was her name," said John. "Brutal. A fantastic runner."

Now he'd made Barbara disappear—or at least from his perspective he had, since he didn't call. Which suggested that the telephone flirtations they had engaged in were analogous to the Saskia fantasy. Which meant . . . ?

The pessimistic interpretation was that for John, Barbara hadn't been entirely real, that there hadn't been a relationship, really. The optimistic conclusion was that John had intended to fail, to lose the contest with Barbara, to break down and propose real sex. Either way, he clearly liked it on the edge.

"And that," said Barbara to her invisible visitor, "is all I know—except that he's physically attractive and physically brave. And hasn't called me. Which is obviously what's called for as he tries to repair his marriage, and his relationship with his daughters."

"Tries?" said the angel who wasn't there. "Repair?"

"Well, I assume there was something wrong or he wouldn't have played along with me, for a year on the phone and an hour in the dungeon."

"Brave?"

"You're right. Boys do foolish things just to see if they can. But there was no . . . immaturity at the end, you know. He was peaceful. He was dignified even, when I was frantic. He didn't say anything nasty or amusing or provocative. He just let me take him to his hotel and undress him and put him in the bath. It was as if it was a ceremony. I was the high priest. He was content with his role, even if his role was to be the sacrifice."

"Sacrifice?"

"I guess he had a need to suffer that was just as intense as my need to get his attention."

"Did you get it?"

"Seems not."

"Perhaps he is still working something out."

"Oh, you are a cruel angel, giving me hope."

"I am giving you practice in accepting whatever comes. You mentioned needing to do that. And hope is a virtue, by the way, if properly deployed."

"Is that what your boss says?"

"Perhaps you should do some more reading," said the voice in her head.

"Wouldn't that be a bit pretentious?" she said. "Or maybe I mean 'preposterous.' Reading my Bible, I assume you mean."

"It's been deemed helpful in the past."

"Well, really, here's a girl who wanted to fuck a guy so badly she arranged to have him tortured in a way that she believed might punch perverted buttons and get him to leave his wife. It would be a bit rich for her to act all holy."

"Human beings are like that."

Barbara had gotten pretty stuck into the Bible when her doorbell rang. She'd been at it for more than a month. It had become a sort of ritual. She came home and took a shower, changed into relaxed but attractive clothes—on the principle that John could show up on any night—ate a simple dinner, settled down in her one really comfortable chair. She didn't pray, just studied. The angel who wasn't there looked in on her from time to time, but generally let her get on with it. She took books out of the library that explained what she was reading, and let her skip over the "begats" without feeling guilty. Guilty, she was made to understand, was a permanent condition, but one that could be ameliorated. Not something to wallow in.

Some nights she felt like a college student working on a term paper. She was "in the zone" as athletes say, jumping between library books and scattered sections of the primary text. She mixed those nights with others when she plodded along, chapter by chapter, unfamiliar name by unfamiliar name. And then some evenings she let the silence wash over her, making her feel clean. Silence was doing that the night the doorbell rang.

Barbara's first thought, which embarrassed her, was that she would be opening the door to God the monster. What would Moses have done? Opened the door. That seemed to have been his job.

It was John. He had a beard. He looked older. He was dressed in blue jeans and a tweed jacket, a blue shirt with a frayed collar and no necktie. "Felicity's kicked me out," he said. "Can I crash on your couch?"

"Why did she kick you out? Come in. Of course you can stay here. You can sleep in my bed if you want. I'd like that. You can whip me with a belt if you need to, though it's quite all right if you don't. There's an angel in my head who's been telling me you'd show up. Are you still a lawyer?"

Barbara stepped back as she said all this and John followed her into the apartment. "Yes to everything," he said. "Except the belt."

"I'm sorry about that . . . episode," she said.

"No, don't be. You broke me open. You broke the spell. Pain let me see past the guilt that prevented me from doing anything about how ghastly I felt."

"What was there to be guilty about? We'd never done anything but flirt."

"I wasn't in love with my wife. And I thought that was a crime. Felicity thought it was just an inconvenience that shouldn't get in the way of the triumphant performance our marriage was supposed to be. She threw me out when I pointed that out." His face clouded up for a moment. "I tried to say it as gently as I could. But we have nothing in common, Felicity and me. Six weeks in Europe proved that—I used all my accumulated vacation..."

So, that's where he'd been.

"... six weeks spending my savings like a man trying to crash his car, putting our daughters to bed and then going downstairs in the hotel each evening to order our dinner and watch the conversation die."

"Your daughters?"

"Lovely little people. They saw seventeen castles and learned to eat frogs' legs. The oldest was just old enough to see that there was some sort of problem. They'll be fine. Most of their classmates' parents are divorced."

"Shall we skip the part where I feel guilty about that and try to make you feel guilty too?"

"That would be good."

"What's with the beard?"

"I'm a new person."

"I think *I've* been born again. Or at least I've been reading about God."

"The angel in your head?"

"Our adventure had an effect on me as well. I seem to be making progress at letting go."

John thought about that for a moment. "What's your position on sex?"

"God invented sex," said Barbara. "Do you have a suitcase?"

"Nope," said John. "There's just me and my beard and..."—he opened his wallet to show her that he had no cash and no credit cards—"... no means of retreat. If you throw me out I will become a street person."

"Did you honestly think I'd throw you out?"

"Couldn't know. I haven't called for quite a while."

"Thank you for that. I needed space." It hadn't occurred to Barbara that he'd been doing her a favor, as well as wrestling with his own demons, but somehow that now seemed obvious.

"What did you learn?"

"Well, I've gotten mixed messages. A lot of what I've read is about waiting, but what my heart has told me is that talking to a person in the middle of the night, the way we did, but never so much as touching that person, is a perversion."

"Which we should put an end to right away," said John.

"I think we can agree on that," said Barbara. "I hope we agree on that. But perhaps we should do a risk analysis first."

"Fuck the risk analysis," said John, still smiling.

"A gratifying suggestion," said Barbara, "but before you fuck the risk *analyst*, she feels a professional obligation to explain a few things to you."

"Could we undress while she does it?" said John. "I need you rather badly."

Barbara began to unbutton the green linen shirt she had on, and as she did so began to talk. "I have an unnatural desire to put myself in situations that hurt me emotionally. I think I know why, but that's not actually important. I *know* it's stupid. If I need to spend fifty thousand dollars having a doctor explain that to me over the next two years, I suppose I can, but I seem to have worked it out for myself."

John began to undo his belt. "And I clearly get something from being . . . frustrated."

"Is that why you married Felicity—sorry, shouldn't open that door."

"It's all right. We're doing full disclosure." He took off his jeans. "I do not enjoy being badly hurt physically, though I like a little bit of that, enjoy the *idea* of it, and it turns me on to show I can take it. It definitely turns me on to take risks. I think I should probably give up skiing. But most of all, I like . . . maybe I can't talk about it yet."

"So we have to be careful," said Barbara, giving him room. She kicked off her shoes and sat down to take off her corduroy trousers. "We're quite alike, you know. I like to train hard, but I don't like to be hurt. And I *especially* don't like being hurt emotionally, though you'd be hard pressed to prove it, given the amount of it I sign up for."

"Would it help if I kiss you every morning and tell you I love you?"

Barbara had started to undo her bra, but stopped. She was about to show John her breasts for the first time, which made her feel vulnerable. "Only if you mean it," she said. "Only if it is not part of a cunning though unconscious plan to break my heart."

"It wouldn't be. Why are you suddenly worried about that?"

"Because I buy into those situations so easily. If I sense heartbreak in prospect, I won't run away. I will go further into that ocean to see if I can drown."

"That was some angel," said John, who was down to his underwear.

"Angels evidently don't believe in white lies," said Barbara. "Can you tell me what you wouldn't tell me a minute ago?"

"No."

"So for example, and to be practical," said Barbara, "if you come home some night from a business trip and I seem distant, it will be because I have convinced myself that you spent an extra night away because you are beginning to tire of me."

Enhancements

"Just as I spent the 'night of Sally,' to give that episode a name, away from Felicity."

"Exactly. So I will unconsciously take actions that communicate a lack of interest. Making you reluctant to initiate. Which allows me to experience rejection. And feel ghastly. Cool, eh?"

"You never seemed distant when we talked on the phone from separate hotels in separate cities," said John. "Should I finish undressing?"

"That's because we couldn't have each other. Couldn't kiss or touch or worse because we were in separate cities. Let's take off the last bits together." They did.

"Yes," said John, "we made a vow of abstinence without ever talking about it."

"You were married. Still are."

"Not really. Never was, emotionally. Stupid behavior for someone who's supposed to be a smart lawyer."

"We found a way of hurting ourselves that seemed so perfect we never needed to discuss it. Or at least I did. Considering my psychological deformities, the situation was ideal. You couldn't really reject me because you were married and in another city and we treated it all as a joke. But I could still get a buzz of rejection because . . . you were married and in another city. If I hadn't turned you over to Sally, it could have gone on indefinitely."

"That phrase you just used," said John. "'Buzz of rejection.'"

"I must get something out of rejection, because I keep finding ways to experience it. I haven't told you about my love life before we met."

"Stop right there," said John.

"You don't want to know about my previous lovers?" she said with a touch of sarcasm.

"No. That's not it. I assume you've had a few—good-looking woman that you are. It's what you said before. About the buzz. I know exactly what you mean. It's like the Japanese who eat fugu—the poisonous blowfish. Or partly poisonous. You have to be trained to be a fugu chef. If you serve the wrong bits the customer dies on the spot. It's some sort of nerve agent. But, here's the rub. Fugu aficionados want to eat the liver, or whatever it is, that's *right next to* the poisonous bit, so that a few molecules of the poison have crossed over. They want their lips to tingle a little."

"The Japanese are weird," said Barbara.

"Human beings are weird," John corrected her.

"My angel would agree," said Barbara.

"Good. My point is that there is pleasure in being just on the edge. Or at least there is for me. If I come home, to continue your example, and you are a bit cool, which is a downer since I've been away for a couple of days, and you say you're going to bed early, so I wander around the apartment doing nothing and flipping through a magazine and, then, finally creep into bed trying not to wake you, and I discover that you are entirely naked and waiting to surprise me, well, that's intensely satisfying."

"So, what's wrong with that?"

"It goes further."

"Yes."

"I tried to persuade Felicity, who I know I shouldn't talk about but I have to, I tried to persuade her to make me wait sometimes . . ."

"Go on."

"I wanted to give her my next orgasm—that's the way I put it—to let her decide when I got to have it, to let her keep me smoldering for a night or two."

"Because that turned you on."

"Insanely."

"Like Saskia."

"She did exist, you know."

"But you've . . . enhanced the story a bit?"

"Sex is enhancement."

"Felicity didn't understand that?"

"She understood the concept. She just disagreed. She thought waiting was inefficient." John fell silent. Barbara waited for him to continue, which he eventually did in a neutral tone. "So, you see what I like. Telephone sex was an approximation. When the girl's in a different city, the fact that she isn't touching you is less intense." He paused again. "Pretty embarrassing, eh?"

"And I completely misunderstood," said Barbara. "I thought you wanted to be hurt, physically."

"I only talked about that because I thought you liked it when I did."

"You did a good job," said Barbara. "Such a good job I turned you over to Sally."

"Sally who turned you over to yourself . . ."

"And forced me to admit in front of God and everyone what I'd been trying to do."

"That night?"

"Oh, the crying and embarrassing myself, telling you how I'd planned to save you, no. The real admissions came later—in my cell here, waiting for you to call."

"If it makes you feel any better, I confronted reality in Florence, with my cell phone in my hand, not calling you."

"That makes me feel a lot better," said Barbara.

"So, let me finish the risk analysis," said John, "and the *mitigations*. I believe that's the technical term."

"It is," said Barbara. It was nice of him to honor her profession that way.

"We'll start with the fact that we are powerfully attracted to each other," said John. "Or at least it should be obvious that I am, standing here naked in front of you and your angel. So, whatever cocktail of self-doubt and self-abuse our subconscious wants to serve us, let's lay down a base... My father used to say that. If he was going to a party where there would be a lot to drink, he always wanted to "lay down a base" of food to delay intoxication. He believed hard-boiled eggs were ideal for that purpose. Russians, or so I understand from spy novels, eat butter for the same reason. Anyway, to avoid intoxication with our inner demons, we should lay down a base of physical pleasure."

"Sex," said Barbara.

"Yes."

"Let's," said Barbara. "And no waiting."

"But as to further mitigations..."

"There aren't any," said Barbara. "Life is one game of chance after another. What was it Sally taught you?"

"That I was lost. That I didn't get to decide what happened."

"I promise I won't hurt you again," said Barbara.

"You can promise all you want but there's no guarantee," said John.

"So, we understand each other," said Barbara.

"And we're right with your angel?"

"He's averting his gaze."

"He's a boy?" said John.

Enhancements

"I thought they were all boys," said Barbara.

"Could I change the subject?" said John. "Do you like to be on the bottom or the top, because I can do either and I am committed to giving you as much pleasure as possible?"

"I think we should start with a bath." She had a sudden thought and smiled. "And while the tub is filling, I could give you a little spanking if you'd like."

"Let's just get in the bathtub," said John. "Both of us this time. We'll leave the graduate courses until next semester. You already get an A for having a fabulous body. You can get another one for washing my back. I hear the professor is an easy grader."

"Well, my angel is not an easy grader," said Barbara, to whom reality had fully presented itself. "Sexual energy travels on an underground river of fantasy and fetish. You need to stay in the boat, but it doesn't pay to ignore the current. If there are games you need to play, let me know what they are. If you can cause me to discover what they are without telling me directly, so much the better. There need be no embarrassment." She paused. "Unless, of course, you . . . enjoy the tingle of embarrassment."

"Fugu," said John.

Barbara started to reply but John came to her and put a finger to her lips.

"There's a prerequisite," he said, "to all the other courses, which I cannot allow you to skip."

"Yes?"

"Kissing 101." He kissed her lightly on the lips. And then a second time, more . . . assertively. Which brought their bodies into contact.

"I'm out of practice," she said. "I will need a lot of tuition."

"We're both out of practice," said John. "Or to be accurate, we're both beginners at what we have in mind, which is an honest relationship."

"You sound so serious," said Barbara.

"I am," said John.

"Oh, I like that," she said.

Youthful Adventure

When Charles was a younger man—before his firm had a gym or he knew what a law firm was, really—he decided it would be interesting to live with two women at once. Having sex with both of them, that is. He had a few months of leisure before law school started. He wanted some fun. So, he ran a classified ad in one of those underground newspapers that seem to exist for the purpose of publishing such ads. "Prideful male professional doing penance desires temporary position as domestic servant to two women."

He got three replies, care of the reference number listed in the ad. He thought about them for a week, thought about the whole thing a second time. He *was* careful, even then. He wasn't sure what he was doing. How much control was he prepared to give up, even in a good cause? In the end, of course, he decided it would be an interesting risk.

The way the system worked, the respondents didn't have to disclose their identities right away, any more than he did. The idea was that you wrote back and forth providing further information until you felt ready to meet. Nowadays, no one would trust that sort of newspaper to protect their privacy, but back then some people did.

"Thank you for responding to my ad," he wrote to each of them. "I should probably tell you more before we decide to meet—and if you continue to be interested, you might wish to be explicit about your expectations. I am twenty-five years old, heterosexual, very fit, a non-smoker, five-foot-eleven, Caucasian, thought to be decent-looking. For reasons I may not be willing to disclose, I wish to submit to a strict regimen of subordination. I wish to live in your house or apartment and keep it clean. I will look after your laundry, iron your shirts, polish your shoes. Having served in the United States Marine Corps, I am quite good at maintenance and neatness, but you may impose whatever standards you like.

"I know how to cook and will do so if you wish, taking responsibility for the shopping and dishwashing as well. I am prepared to be your waiter in the evening and serve you breakfast in bed. I will wear any form of servant's uniform or other apparel you direct me to.

"I do not expect to have any personal privacy."

Let's see what that elicits, Charles said to himself. The first answer came in almost immediately: "Pain?" He put that couple in the discard pile. They probably lacked finesse.

The second response was interesting, but not a good fit. "We are lesbians," it said. "We dislike men. We like the idea of having a man serve us, and we can probably make the job unpleasant, which you seem to want, but it is only fair to warn you in advance that there will be no sex." When he was eighteen, Charles might have seen that as a challenge, but at twenty-five he had more sense.

The last letter came a week later. "We may be what you are looking for," it read. "We are 'neatniks.' Each of us has her own bedroom; you will have to sleep on the couch—and of course get up and put away your blankets before our alarms go off. We have demanding jobs, so we have to stay fit. In your capacity as a cook, that will mean very careful attention to calories and fat grams. If you learned about exercise in the Marines, and could act as a personal trainer, that would be good.

"We think it would be nice to have you serve dinner. We can talk about a uniform.

"We are not looking for sex," they concluded. They gave their names as Sigrid and Stephanie.

Perfect, said Charles to himself.

"In the Marine Corps," Charles explained to his new employers—for some reason Sigrid and Stephanie insisted on paying him a dollar a week—"the correct form when being instructed or corrected is to stand at attention and look straight ahead into nothingness. In other cultures, one indicates submission by looking down."

"A cat may look at a king," said Sigrid, who had a feline sinuousness to her.

"Meow," said Stephanie without missing a beat.

"You two seem to know each other well," said Charles.

"That's none of your affair," said Stephanie. Not clear what that meant.

"But we *are* a bit competitive," said Sigrid.

He guessed they were in their late twenties. Not glamour-puss beautiful, but more than presentable. Bodies their contemporaries would envy in ten years. From the quality of their furniture, he judged that they earned good salaries.

"In answer to your implied question," said Stephanie, "you may look at me all you want, so long as you do what I tell you to."

"Likewise," said Sigrid slowly, "so long as I may look at you. And you're obedient, of course. From time to time it might be interesting to have you stand at attention, though. Can you stand at attention for an hour?"

"As you wish, mistress."

"Umm," said Sigrid.

The innuendo seemed to make Stephanie uncomfortable. "Now get to work on the kitchen," she said sharply. "The cupboards haven't been emptied and cleaned for at least two weeks. The oven is embarrassing. We'll be back after lunch to inspect."

It was a Saturday. He'd presented himself as agreed at nine o'clock for what was supposed to be an interview, but they'd told him—nice touch, he thought—that having been engaged, he must start work immediately and wasn't to go back to collect his belongings. "You belong to us now," said Sigrid.

"As you wish," said Charles. He could exist in the running shorts and polo shirt he was wearing. He didn't have a cat that would starve. "I can wash my clothes when you are out."

"Or when we're here," said Sigrid, "if we decide we like looking at you."

Stephanie gave her apartment-mate a severe look.

"What's your name again, servant?" said Stephanie.

"Oliver," said Charles.

As soon as he heard the elevator depart, Charles inspected the apartment. Granola in the cupboard. White wine in the refrigerator. Professional suits and dresses in their closets. Pictures of what could have been parents in what must have been Stephanie's bedroom. Medals from college swim meets hanging on the mirror above Sigrid's dresser.

Youthful Adventure

Why did he assume whose room was whose? Interesting that he was so sure. More silk in Sigrid's wardrobe? More serious books beside Stephanie's bed? Well-reviewed Egyptian novel beside Sigrid's, though. And Stephanie had a fur coat. Must come from a grandmother. No one wore mink anymore. It made too many people angry. Charles wondered what would make Sigrid and Stephanie angry. That could be important. Anger meant passion.

Charles took off his running shoes and lay down on Stephanie's bed. He rolled over to the other side, turned over on to his back, rolled back again. Then he went into Sigrid's room and did the same. Then he stripped the sheets off both beds to see what odor they gave off, if any.

So they weren't sleeping together. Depressions on one side only of each queen-size bed. Different perfume—and Sigrid used more of it. Stephanie's sheets smelled primarily of soap.

Charles collected the sheets and took them to the tiny laundry off the kitchen. Then he went back to get the towels from the single bathroom. Ah. Twin college diplomas: same year, both with honors. Stephanie had majored in psychology, Sigrid in math. So maybe she didn't read as many books because she liked numbers.

And "Sigrid" and "Stephanie" were their real names. They were new at this sort of thing, Charles decided. In due course, he would have to talk to them about risk.

His employers came back at one o'clock. "Where's lunch?" said Stephanie.

"I might ask the same question, mistress," said Charles, looking straight at her. "You said I was to serve breakfast and dinner. You didn't mention lunch. But if you wish, I can make a salad in a few minutes."

"Do that," said Stephanie.

As they walked down the hall to their respective bedrooms, Charles could hear Sigrid laughing and Stephanie telling her to hush.

Sigrid was back in a minute. "You've changed my sheets."

"Yes, mistress."

"I didn't tell you to do that."

"Clean sheets are part of a very clean house, which I believe is my explicit responsibility. The ones you slept in last night are in the wash."

Sigrid thought about that for a moment, looking around the sparkling kitchen. "Did you clean behind the refrigerator?" she said.

"I found the apple core."

"I told her you would."

"She needs to test me?"

"She wants to get her money's worth, I think."

"A dollar a week?"

"She says you are getting *psychic* income. This game presumably does something for you—or so she tells me. Does it?"

"Yes, mistress."

Charles waited for her to ask the obvious question, but she didn't. There was a hint of passive-aggressive about Sigrid. She was definitely angry about something.

Stephanie reappeared in running clothes. "I want you to take me for a run, Oliver. We'll go to Central Park."

"Not until you have let your lunch go down," he said. "Speaking as your person trainer, that is. Would you like me to serve you at the table in the dining room?"

"Serve us both in there," said Sigrid.

"I will have to make a second salad, mistress."

"Wasn't it obvious that we'd both want lunch?" said Stephanie.

"You must ask for what you want," said Charles.

"Aren't good servants supposed to be mind readers?" said Stephanie.

"I promised you obedience," said Charles. "But you must be explicit about your desires."

"I see," said Sigrid.

"Which means you have to know what they are," said Charles, looking at Stephanie, who quickly looked away.

He made the second salad, making use of the rest of the canned tuna from the cupboard and the array of vegetables in the refrigerator, and served them both.

"It would be helpful if you made lists of what you like to eat," said Charles "so I can give you what you want." He was standing in a corner of the dining room, which clearly made the women nervous. And telling them what to do, whether they realized that or not. It would be interesting to discover how malleable they were. "Also, if I am to do the shopping, I will need a key to the apartment, so I can get back in with the groceries."

"Sounds reasonable," said Sigrid. She looked at Stephanie. "There's that hardware store on the way to the Park. It will give you a way to digest your lunch, as Oliver suggests."

"I thought I might also get him more pairs of shorts and polo shirts. Is there a color you'd like for his livery, Sig?"

They were practicing talking about him in front of him, as if he weren't there, as if they didn't care that he was there. They were finding that hard to do.

"Red. Chinese red if you can find it?" said Sigrid. "That just slightly orangey red."

Charles had the sudden thought that Stephanie might be color-blind. If she was, Sigrid would dance on her weakness exactly that way. But mostly it was boys who were color-blind. Nevertheless, the beginning of an insight?

"Won't that make him a bit conspicuous in the neighborhood?"

"Don't you suppose he'd like that—at some level? Do you want to be conspicuous, Oliver?,

"What I want is not an issue, mistress," said Oliver, looking straight ahead. "The Marine Corps is partial to red, mistress."

"A question," said Stephanie suddenly. Something was rubbing her the wrong way, which was good. "If you insist on calling us both "mistress," how are we supposed to know which one of us you mean?"

"Context, mistress," said Charles.

This made Sigrid laugh.

"What is that supposed to mean?" said Stephanie.

"The servant means it will be obvious," said Sigrid. "Aren't you going to inspect the kitchen, Steph?"

"It's obviously clean," said Stephanie, sounding peeved.

"Don't you want to look for the apple core?" she said.

"I suppose he's found it," said Stephanie, "just like you said he would. It's annoying how often she's right, Oliver. And I'm the one who took psychology. So, OK, did you clean behind the refrigerator?"

"Yes, mistress."

Stephanie took a couple of deep breaths.

"You'd better go for your run," said Sigrid. She turned to Charles. "And run her into the ground, Oliver. She's impossible if she doesn't get enough exercise."

Stephanie didn't argue.

Pick up some lamb chops on the way home," said Sigrid. "I think we have plenty of vegetables."

"Yes, mistress," said Charles.

"Or are you a vegetarian again?" said Sigrid to Stephanie.

"No," said Stephanie, a bit too loudly.

"It's OK," said Sigrid in a soothing voice. "There's nothing *wrong* with carrot juice."

Stephanie is the real neatnik, Charles told himself. And the health and fitness nut. Sigrid is a natural athlete, has perfect skin, obedient hair. She has a streak of laziness, hard as that is to believe of a competitive swimmer. But maybe the league she swam in wasn't that tough. Stephanie, on the other hand, has to work hard at everything. Sigrid is genuinely fond of Stephanie, but treats her as a younger sister who needs to be reminded of things. She gets pleasure from needling her. Probably leaves dishes in the sink to annoy her. Or makes her late for work somehow. At some level, Charles told himself, Sigrid probably regards aggravating Stephanie's foibles as a form of affection.

They went to Central Park. "We'll just walk there to warm up," said Charles. It turned out that Stephanie was a good athlete, which was not a surprise, even if she had no medals in her bedroom. She was driven. He pushed her, as instructed, but she didn't get tired until the fourth mile. They did five.

They left the Park and went to one of those Madison Avenue "yuppie stores," as Charles thought of them, with shirts and trousers in a range of self-confident colors. "What color would *you* like, Oliver?"

"It is not for me to decide, mistress."

Another woman standing nearby must have overheard him. Charles could see that she was edging closer trying to eavesdrop. "You must do what pleases you," he added.

"Keep your voice down," Stephanie said in a whisper.

Charles realized how easy it would be to keep Stephanie on edge, what thorough training Sigrid had given her in being stressed out. "Yes, mistress," he said in a whisper just loud enough that the other woman would have heard him. Fantasies to last her a week, he said to himself as he followed Stephanie to another part of the store.

In the end, Stephanie decided the red the store offered was close enough to what Sigrid wanted. She also decided that while red would be all right above the waist Oliver needed chino long trousers. The store offered a monogramming service. She wanted to have something embroidered on the shirts, but what should she choose?

"There are various possibilities, mistress." He could see that offering suggestions was the best way to serve her in this matter. "You could list your names. You could use my name. You could use your address. You could use a non-existent address on your block, or a non-existent apartment number in your building. Or just the words, 'Sleeping on the Floor.'"

It took Stephanie a moment to register—and then she was confident and in charge again. Maybe it was because they were out of range of the eavesdropper. "A non-existent address because you're a fantasy creature," she said. "I see. And rest assured, Oliver, we will winkle out your fantasies soon enough. But you're supposed to sleep on the couch."

"Not hard enough," he said.

"Do you like being uncomfortable?"

"I like discipline," said Charles. "'Sleeping on the Floor,' embroidered on a yuppie polo shirt, would be an emblem of my subordination, and your control." Not a lot of winkling necessary.

"What if our friends saw it?"

"Will you be having friends come for dinner, mistress?"

"Well, we sometimes do. And they are bound to ask what the emblem, as you call it, means." She paused, and acted out having a sudden thought. "Come to think of it, they are bound to ask about you. What would you want us to tell them, Oliver?" She was riffling through a display of men's brightly colored neckties as they talked.

"'Sleeping on the Floor' would be the answer," said Charles. "You could tell them you won me in a charity auction. I understand such things are not unknown in New York. Half a dozen presentable young men make themselves available for household chores and a dinner date. Do they make themselves available for anything else? Read my shirt. If your friends ask questions, I would recommend you simply smile. But understand, mistress, you may say or do anything you like. *My* comfort, or embarrassment—for that matter, my fantasies—are nothing for you and your friend to be concerned about."

Stephanie thought about that for a moment. "I will take your advice," she said, effectively closing the subject. She ordered three sets of his new uniform. Charles could see that she was pleased with herself.

On the longish walk back, which included visits to hardware and grocery stores, Stephanie asked Charles a series of questions. You didn't have to be a psychologist to know that they weren't about him, really. They were about Stephanie—though she didn't appear to know that.

"Have you ever done this before?"

"No, mistress."

"Were you really in the Marine Corps?"

"Yes, mistress."

"Did you ever shoot anyone?"

"Yes, mistress."

"Are you troubled about that?"

"No, mistress."

"I thought you might be punishing yourself for having done that—killed someone. I mean, what you've undertaken with Sigrid and me is not a normal thing to do. And you won't say why?"

"No, mistress."

"There isn't some girl you've jilted, or who won't forgive you for something? You did mention 'penance' in your ad." Charles made no reply. They walked a while in silence. "So, what are the limits?"

"I will not let you kill me, mistress."

Stephanie laughed. "Well, that's a relief. How about hurting you—no, forget that."

"If that is something you want to do, mistress, I will accept it as well as I can. Marines are tough. Any man may be broken. But the important thing is for you to discover what *you* want."

Half a block of silence. "Well, I'm not going to hurt you. Unless you misbehave. If you fail to keep the apartment clean, I might make you do push-ups."

"I am extremely comfortable with push-ups, mam. Excuse me. 'Mistress,' I should say. 'Mam' is Marine Corps language. We are not in the Marine Corps. In the Marine Corps, you do not have personal desires. You have duties, and standards, a tradition to uphold. It is all quite easy, actually. But in this situation you and my other mistress have put yourselves in, there is no field manual. There are no standards. There is no tradition. You must chart your own course."

"Sigrid is an actuary, you know," said Stephanie, as if that followed.

"And what are you, mistress?"

"Human resources."

"Is it interesting work, mistress?"

"Sometimes it is. People are interesting to study. But the job requires you to be objective all the time."

"By which you mean firing people?"

"If their managers are gutless, yes. That makes me tired sometimes. I may be too soft for the career I have fallen into. It is not normal human behavior, if you think about it, being quote, objective about everything."

"Civilization is an argument with our baser instincts, mistress."

"The Marine Corps taught you that?"

"The Marine Corps is very clear-eyed about human weakness—and the strength of groups."

"Oh, yes," said Stephanie. "Groups. A large corporation is a forest of groups. It is like a science fiction horror movie, with fast-growing plants trying to strangle each other."

"And this interests you, mistress?"

"I hate it. I have watched the movie over and over again. There is also a lot of human weakness to come to terms with."

A block of silence. "Are we a group, Oliver—you and me and Sigrid?"

"Inevitably we will be, mistress."

Stephanie took a deep breath and then let it out. "Sorry. My issues are not your problem."

"If you wish to talk, mistress, I will listen."

"This was Sigrid's idea," said Stephanie. It was all she said until they got home.

When they did get back to the apartment, Sigrid was sitting on the couch, reading the well-reviewed Egyptian novel from her bedside table. "Did you two have fun?" she said. "And Oliver, I need a cup of tea. The Earl Grey. No milk. No lemon."

"The same for me," said Stephanie, suddenly brightening up. "And yes, it was a good run." She explained about the color of the red shirts and the chino long trousers. "Shorts could be misinterpreted. And we should have some people over soon."

"To show him off?" said Sigrid.

"Why not? He says he wouldn't mind. You'd like him to mind, though, wouldn't you, Sig?"

"You seem more comfortable with this situation than you were before," said Sigrid. Charles was in the kitchen preparing the tea, but could hear her clearly. He assumed she was speaking for his benefit.

"He's quite nice, you know," said Stephanie. "You should talk to him."

"You can have first go," said Sigrid.

"Oh, nothing like that," said Stephanie. She explained about "Sleeping on the Floor."

Charles took in the tea things, poured out two cups, and took the teapot back to the kitchen.

"I'm really stiff after that run," said Stephanie to Sigrid.

"Have him run you a bath," said Sigrid. Charles was certain she intended to be overheard.

Stephanie gave a little gasp.

"Indeed," said Sigrid. "And you could have him wash your back."

"I couldn't," said Stephanie.

"I thought we'd talked about all this. Why did we answer his ad if we didn't want to have some fun? Why do you buy that newspaper if not for the ads?"

Youthful Adventure

"I buy it for the movie and restaurant reviews," said Stephanie.

"Right. And you just happen to glance at the 'Personal' section—for an hour and a half. You're repressed—which you ought to recognize, being a fucking psychiatrist."

"Psychologist. A not-fucking psychologist by your lights. And by the way, when was your last date?"

Charles was riveted. He had nothing left to do in the kitchen but listen. He was living with two good-looking women, who were having a fight because they weren't getting enough sex. There was only one solution. He took off his clothes, put them into the washing machine, and walked into the living room with a refilled teapot.

"Oliver!" Stephanie exclaimed.

"My clothes are in the wash, mistress."

"And you look very good without them," said Sigrid. "Turn around and let us look at you."

"Sigrid!" said Stephanie.

"We had to get to this," said Sigrid. "You don't mind being naked, do you Oliver? You probably quite like it."

"As you wish, mistress."

"So as long as you are comfortable with nakedness," said Sigrid, "run a bath for my inhibited friend. Kneel on the floor and wash her back. And be thorough. She likes to be clean."

Stephanie was blushing. "Oh, all right," she said.

Charles turned on the faucets in the bath, adjusting the temperature as it filled. It was a large bathtub, but there was plenty of hot water.

Stephanie went in and closed the door. "Come in," she called out after a few minutes. She had poured in bubble bath. She was leaning forward, holding onto her knees, with her back exposed.

"Leave the door open if you want a chaperone," said Sigrid. It wasn't clear whether she was talking to Stephanie or to him. The bathroom was down the hall from the living room, so it didn't matter, really, but Stephanie asked him to close it.

Charles immersed a washcloth in the water and started to rub Stephanie's back. "Soap first," she said. "And just use your hands."

"Tell me everything you want, mistress," said Charles, as he explored the tension in her shoulders.

"I'd like it if you'd call me 'Stephanie.' And I'd like you to make the decisions."

"That isn't really the agreement," said Charles after he'd worked on her back for a while, "but I'll take that as an instruction to wash more of you. Lean back and let me have a leg."

Stephanie raised one leg out of the water.

"Nice calf," said Charles, running soapy hands down from her ankle. "Nice thigh. Nice girl, in fact."

"Pretty messed up in the head," she said.

"Who told you that?"

"My honors degree in psychology told me that."

"Did it tell you what to do about it?"

"No." There was genuine sadness in her voice.

"I recommend an orgasm," said Charles, as if he had been suggesting a cold remedy. "Releases endorphins, same as exercise. Makes the world less complicated." Under the bubbles his hand explored further. Stephanie stiffened but didn't tell him to stop.

This part of the dance always made Charles smile, remembering the first and probably only sex lecture he had ever had—delivered when he was eleven by a worldly wise fifteen-year-old cousin: "There's a little nubbin down there," he'd said grandly, "and if you touch it the right way, the girl goes batshit."

Stephanie did, biting her lip to avoid making any noise. "Get in the tub," she said finally. "Behind me. I need to be held."

"Yes, mistress," said Charles, getting up off his knees and complying.

"Please," she whispered. "My name."

Charles lowered himself into the warm water and put his arms around her. "Stephanie," he said softly into her ear.

After a few minutes they got out. Stephanie ran the shower to rinse herself off. Charles dried her with a fluffy bath towel, and then began to dry himself. "We need to get you something to wear," she said.

"As you wish," said Charles. His only clothes would still be wet and need to go into the drier.

"I have an oversize man's shirt you can use. Oversize for me, that is. I got given it at an office picnic last year, when it suddenly got cold and I had on a topless dress."

"I assume you mean 'sleeveless,'" said Charles.

"Oops, yes, of course," said Stephanie. "And he had a tee shirt underneath. What have you done to me?"

"Nothing hundreds of other men in New York wouldn't be pleased to do," said Charles. "And you still have the shirt rather than calling to thank him because . . . ?"

"Don't be like Sigrid."

"As you wish . . . Stephanie."

She gave him a kiss on the cheek and went to get the shirt, which had reassuringly long tails.

Two hours later he served his employers dinner, wearing his own clothes again. Lamb chops, baked potatoes *without* butter or sour cream, broccoli, tossed salad, red wine from a 24-bottle rack in one of the cupboards, a slice of melon for dessert. Stephanie gave every impression of wanting to get drunk.

"So, how was your bath?" said Sigrid when the fruit had been served. "Shall I have one after dinner?" Charles was in the kitchen but again he could hear the conversation clearly. He had to assume they knew that.

"I'm not going to share him," said Stephanie.

"I thought we were in this together," said Sigrid.

"It wouldn't be sanitary. And if one of us got pregnant we wouldn't know who the father was."

"You're not making a lot of sense, Steph."

"Never mind. Getting pregnant isn't an issue. But he's mine."

Oh my, said Charles to himself. He went into the dining room to clear away the dishes. Sigrid took advantage of his presence to tell Stephanie she should go to bed. "Eventful day," she explained to Charles.

Stephanie did as her friend had suggested. Even after four glasses of wine, she seemed reluctant to look Charles in the face.

"I'll read in my room," said Sigrid, "so you can go to sleep out here."

Three hours later Charles woke on the living room floor, underneath a blanket he had found in the linen closet and with a rolled-up bath towel for a pillow. During the more interesting parts of his time in the Marine Corps he had acquired the habit, when he woke, of lying very still with his eyes only half open and assessing the situation. There was someone squatting beside him in a dark long-sleeve tee shirt and leggings. It was Sigrid. "You're a ninja?" he said very quietly. Actually, what she called to mind was tribesmen squatting around a cooking fire. Men from a culture without chairs—or mercy, for that matter.

"You're common property," whispered Sigrid. In a previous life she had presumably lived in such a culture. And been a man.

"If you're so confident, why haven't you got your own boyfriend?"

"They always want a relationship."

"Like Stephanie."

"Well?" said Sigrid—by which she presumably meant, are you going to have a tumble with me or not?

"I only do one woman in any 24-hour period," said Charles—which of course wasn't true. "Start a sign-up sheet." For some reason he wanted to see how hungry she was.

"You didn't *do* her and we both know it." Sigrid stood up. She reminded him of a heron unfolding, transforming itself from a jumble of feathers into the lean creature it was, able to defy gravity, just as Sigrid defied her hunger. "My door will be open if you change your mind."

Charles thought about the situation for a quarter of an hour and decided that, as Sigrid had been pretty clear about her desires—as he's told them both they had to be—honor required him to "do" Sigrid. Also, he rather badly wanted to. She was his type: self-sufficient, strongly muscled under a smooth surface, a pusher of boundaries.

"Leave the door open," she said as she sat up in bed and began to take off her ninja outfit.

"You want her to hear us?"

"If she does, she does."

"She's a bit fragile."

"Yes, and it pisses me off. She gets herself in ridiculous situations, emotionally. Falls in love with the wrong guy. Doesn't have a date for three months and then manages to accept two for the same night and decides she has to call both men and pretend to be sick. Did she even manage to have an orgasm?"

Charles didn't answer.

"I'll take that for a 'no.'"

"Believe what you wish to believe, mistress."

"Oh, I see." And then, "well done."

Silence.

Charles was still standing beside her bed. Sigrid lay on her side, looking at him. Both of them were now naked. The only light came from the red numbers on the digital clock radio. "Do you have any special requests, mistress?"

"Just get in the bed," said Sigrid.

He got under the covers. He touched her in various places to see what she liked. She pushed his hands away a few times, but it was clear she liked everything.

"It's been a while," she said, letting down her guard a bit.

"You're sure it wouldn't intensify your pleasure to wait another couple of days?"

"Absolutely unnecessary."

"You're sure you don't need to talk to Stephanie first?"

"Not her decision."

"Why do the two of you share an apartment?"

"Not relevant, but if it will make you get on with it, we've been roommates since the first year of college."

"Do you think you are well matched?"

"No, of course not. But we understand each other. Pleeese, stop asking me questions."

"May I tell you then, that you are very beautiful, that I admire your directness, that I love your skin . . . ?"

"Not relevant."

"Yes, mistress."

Charles knew how to be a tease in bed, but he regarded it as discourteous to seek his own pleasure before he had given a woman everything she wanted, which required a man to pay attention. Another lesson from his older and wiser cousin. What is "the right way?" he'd asked. "Depends on the girl," was the answer.

In Sigrid's case, pleasure took a while. When they both were finished, he rolled over on his back.

There was a ghost in the doorway. It gave Charles a start. A nightgown illuminated by Sigrid's clock radio, the face and arms less distinct. He realized it had to be Stephanie. Sigrid laughed.

"Do you always watch each other?" said Charles.

"When we can," said Stephanie.

"You owe me a show," said Sigrid to Stephanie.

"If Oliver is willing, I'll square accounts tomorrow," said Stephanie.

"As you wish, mistress."

"Can I keep him for the rest of the night?" said Sigrid.

"Of course you can, sweetheart." She walked into the room, around the bed to where Sigrid was and gave her a kiss. Then she turned and went back to her own room, closing the door on the way out.

"Is this some kind of ritual?" said Charles. There was something practiced about it.

"Yes and no. She pretends everything is my idea but she sets it up."

"I mostly thought she was insecure."

"She is. That's why she's a chameleon. Some games she's an ingénue, sometimes she's a vamp. She'll bring a boy home from a bar and—no, I'm not going to tell you that."

"Have you answered a lot of those ads?"

"Yes. They're addictive."

"What happened to the boy from the bar?"

"I said I wouldn't tell you."

"Doesn't mean you don't want to," said Charles. "You two said you weren't looking for sex."

"Everyone lies—as Dr. House reminds us."

Charles let his hands wander a bit, in case that was what she wanted.

"Just hold me," said Sigrid. She was silent for a while. "That boy. Younger than you. She got him to cry."

Charles stayed another week. He liked them both, actually. They were gratifyingly responsive to every sexual thing he did. Sigrid could be goofy as well as slinky. And Stephanie cried real tears. But eventually they ran out of games to play.

"Thanks for the memories," he wrote in the letter he left on their kitchen counter, along with the key to their apartment. "I'm keeping one of the red polo shirts." It sounded like a line from a trashy novel. If you thought about it, the whole thing had been a trashy novel—except for the fact that actual women had been involved.

"I've never been with anyone like you two," he'd continued. "You're desirable, unexpected, courageous, kinky in manageable ways—all good qualities. But I must tell you that each time I finished with either of you—when the performance was over and we were alone—all you wanted was to be held. Sex as a performance is a way of holding back. Both of you are closing in on thirty (I read the dates on your diplomas), so perhaps it is time to give up emotional hide-and-seek. All the best, Oliver (not his real name)."

His time with Sigrid and Stephanie also taught Charles a lesson. Never assume you are in control, he thereafter made it a point to remind himself. Where women are concerned, never even assume you know what's going on. Long-term, the only sensible strategy is love.

"Such Wilt Thou Be To Me"

Perhaps there is a language that has a word for the relationship that exists (or doesn't) when two people share an apartment but not a bed. If Lilac had taken anthropology instead of art history she might have known what it was. Might know the word.

Lilac had these thoughts some mornings (many mornings) as she rode the subway downtown, where her name was "Lil" and she was a paralegal. She found her actual name embarrassing, evidence of an uncool romanticism in her midwestern parents. Her workmates assumed her name was "Lillian," which was fine.

Of course, "Lilac" was nothing to her sister's name, which was "Freesia." But *her* name didn't bother Freesia at all. When guys hit on her sister in a bar, for example, and asked her name, she stretched out the "ee" a bit, presumably to show she wasn't embarrassed. And if someone then asked her, "So, does that mean you're free or freezing?" she'd just laugh. Freesia was cool.

Lilac's sister lived in California (of course) and did some kind of logistics in the movie business. Lilac had seen Freesia's name in the crawl a couple of times. She supposed people thought it was a made-up name—"Freesia Conroy." And to be brutally honest (or bitchy?) there was an imaginary quality to her sister: slender, uninhibited, generous and supportive, but on her own terms. *Blade Runner* meets *Mary Poppins,* Lilac had once said to herself. That was after the surprise birthday dinner Freesia had cooked for her where most of the men turned out to be gay.

Lilac was excited when Freesia called from JFK and asked would Lilac be there when she got to her apartment, which was where again? Lilac was there.

So was Bob, the guy with whom Lilac had the relationship that had no name. Bob wasn't exactly cool. Cool was difficult for an analyst at a private equity firm to be because they made you work too hard. Like eighty hours a week, as far as Lilac could see. Bob didn't seem to mind, though there were nights when he stumbled in after midnight—Lilac could hear him come in—there were times she wished she could comfort him or something. Just a hug it would have been, you understand.

Anyway, Lilac hoped her sister would like Bob. Or actually maybe the other way round. Lilac hoped Bob would be impressed with her sister. She'd always believed that her sister made her more interesting. She sometimes wished Freesia lived in New York so she could go out to dinner with her and meet more of Freesia's interesting friends, even if they were gay. Freesia would see to it that Lilac sat next to someone who was at least interesting. Freesia was good at organizing where everyone sat, and had no hesitation about *re*organizing an entire table of twelve people in a crowded restaurant. That had happened once when Lilac went out to California to visit her sister.

Bob did like Freesia. He volunteered to go out and get Indian food when she mentioned liking it. "Oh, thanks," said Freesia.

And Freesia seemed to approve of Bob, which surprised Lilac a little. Freesia had some sort of radar that identified uncoolness immediately. "Polite," she said, after Bob had gone out, which was not a Freesia kind of word.

You aren't really supposed to drink wine with Indian food, but it has other benefits, which was presumably why Bob brought back two bottles of Chardonnay. The three of them drank all of it.

What did Bob, do, Freesia wanted to know? Too boring to contemplate, said Lilac quickly, which probably wasn't true. Did Bob know what Lilac did? Freesia certainly didn't, or at least claimed not to. She referred to her sister's job as "paragliding."

Yes, Bob knew exactly what Lilac did downtown. "Law and finance are kind of cousins in New York," he explained.

"Do you help each other with your homework?" said Freesia.

"No," said Lilac.

"Can't," said Bob. "Most of it is confidential."

"Who does the dishes?" said Freesia.

"I will," said Bob. "Your sister did yesterday."

"You have dinner together every night?" said Freesia.

"Can't" said Lilac.

"I work too late," said Bob.

"They were kind of two-day-old breakfast dishes that I washed yesterday," said Lilac.

"Yuk," said Freesia.

"I do the laundry for both of us," said Lilac. She supposed she wanted to stake a claim for household cleanliness.

"Does she ball your socks?" said Freesia.

"Yes, actually," said Bob, and then tuned around quickly and went into the kitchen.

"But you're not balling him?" said Freesia under her breath to her sister.

Lilac decided not to explain about the word that didn't exist in English. "No," she said.

When Bob came back to the table and poured the last of the wine into Freesia's glass, Freesia made a little speech. "Listen," she said, "it's nice of you to let me stay here. I've got about five days of business to do, some people to catch up with, and a show at MoMA to see, but I'll take you out to dinner tomorrow. Girlfriend of mine has a new restaurant on 10th Street."

"Can we make it late?" said Bob. It occurred to Lilac that coming back to the apartment in time to greet Freesia had probably put him behind on whatever work he had to do. She'd called him and asked him if he could be there.

"Ten?" said Freesia.

"That works," said Bob.

"It's a kind of fusion place. Mexican and Vietnamese, but not actually mixed. Just both available. "Ping Pong," it's called.

Lilac had heard of the restaurant. It had been reviewed in the *Times* the previous week. It was typical of her sister that it was run by someone she knew. Bob would have to be impressed. "It was in the *Times* last Thursday," she said.

" 'Fraid I don't read the arts and culture bits of the paper," said Bob, addressing Freesia.

"No time," said Freesia, to indicate that she understood. And then to Lilac: "So who am I supposed to sleep with?"

There was a brief silence.

"No sex," she added helpfully. "I promise. I'll even wear pajamas."

"Bob has a bigger bed," said Lilac, trying to be sophisticated.

Freesia looked at Bob. "No sweat," he said.

Freesia got up ridiculously early and disappeared. Lilac encountered Bob in the kitchen. "Did you have sex?" she asked. It seemed like the only honest thing to say.

"She lied about the pajamas," said Bob.

"She lies a lot," said Lilac. (Not true, actually.)

"She calls you 'Lilac,'" said Bob.

"That's my name."

"I didn't know."

"I try to keep it a secret. It seems like a dorky name—that is, if a girl's name can resemble a penis." Lilac was determined to be cool about the sex that had happened in the bedroom at the other end of the apartment from hers.

"So you shortened it?" said Bob.

This made them both laugh.

"I don't want to be a lilac," she said finally.

"Oh, I like the name," said Bob. "I'd really rather call you that than 'Lil.'"

"I suppose you can," said Lilac. "Just don't tell anyone else."

Ping Pong at ten o'clock in the evening was full of people who looked like you should recognize them. Several of them recognized Freesia. She introduced Bob and her sister to a minor movie star. "This is my little sister, Lilac," said Freesia. "She does something mysterious and boring on Wall Street. And this is her gorgeous roommate."

Freesia's girlfriend the chef came out of the kitchen to make recommendations. "Do you like hot or very hot?" she asked.

"Hot," said Lilac.

"Such Wilt Thou Be To Me"

"I'll bet she is," said the chef to Freesia.

"Hands off," said Freesia. "She's mine tonight."

"Well after your bossy sister leaves town," said the lady chef, who could have had some Mexican blood, Lilac decided, "you sneak down here some night and I'll test your limits." It hadn't occurred to Lilac that her limits needed testing, but maybe they did. Having Freesia around always made Lilac want to loosen up.

Someone ordered a lot of wine. Lilac couldn't decide whether her sister was flirting with Bob or with everyone in the restaurant or with her. The taxi ride was a bit of a blur. When Freesia climbed into her single bed she didn't object.

"We used to sleep together when you were four and I was six," said Freesia. "Do you remember?"

"You used to tickle me."

"Shall I do it again?"

"I'll probably throw up?"

"I'll risk it," said Freesia, but Lilac pretended she was asleep.

Next morning, Freesia pulled the covers over her head, pleading a hangover. Lilac felt a little wobbly herself but reckoned she had to get to work. Bob greeted her in the kitchen. "Pajamas?" he said.

"I think I was drunk," said Lilac.

"We were all drunk," said Bob. "Would you like a Coca-Cola?"

"That would be most kind," said Lilac.

"You're welcome, Lilac," said Bob, reaching into the refrigerator. And then, unaccountably, he blushed.

"You know what?" said Lilac. "One of the people at our table last night had heard of your firm."

"I didn't think you knew its name."

"Of course I do," she said, and proved it. "And the person was very impressed. Said it was small but incredibly successful. Do they pay you vast sums?"

"I'm hoping they will eventually," said Bob. "Or at least enough to buy us some comfortable chairs."

The apartment Bob and Lilac shared was the product of a warehouse conversion that had lost its bearings in the last stock market crash. Bob said the developer must have run out of money and finished the project off as quickly as possible. The rooms, of which there were too many, were all in a line except that there was a 90-degree bend in the middle. The two bedrooms were at opposite ends of the apartment. The string of "living" rooms from Lilac's bedroom to the kitchen opened into each other and in a sense formed one enormous "hall," such as one might find in a medieval castle. The front door was roughly where the bend was. There weren't enough windows, except in the kitchen, which gave access to the fire escape, and the single bathroom, which was ridiculously grand. The bathroom was located off the normal hall that ran from the kitchen to Bob's bedroom—a situation that could create surprises. (Had once.)

Bob and Lilac tended to tell people they'd agreed to share the apartment because they'd essentially have their own spaces. They'd bought beds and dressers but didn't have enough money to do much with the living room/dining room/library/whatever middle of the apartment. Every so often one of them would be given a lamp or a used couch by a friend or an aunt and shyly extend their territory, but there was nothing on the walls and the whole place looked like they were in the middle of moving either in or out.

Lilac pretended that she didn't mind living in a half-empty warehouse. She told herself it was part of the "adventure" of "starting out." Whether Bob minded was something she regularly asked herself. She couldn't tell. He worked so hard that Lilac vaguely felt she ought to be the one who made the apartment homier. But she owed money from college that she had promised herself she would pay off as quickly as possible. As an art history major, she knew what "style" was, and there was no way she could afford it.

One Saturday, Bob went to Ikea and bought a small table and four chairs for them to eat at in the kitchen at the end of their medieval "hall." These items took a couple of hours to assemble, so maybe he did care. Lilac went out at lunchtime on Monday and bought some colorful placemats and cloth napkins. "Nice," he'd said. Which told her nothing.

Lilac had adopted the view that Bob was shy, that he didn't know how to deal with having a girl for a roommate, that he wasn't particularly "experienced." She preferred this to the equally plausible theory that he just wasn't that interested in her.

Lilac didn't have a lot of "experience" herself. She wasn't good at reading people, she felt. For example, what did the whole pajamas thing mean? As usual, Freesia was stirring things up.

Bob and Lilac hadn't known each other at college. They'd had friends in common, who'd said, if you're going to work in New York maybe you should share. "Um," said Lilac. "OK, sure," said Bob. This at an impromptu dinner during graduation week. (Graduation is when things are supposed to happen, right?) The next day, Bob had called up and said, "Did we agree to something or were you just being polite?" and Lilac had said (thinking of her sister), "We're grown-ups." And he'd said, "I've got a lead on a place that kind of quirky but has a lot of space." So there they were.

When Lilac got home from work the third evening of Freesia's visit, her sister had taken over the "hall." There was a stack of plastic boxes filled with glasses and silverware. There were long folding tables leaning against the walls. One had been set up and had pots and pans on it. There were what must have been two dozen folding chairs. Freesia was sitting in one of them looking at a clipboard.

"Your refrigerator isn't big enough," said Freesia.

"Well, I'll run right out and get two more," said Lilac.

"Sorry. We can cope."

"You can always 'cope,' Freesia, but what are we coping with?" As usual, Lilac couldn't decide whether she was annoyed with her sister or wished she could be more like her.

"We're having a dinner party."

"You and I?"

"You and I and Bob," said Freesia. "And Monica."

"Monica who owns Ping Pong?"

"Owns twenty-five percent of it, but you don't want to know her backers."

"Oh good. And I suppose this is her stuff. And someone will show up at midnight wanting it back . . ."

"No problem. It's all rented. Movie people know how to rent stuff, remember? And Monica will bring her own knives, of course."

"And this party will be?"

"Tomorrow. And Bob's got to come. And actually, you've both got to invite a few other people. The party won't look right without at least eighteen people sitting down. Twenty-two would be better."

"This is a dinner party?"

"Monica's cooking. She's going to leave the sous-chef in charge. A risky thing to do on a Friday night, but she doesn't think anyone will notice."

"And Bob and I are decoration?"

"'Extras' would be the technical term," said Freesia.

"Tomorrow?"

"Right," said Freesia. "No, look, let me explain. You and Bob need some glamour in your life. We can't say that . . ."

Uncool, Lilac said to herself.

" . . . so I've found a reason for a party that has nothing to do with your needs, but will meet them perfectly. And is also a nice thing to do. An important thing to do."

Lilac looked blank. She was thinking about how to persuade Bob to leave work early again tomorrow.

"Geraldine Fisher, the novelist . . ."

" . . . and her husband Max, the Columbia professor."

"How do you know that?"

"I read the arts and culture section. I studied art history, remember?"

"Oh, right. And got highest honors. Anyway, Gerry is dying of some wasting disease."

"'Gerry?'"

"That's what she's called by people who know her."

"Oh."

"So she can't cook any more, which she used to be famous for, along with her wonderfully sad and evocative novels . . ."

"Which you've never read."

"I didn't say I had."

"You wanted me to think you had."

Freesia put her hands in the air as if in surrender. "I'm in the movie business, remember. I'm an illusionist."

"You're a wonderful sister," said Lilac. (This was true.) "But what do we have to do with Geraldine ... Gerry, that is, and Max?"

"It's his birthday tomorrow."

"Oh."

"But for the first time Gerry feels unable to cook him a birthday dinner—at least not as fine and memorable a meal as she has always produced in the past. With a bunch of friends."

"So you thought, my little sister has an apartment that looks like the set of a Samuel Beckett play, so why not have the party here?"

"Um ... yes."

"And Monica is willing to desert her newly opened restaurant to cook said dinner because?"

"Gerry's her godmother. Her father is Gerry and Max's gardener."

"Will he be coming too?"

"Oh, I assume so. His name is Pedro, by the way. Monica's mother was a gringo, but she disappeared when Monica was two. So Pedro took to gardening, for which he turned out to have considerable talent, because he could live on the grounds and keep an eye on Monica, or ask one of the maids to do so. Max comes from money, you know? Big estate out on Long Island, which they don't get to very much, I'm told. They stay in Manhattan to be close to her doctors."

Lilac paused. Maybe she had heard that. "And the other guests will be?"

"Gerry and Max's friends." Freesia reeled off the names of poets and painters and actresses Lilac had definitely heard of. "And you and Bob. And a couple of your friends, I hope."

"Provided they are cool or good-looking or both."

"It would also be good if they could perform in some way. That's sort of a tradition at Max's birthday parties. People read poems. People write poems for the occasion. Musicians bring their instruments and jam. Saxophone and cello. Improbable combinations. According to Monica, that is. I've never been."

"And you need Bob and me to find some younger guests—I know, I know, who have the appropriate capabilities—because Max and Geraldine's friends are in their sixties and the 'look' you want for the party has to be diverse and multi-generational. A Veronese banquet, perhaps?"

"You could do my job, little sister," said Freesia, smiling broadly.

"How do you know Monica?"

"Later," said Freesia.

For some reason (and to be honest, as usual) Lilac was suddenly very happy to be Freesia's sister. "Well, if it will make a dying famous novelist and your lover's godmother happy, why not?"

Freesia didn't respond to Lilac's probe. "It will do a lot for you and Bob, as well," she said.

Lilac went to her bedroom (which Freesia was now sharing) and called Bob on her cell phone. She assumed he'd still be in the office. She supposed she wanted his permission, though she knew the party was going to happen no matter what he or Lilac said. (Freesia was like that.) Even more, she wanted Bob to invite someone who was cool or good-looking or both. And who could perform in some way. She wanted Freesia to approve of Bob. She wanted Freesia to approve of Lilac. She wanted Bob to *notice* Lilac.

"A friend of mine dates an interesting-looking model," said Bob. Lilac said that should pass muster.

The only glamorous person Lilac knew was the partner she worked for, Charles. He was funny and gorgeous and half the young women in the office had crushes on him. He was alleged to be engaged to the managing partner, Alice O'Malley, but you'd never have known it from the way they treated each other in the office, which was very professional. Lilac's desk was fairly close to Charles's office, and all the offices had glass front walls (except of course Mr. Franklin's), so she saw them interact fairly often. They never touched each other. They maintained a neutral tone when they spoke. They could have been Lilac and Bob, in fact, for all you could tell, working in the same office, but . . . anyway.

Lilac figured there was no reason not to invite Charles to her party. Geraldine was famous. Monica was a hot new chef. Maybe he'd come.

"Sure," said Charles. "Tonight?"

"Do you want to bring a date?" (Oh, God.)

"You mean Alice?" he said.

Lilac nodded.

"I'll see if she's free," said Charles.

When Lilac got back to her apartment at six, there was chaos. (Purposeful chaos, to be honest.) Monica and a couple of helpers had set up one of the folding tables, as a supplement to Bob's Ikea one, and had what seemed like fifteen dishes in progress. Two waiters from Ping Pong were setting the table—four folding tables actually, arranged end to end, with white cloths covering them. They extended into all three rooms of the "hall," with lots of space around them.

The doorbell rang and it was a middle-aged Mexican-American looking gentleman with a lot of flowers.

"This is my daddy," said Monica. "Pedro, this is Lilac."

"Welcome," said Lilac.

"I bring these in your honor," he said.

"Lilac," said Lilac. (Rats.)

"Only time of year," said Pedro, whose helper was bringing in buckets of blooms. "Beautiful flowers. Beautiful name."

Lilac smiled—graciously, she hoped.

"I brought this too," said Pedro, indicating a guitar case.

"Oh, Daddy," said Monica. "I didn't want to ask, but I was hoping you would."

"It makes her happy," he said. "When she is very tired. I haven't played for her in six weeks."

"Will she be all right tonight?"

"I think so. She will make a big effort. She is very, very happy you are doing this. We speak yesterday on the phone. 'My little goddaughter,' she says." Pedro turned to Lilac. "No children," he said, as if in explanation. "Just books."

Bob arrived.

"Thank you for being early," said Lilac.

"Is there a dress code?"

"Only an undress code," said Freesia.

Lilac gave her a quizzical look.

"Later," said Freesia.

"Evidently not," said Lilac. "I plan to wear a dress."

"I have some freesia too," said Pedro.

"Oh, thank you," said Freesia. Lilac realized that her sister and the gardener had up to that point avoided looking at each other directly.

"You are beautiful," he said. "Same as my daughter."

"Thank you twice," said Freesia, looking down.

"I need a shower," said Bob.

"So do I," said Lilac.

"Well, take one together," said Freesia. "Get into the spirit of the evening."

Bob and Lilac looked at each other. "You go first," he said.

Max and Geraldine arrived at seven-fifteen, a quarter of an hour before the other guests were bidden. She was in a wheelchair. "This is so very kind," she said to Freesia. Monica came out of the kitchen and received a kiss.

"This is Lilac and this is Bob," said Monica. "They are your hosts."

"Freesia's sister," said Geraldine, giving Lilac a warm smile.

"It's an honor to have you here," said Lilac.

"Fiddlesticks," said the famous novelist.

"Be good, sweetheart," said Max.

"I've read three of your novels," said Bob unexpectedly.

"Which ones?" said Geraldine greedily.

"I thought you were a Wall Street blood-sucker," said Freesia.

"A cultured blood-sucker," said Bob.

"Then we come from the same stock," said Max.

Bob listed the titles he had read. "I wrote the first one the summer I met Max," said Gerry. "Could you tell I was in love?"

"Yes, to be honest."

Lilac found herself looking at Bob with new curiosity, but pretty soon the doorbell rang, meaning that Max and Geraldine's famous friends had begun to arrive. Lilac wasn't sure what to do. She felt superfluous. Geraldine tugged on her sleeve. "Be the one to open the door," she said in a hoarse whisper. "Tell them your name and invite them in." Lilac did as she was told and found herself face to face with a full-fledged movie star, who stuck out her hand and said "Anne," in her famous mezzo-soprano voice.

"Please come in," said Lilac. "Max and Geraldine are already here."

"Gerry," the famous novelist corrected her.

"Champagne?" said Freesia.

And so it went.

Lilac was startled when the "model" Bob's friend showed up with turned out to be Sandra, the stylish litigation partner. "Hello," she said. "This is Stephen. And I thought your name was 'Lil.'"

"I'm using 'Lilac' now," said Lilac.

"To match the decorations," said Sandra. "Good decision."

Lilac had no idea what that was supposed to mean. The word in the office was you never knew where Sandra was coming from, but she supposed litigators were supposed to keep you off base. Sandra's "date," if that's what he was, looked to be approximately Bob's age. They seemed to know each other from Yale—or maybe it was the Yale Club.

Dinner was served pretty much on schedule. There was an unspoken recognition that Gerry wouldn't last that long.

"Eat fast," said Freesia to the most famous political cartoonist in the city soon after the starter was served. "We're up first."

"Ready when you are," he said.

Lilac had known her sister would need to make a splash, and sure enough, she stepped up on a box, one of several scattered around the room and called the seated guests to attention.

"I want to thank my little sister, Lilac, and Bob, of course, for helping Monica and me make this birthday party for Max. And I want to thank you all for coming.

"Monica tells me that Gerry and Max have a tradition of performance at their parties. Many of you are in the arts, so you will feel comfortable with that. I understand that some of you will probably be willing to sing or do scenes from famous plays. I want you all to feel free to do that here.

"Monica's performance is the meal you are about to eat. Be careful. She is an uninhibited chef. Her food is as warm as she is. There are beers in the ice buckets if anyone has a sudden need.

"I work in the movie business, so I understand performance, but I am not a performer. I do wardrobe and properties, that sort of thing. So I asked myself, how can I contribute?

"As you may have noticed, Lilac's apartment is a little bare. Its walls are empty and white. So I said to myself, perhaps I should let myself be drawn or painted, as a way to make the walls less empty—and as a way to give some of the artists present an opportunity to display their craft. Movies are a collaborative art form after all."

At this point, Freesia began to remove her clothes, which she did quite gracefully without getting off the improvised plinth on which she was standing. "I suppose this makes me an un-wardrobe mistress," she said, eliciting a ripple of laughter.

As usual, Lilac could only marvel at her sister's self-confidence, her preparedness to do things that would have made Lilac die of embarrassment.

The best political cartoonist in New York took a handful of marker pens out of his jacket pocket and began to sketch a life-size Freesia on the wall. "One arm in the air," he said. "And fluff your hair to make it fuller if you can."

On the other hand, perhaps Freesia *liked* being embarrassed, just as people who bungee jumped evidently liked being afraid. Perhaps Freesia found embarrassment self-affirming. She had always been a *transgressive* personality. Lilac had only recently acquired that word and she liked it.

"Please go on with your meal," said Freesia to the table as she complied with the cartoonist's instructions. "It isn't fair to Monica to let the food get cold."

Lilac liked the *idea* of transgressive behavior, of doing unexpected things as if they were normal. And getting away with it. For example, what if she just started kissing Bob when he left in the morning? Maybe they'd turn into a couple.

"This is good," said the man on Lilac's left. She knew who he was: a commentary writer for the arts section of the *Times*. "Are you also in the performance business?"

"I fear not," said Lilac. "I'm Freesia's boring sister. But I read your column in the hope of being less boring."

"What did I write about today," he asked immediately.

"Canaletto," she shot back. "What are his dates?"

"Who cares about dates?"

"You were testing me, so I thought I'd return the compliment."

"You are not as boring as you think," he said. " And the answer is 1697 to 1768," he added. Lilac liked not being boring. Maybe if she had just enough wine . . .

Freesia was taking a break and eating her first course. Monica had brought her a robe. There was a sound of knocking at the other end of the table.

"What comes next?" Lilac asked the arts columnist. She gathered he'd been to a lot of Max and Gerry's parties.

"This," he said.

A rumpled man with a Royal Shakespeare Company accent stood up across the table and began to wander in the direction of the sound, which another guest was producing by thumping the table. "'Here's a knocking, indeed,'" said the Englishman.

"Drunk porter scene from *Macbeth*," said the columnist helpfully. "Does it at every party."

"Duncan has just been murdered," said Lilac.

"I thought you were an art historian."

"Not sure what I am," said Lilac.

"'Here's a farmer that's hanged himself on the expectation of plenty,'" said the rumpled actor, who was beginning to look familiar.

"Are you going to take your clothes off?" said the columnist.

"Probably not, but Freesia's getting ready to again." Her sister had indeed stood up and taken off the robe.

"Nice touch," said the columnist, "letting the two scenes overlap."

"She's in the movie business," said Lilac. "She understands pacing."

After Freesia had been posing for another ten minutes, with the marks on the wall beginning to resemble her, Alice-who-runs-the-place (as the associates at Lilac's firm called her) stood up. Everyone looked in her direction. "I can never resist a challenge," she said. "Are there any other artists here?"

"There are three," said Lilac's companion, "but only two of them can do decent figure drawing."

Two men stood up, followed more slowly by a woman. "Sit down Joe," she said. "You couldn't paint a house."

"Abstractionist," said Lilac's neighbor. "Genius, but not a draftsman."

The housepainter sat down. "How do we decide?" said the other male painter, who remained standing.

"Maybe I can help," said Sandra, rising from her chair and reaching behind her back to unzip her dress. "Help me, Stephen," she said to Bob's friend.

"I'll take you," said the woman painter to Sandra. "But you need to leave some article of clothing on. It will make you nuder."

"I'll make a paper hat," said someone. "Have we got any newspapers?"

"Who *are* these women?" said the columnist. "I like them."

"They work at my . . . company," said Lilac hesitantly. She wasn't sure she wanted to identify Alice and Sandra. "They're sort of here to fill out the numbers."

"Must be an interesting place you work at."

"I wouldn't have said so," said Lilac, "but I must not be paying attention."

The two painters "just happened" to have paints and brushes with them. Sandra and Alice mounted their respective plinths. Alice removed Charles's red and yellow striped necktie and made a headband of it. "A girl needs some color, right?" she said.

Alice and Sandra posed for fifteen minutes. "This is hard," said Alice.

"Everything worth doing is hard," said Gerry.

Sandra turned her head and smiled at her.

"Don't move," said the lady painter. "I'm working as fast as I can."

"You may be finding something new," said the columnist in a serious voice.

"You know, I think you're right," said the lady painter. She stepped away from the wall.

"Working faster is giving your line more energy," said the columnist. Lilac didn't know the woman's work, but there was certainly electricity in the figure that was taking shape on the bare wall.

"Maybe some music," said Max. Several individuals reached for their instruments. "Ragtime," said Max. The models need encouragement.

When Alice and Sandra took a break, Charles stood up. "What a totally beautiful man," said the columnist.

"My boss," said Lilac.

"I would play the piano for you," said Charles, "but fortunately you don't have one, as I stopped my lessons in the fourth grade." Everyone laughed. Charles could always make people laugh. "I would take my clothes off," he continued, "but I'm shy." More laughter. "So I will sing you a song. Are there any other marines here?"

Max stood up.

"The Marines' Hymn," said Charles.

"Excellent," said Gerry.

At this point, the mezzo-soprano movie star joined them, to considerable whispering and questioning around the table. "I can't sing, really, but I know the words," she said.

"Are you a marine?" said Charles.

"No," she said slowly. "But I've slept with a lot of them."

Everyone laughed. The three of them sang about the halls of Montezuma and the shores of Tripoli pretty well, actually.

The painters finished. Three quick but reasonable likenesses looked down from the bare walls. Dessert was consumed. There was the sort of pause that sometimes happens in a noisy restaurant or a successful dinner party, when everyone happens to stop talking at once.

Geraldine Fisher pushed her wheelchair back from her place at the head of the table, looked at Max, who was sitting on her left, and began to recite: "'As virtuous men pass quietly away and whisper to their souls to go . . .'"

"Donne's 'Valediction,'" said the columnist under his breath. "I may have to cry."

Lilac turned and looked at him and saw that he meant it. "Is this another favorite?" she asked.

"No," he said simply. "She has never done this before, and it gives me a chill."

Gerry paused and Max continued the poem: "'. . . while some of their sad friends do say, "The breath goes now," and some say "no" . . .'"

"'So let us melt,'" said Gerry, "'and make no noise, no tear-floods or sigh-tempests move.'" She turned the wheelchair on its axis and began to move slowly behind the line of diners, all of who turned to watch her, and one or two of whom touched her on the arm or shoulder as she passed. "'T'were profanation of our joys to tell the laity our love.' Max gives a very good little talk about this poem." This addressed to Sandra. "And, oh, you are a wonderful color."

"Thank you," said Sandra in her paper crown, seemingly unconscious of her continued state of undress. As Gerry continued her progress, three of four of her friends around the table were beginning to tear up. This will be a famous evening, Lilac said to herself, and then felt a stab of unworthiness for having even had that thought.

"'Dull subliminal lovers . . .' No, that's not right. There was nothing subliminal about Jack Donne." She had stopped at Bob's chair. "I always have trouble with this stanza. There is an internal rhyme that throws me. Can you help me, polite young man who had read three of my books?"

Miraculously, Bob could. "'Dull, sublunary lover's love, whose soul is sense, cannot admit absence because it doth remove . . .'"

"'Those things that elemented it,'" Gerry interrupted. She patted Bob's shoulder and rolled on.

"How do you know that?" Lilac whispered to him across the table.

"Just do," said Bob.

Gerry got to the end of the table and put her arms around Monica's shoulders. Max took up the recitation: "'But we by a love so much refined that our souls know not what it is, inter-assured of the mind, care less eyes, lips and hands to miss.'" Tears rolled down his cheeks.

"Oh, Gerry," said Monica, as the older woman turned her wheelchair to continue.

"'Our two souls, therefore, which are one,'" she recited, "'Though I must go, endure not yet . . .'"

"'. . . a breach but an expansion, . . .'" said Max from what was now the far end of the table. "'Like gold to airy thinness beat.'"

Gerry had gotten as far as Alice, sitting triumphantly naked except for Charles's necktie. "That was very brave of you and your friend," she said. "I like brave."

It occurred to Lilac that Gerry was gathering her strength for the end of the poem. The ending reminded Lilac of the winding up of one of Bach's great fugues. She did know the poem, though she could not have plucked out a stanza the way Bob so wonderfully had.

"Are the two of you really models?" said Gerry to Alice. "I read all the magazines, you know, and I've never seen your pictures."

"We're lawyers," said Alice. "And, therefore, shameless."

"Such Wilt Thou Be To Me"

Gerry looked carefully at Alice, and then across the table at Sandra. "Lovers?" she asked. "That would be all right, you know."

"Conventional," said Sandra.

"But not boring," said Gerry. "I am anti-boring." She began to recite again, and wheel herself slowly down the other side of the table. "'If they'—that means our two souls, Max's and mine—'if they be two, they are two so, as stiff twin compasses are two. Thy soul, the fixed foot, makes no show to move but doth if the other do.'"

"'And though it in the center sit,'" said Max, "'yet when the other far doth roam, it leans and harkens after it, and grows erect as that comes home.'" She was almost within his reach. "Oh, sweetheart," he said. It was a cry of pain.

"'Such wilt thou be to me,'" said Gerry softly, "who must, like the other foot obliquely run. Thy firmness draws my circle just, and makes me end where I begun.'" She put her hand on his. "It's time to go home, Max," she said.

Lilac woke up in Bob's bed. No pajamas was her first thought. The memory emerged of Freesia telling her Monica needed physical contact. "I can't let her leave," her sister had explained.

Bob came in, wearing boxer shorts and juggling the *Times*. "We made the paper," he said, tossing a handful of lilac branches on the bed beside her.

"How?"

"The party broke up pretty early, if you remember," said Bob, sitting down on the end of the bed.

Lilac did remember. She was suddenly remembering all kinds of things, some funny, some exciting, some sad.

"The arts columnist who sat next to you?" said Bob.

"Umm," said Lilac. Bob looked very good, sitting on the end of the bed in nothing but his boxer shorts—sitting there as if there was nothing unusual about Lilac being in his bed.

"He managed to file—I think they still use that term—for the last edition. 'Party of the Week.' It's usually run on Sunday or Monday. 'A heart-stopping evening,' they call it." He was reading from an inside page. "At the stylish home of Lilac Conroy and her partner, no name given. My firm doesn't like us to have our names in the paper."

"You spoke to the columnist?"

"Charles did. Freesia and Alice and Sandra's performances were described but they weren't identified."

"What about me?"

"It was the best Charles could do. They evidently have to say who gave the party. He texted me at five in the morning. He went out to get the paper then."

"I didn't give the party. Freesia did."

"The hostess gives the party, even if other people do the work."

"You *must* come from money," said Lilac, "just like Max said."

"I try not to make a point of it."

"So we see," said Lilac, looking around the almost unfurnished bedroom. "But you know the rules—about hostesses and such."

"Anyway, you'll be famous," said Bob. "I think famous will suit you. Just because your sister is outrageous doesn't mean you have to be invisible."

"Famous for fifteen minutes," said Lilac, suppressing the pleasure that the idea of being famous was giving her.

"More than that," said Bob. "You can read the story. It's all in there, minus *some* of the names. There's Pedro playing and that woman who's just won a Grammy singing. It names the painters, if not the models."

"The paintings are still there? Are they as beautiful as I remember them?"

"You will have to decide for yourself. You're the art history student, remember."

"I don't want to be a lawyer."

"I wouldn't have thought so."

"What shall I do?"

"We'll figure that out." (We?) "And there's a beautiful description of Gerry and Max reciting the 'Valediction Forbidding Mourning.'"

"And you helping?"

"It wasn't about me," said Bob. "And no, fortunately, I'm not mentioned. It was about Gerry and Max—the article and the poem and the whole evening. It was her way of telling him she was ready."

Lilac had a scary thought but was unable to voice it.

"Gerry died soon after Max got her home. Your party will be literary history."

"Does Monica know?"

"She got a phone call from Max after we'd gone to bed."

For a moment, neither of them spoke. "I'm glad she stayed here last night," said Lilac.

"So is Freesia," said Bob.

"She's awake?"

"She and Monica are washing dishes."

"We should help them," said Lilac.

"We should give them space," said Bob. "May I get back in bed?"

"Of course."

He handed her the paper and she read the story twice.

"Do you think he helped her?" Lilac asked.

"Maybe," said Bob. "Would have if necessary. *Semper fi*, you know."

"The Marines," said Lilac.

"Love," said Bob. "But twenty of us saw how little strength she had by the end of the night. I don't think there will be an issue."

Lilac thought about that for a while. "Are you my partner?" she asked him finally. "Like the article called you."

"I'd like to be," said Bob.

"You didn't act that way last night."

"You'd had a lot of wine," said Bob.

"Yes," said Lilac, remembering hugging a few departing guests she had barely spoken to. "I was running a bit obliquely at the end."

"I'm a pretty good fixed foot," said Bob.

"A good quality in a man."

"And there are rules."

"But not in the morning," said Lilac. And she surprised herself by rolling over to kiss him.

"Well, yes there are, of course," said Bob, treating the kiss as if it were normal behavior. "Even in the sunshine. Even in the dark."

"Do you think Gerry would mind our marking her passing by making love?" (How could she say such a thing?) "That is, I mean . . ."

"I'm sure she'd be pleased," said Bob. "As an appreciator of Donne's poetry, she would have to be."

There was probably a word in English, or at least in some language, for being inappropriately happy, but Lilac didn't know it. Being inappropriately happy and not caring.

Bob got out of bed and took off his boxer shorts.

"Oh my," said Lilac. And then, to be casual, to regain control: "You know, I saw you walking from the bathroom to your bedroom once."

"I know."

"You didn't say."

"What was I supposed to say? It was a lapse. It was a Saturday morning. Maybe seven-thirty. I'd taken a shower and was going in to work. I'd assumed you were still asleep."

"Did you ever see me—by accident, that is."

"Never."

"And even if you had, you'd pretend otherwise."

"Yes."

"Another rule," said Lilac. "Well, I did take a few risks, thinking perhaps you'd see me."

"I admit I did think about that possibility." He was lying beside her and had begun to touch her shoulders and the part of her chest between her breasts. She supposed her heart was approximately where he was touching her. Why did this feel so natural? "I said to myself, Lilac probably has very pretty breasts. I wonder if she'll find a way to let me see them—accidentally, of course."

"I'm beginning to wonder when you're going to *touch* my breasts," said Lilac.

"In due course," said Bob. "My grandfather—the one who made the money I'm supposed to come from—he had three pieces of advice. He took me to lunch at his club when I was seventeen and beginning to look presentable."

"More rules."

"No. Advice. Recommendations. Lessons from the master. Lessons for life, really. Which of course had greater impact on a seventeen-year-old than being told what to do."

"And his . . . recommendations were?"

Bob sat up and stopped touching her, which at some level of consciousness Lilac regretted, though she was quite curious to hear his answer, which seemed to require one's undivided attention.

"*Never* be in a hurry."

"We've been pretty good at that," said Lilac.

"Beautiful slow motion," said Bob.

Lilac waited for him to go on. She realized that waiting was part of the game, part of pleasure itself.

"*Always* keep it a secret," said Bob.

"Very wise," said Lilac. Considerate, she said to herself. Loving, actually. And sly because it gave a woman the confidence to let go. This woman at least. "And . . . ?" she said.

"Count any day a loss on which you do not give a woman pleasure."

"Oh my God," said Lilac, for she had a sudden vision of being touched and protected and made to wait and then, in accordance with the rules, which seemed to exist for her personal benefit, being overwhelmed with pleasure, day after day, for the rest of her life.

"I think I'll start with my tongue," said Bob matter-of-factly.

This was not something with which Lilac had personal familiarity. To be honest, she was a bit ambivalent: interested but unsure. "What . . . what do I do?" she said.

"Absolutely nothing," said Bob. He moved her around on the bed a bit, very gently, slid his arms under her thighs and brought his arms around her body so that his hands could reach her breasts and *finally* touch her nipples. "I will take full responsibility for our crimes," he said.

He took his time about it. He licked Lilac's satisfactorily flat belly, explored her belly button. Lilac calmed down a bit.

"Such Wilt Thou Be To Me"

He licked the places where her thighs met her torso, which seemed to release tension even as it excited her.

She realized that she could hear her sister and Monica laughing, down the hall in the kitchen as they washed dishes. It was good Monica was laughing. It was good that Freesia had come to visit on this particular week. Lilac had never really believed Freesia and Bob had had sex that first night. And Bob hadn't denied it because he believed in secrets. He wouldn't have said so even if he had, so to be consistent he had to leave it ambiguous.

Bob was beginning to lick her in less ambiguous places. And squeeze her nipples just a little. Ambiguous was good. The word sounded like it felt. Bob might have taken responsibility but Lilac was implicated.

Lilac wondered whether she could hear Monica and Freesia laughing because the door to Bob's bedroom had accidentally come open a crack. There was no way to lift herself up enough to check. Maybe she didn't want to check. Maybe she didn't need to. Bob wouldn't let her be exposed.

Of all the dreams and fantasies Lilac had ever had, from childhood through adolescence to whatever suburb of maturity she had now come to live in—and this morning she had clearly arrived in a new place—in all that time nothing had prepared her for the contentment of being made love to, slowly and skillfully, to the sound of her sister and Monica's honest laughter. Laughter despite loss. Laughter because we are all human beings, who fear death, believe in sex, know the rules. Count no day lost on which you have given pleasure. Was that how it went? Rational thought was becoming difficult. In any event, Bob's grandfather was not going to be disappointed.

Extremely not disappointed. (Oh God.)

"What about you?" said Lilac, finally.

"We're not in a hurry, remember."

Lilac suspected there was no word for feeling sexy and safe at the same time. But who needed words?

Alice Who Runs the Place

She'd proposed. He'd agreed. They weren't living together, though they had a lot of sex. She didn't have a ring.

Alice and Sandra were having lunch. Posing at Lilac Conroy's party had made them sisters—or co-conspirators, as Sandra liked to put it. They got together fairly often now and talked about things neither had previously had a girlfriend to talk to about.

They were a pretty scary pair. They knew that. Other partners who saw them in a restaurant, or having mid-morning coffee at the shop around the corner from the office, tended not to approach, waved from a distance, pretended not to see them.

The fact that they had posed at Lilac's party enhanced their aura. If they were willing to do that, what wouldn't they do?

Alice had briefly speculated on how Sandra's and her "performances" that Friday evening had become known within the firm. Charles wouldn't have said anything to anyone. She was confident of that. He'd been the one who persuaded the arts columnist not to identify them. He hadn't, to give him his due, even told people they were a couple. She'd been seen hugging his arm late one night as they left the building, and assumptions got made.

Lilac herself seemed disoriented by her fame—*everyone* had read the article—and Alice's intuition was that the girl would not have provided further details. Lilac had never seemed comfortable at the firm—as if there were rules she didn't know and was afraid of breaking. She was definitely a girl who wanted to obey the rules.

And Lilac worked for Charles. "I made it clear right away on Monday morning that we wanted to let the story fade away," he'd said. "I told her, if anyone asked her questions, either inside or outside the firm, to say it was a private party, organized by her sister, and that it wasn't appropriate to talk about it. That seems to have worked, so Lilac tells me."

"Face it," said Sandra. "Our partners have seen us in the shower. They know we have balls. We're assumed to have done it because we *could have* done it. But does it matter?"

"Not really," said Alice. Vaguely gratifying, in fact, she said to herself. And useful. The trick to being managing partner, she had found, was to get people to do things without asking them to, let alone *telling* them to. If they cared enough about what you thought, which at the margin meant *feared* you in the right way, they would devote themselves to figuring out what you wanted. Sad, really.

But that wasn't the issue of the day. Sandra had been seeing Stephen for seven months now. It had started as a lark, and been entirely his doing. What the hell, she'd said to herself. If he wants to sleep with an almost middle-aged lady, why should the lady complain? A hundred and twenty orgasms later, as she put it to Alice . . .

"You've counted?"

"Not really," said Sandra, "but he's pretty diligent."

"Umm," said Alice.

"Anyway, I gradually realized that he made me laugh, made me happy, made me breakfast when he slept over. I wanted him there all the time. So I told him that."

"And he accepted?"

"On the spot."

"And now you're having second thoughts?"

"No. But he says he's worried that I will, that I've most likely had a lapse in judgment I will soon regret, that we need a cooling-off period."

"So you're not seeing him?"

"On the contrary."

"Still making you breakfast?"

"And everything that goes with it."

"Do I detect an incongruity here?"

"Stephen says he wants to marry me. Age doesn't matter. I'll be a 'hot ticket' when I'm seventy."

"So he's 'pressing his suit,' as the Victorians would put it, while urging you to reconsider. I suppose we could see this as a form of chivalry."

"He says he's doing exactly what companies do when they sell securities: print the risk factors in bold type and then sell hard."

Alice considered this for a moment. "Perhaps you should elope."

Sandra laughed. "How do I persuade him to do that?"

"You don't. I'm talking about eloping in the old-fashioned sense, as in kidnapping."

"Right," said Sandra. "I have Millie get Mike Forrest to recruit some off-duty cops. They bundle him into an unmarked van and drive him to a church, where you and I are waiting at the altar holding bouquets. It has possibilities."

"And I'd be honored to be your maid of honor," said Alice. She glanced at her watch. "Oh, God. I'm late. Can you pay and tell me later what I owe you?"

Alice walked the three blocks to the office laughing. People will think I'm a crazy woman, she told herself. And I am a crazy woman. I'm in exactly the same ridiculous position as Sandra, but I'm not doing anything about it.

Well, not *exactly* the same situation. Stephen was an investment banker. He worked at a different firm. Charles and Alice were partners. And their firm had a rule against nepotism. An unwritten rule. They'd *encouraged* that librarian girl to resign right after they'd un-fired her, when Thomas announced they were going to get married. Alice herself had had a difficult conversation with Fred, the previous week, when he called to say he was ready to come back from paternity leave. Mary was in the zone for partner, she'd told him—"so think about it, Fred."

Alice and Charles had talked about it in the bath. He gave her one most Friday nights. The night of Lilac's party had been an exception. Alice decided she'd probably undressed there to make up for not being able to do so at home. She was pretty addicted to their Friday nights.

"You have a hard job," he'd say to her, as he unzipped her dress for her or unbuttoned her blouse. "You need to be attended to. Your fingers are too tired to cope with all these little hooks and snaps and fasteners."

She would let out a sigh and stand perfectly still as he did everything for her. "But we're not married," she'd say as he took the last of her clothes off.

"You are correct, Miss O'Malley," he'd say, as he led her back to her living room and seated her on her couch. "We have an *irregular* relationship. And that suits us, because we are not conventional adults."

Then he'd go start the bath while she watched the news. If it was cold, there was always a throw on the couch she could wrap around her, but Charles seemed to like it best when she didn't, when he came back naked himself and she was wearing nothing but her wire-rim glasses.

"Let's not worry about the rest of the world," he'd say, turning off the news. "Let's help Alice relax."

Charles was a genius. He had created a ritual, which was comforting, but with just enough variation to keep it fresh. He'd take her hand as she stepped into the tub. She'd settle in. He'd put a towel on the floor to kneel on, and wash her back. She'd eventually ask him to get in behind her. She'd lean back against him and they'd talk.

"John called me earlier this week," he said. "We had lunch today."

"Yes," said Alice—by which she meant, so go on. Charles had this lovely way of never overwhelming her with information. He'd introduce a topic, or a story, and wait for her to indicate he should proceed. Since she was often already thinking about three things at once, this was considerate.

Charles was unfailingly considerate. "So you've really never dated anyone at the firm," she'd asked him, as they stepped carefully through each other's histories, a process that had taken more than a year. "Why not?"

"No," he'd said. "They might have fallen in love with me."

"Of course they would have," Alice had said. "But aren't you dating me?"

"Worse than that, Miss O'Malley. I am sleeping with you. And as to falling in love, I very much hope you will."

"I have already—which is a problem," Alice would say.

"Not really," Charles would say. "I have a plan."

Because she wanted his plan to work, she never asked him what it was. And also, at this point in the conversation he typically began to do things that distracted her. Charles was extremely good at getting her to stop worrying when he set his mind to it.

Going back to John, it seemed he had a beard. "Henry won't like that," said Alice.

"John doesn't think you'll like it either," said Charles.

"That can't be why he wanted to have lunch. His holiday is almost over, right?"

"It seems his marriage is also over."

"Oh. Wife's named 'Felicity,' right? Couple of children."

"Three daughters. And a father-in-law who used to be a big cheese here."

"Of course."

"And John's always believed he was made a partner because of that, because he was married to Felicity Cheese. So, he wants to know, do we want him to quit. Sorry to let work invade our Friday night, but he may call you over the weekend."

"Of course I don't want him to quit. He's good. I'm counting on him. We're at full capacity already. And this isn't the Middle Ages, for Christ's sake. His partnership isn't entailed. When does he plan to see Henry?"

"He wants to talk to you before he does anything else."

"Whatever for?"

"He reckons you run the place now."

Alice let that pass. "I'm beginning to remember Felicity," she said. "They were at our table at the Partners' Dinner last May, remember? She's pretty."

"I only have eyes for you, Miss O'Malley."

This appeared to be true, actually. Charles was quite straightforward—honest to Alice and honest with himself. If another man had claimed to be circumspect with the female associates *so they wouldn't fall in love with him*, she would have written him off as an egotist. Charles was simply telling the truth—and didn't seem to regard his quick wits and physical attractiveness as achievements. "You are the love of my life," he'd told her, and she believed him.

"But why," she'd asked him. She asked him over and over again. She liked listening to his answers.

"Because you are brave and wise and beautiful," he'd say. "Because you think before you speak. Because the little boys want you to be their mommy and the old boys want you to be their daughter. Because we treat each other as equals. Because I'm never completely sure what you'll do next."

"So you liked it when I went into the gym?"

"I'd fantasized about it for three years—ever since you made partner, in fact."

"But you never hit on me."

"That wouldn't have been fair."

"Should I call John?" said Alice.

"I have his new cell phone number," said Charles.

"OK, I'll deal with him. And would you, please, talk to Stephen?"

"Sandra's Stephen?"

"The very same. I want to know if he's suitable. Take him to your club, if that's the form." Alice was a bit touchy about "clubs that require penises," as she called them.

"He's suitable," said Charles.

"You've had lunch with him already?"

"Twice. And a game of squash. I wanted to get to know him. We share an interest. We both have girlfriends who take their clothes off in unexpected places. I assumed you'd be worried about Sandra."

"You weren't worried yourself? I mean he's fourteen years younger than she is."

"Worrying about Sandra is part of *your* job description, Miss O'Malley. I just figured you'd ask me about him eventually."

"And?"

"He's been an adult since he was fourteen, which is a dozen years before most boys begin to become men. So if you add twelve to his calendar age, he's forty. Sandra's forty-one. They're contemporaries. She'll be in good hands."

"You think Sandra is a grown-up?"

"She's a litigator."

"I know. I know. You think they're all mad."

"What I think, Miss O'Malley, is that our whole profession is mad. Litigators just have a more virulent strain of the disease. To be fair to Sandra, she's always struck me as having the fever under pretty good control. At least she did until she fell in love."

Alice suggested it was time to get out of the bath. They dried off and got dressed. Charles began to open the take-out Chinese food they'd picked up an hour before.

"Are you falling out of love with me, Charles?" She couldn't prevent herself from asking the question. She'd asked it before.

"Not in the least degree," he said. He stopped what he was doing to look directly at her. She was reassured.

"Are you falling out of love with the law?"

"It's a game," said Charles.

"Don't you like winning?"

"I think I've forgotten how to keep score."

"Sandra keeps track of her orgasms."

"You're kidding."

"Not literally. Twenty a month, she says. And Stephen's out of town on business some nights."

"Good gracious. No wonder he can beat me at squash. I've been neglecting you, Miss O'Malley."

"If anyone has been neglecting anyone, it's me," said Alice. "I fell asleep in your arms on Tuesday, if you remember. You were saying lovely things to me. You were about to *do* lovely things to me. Next thing I knew it was 6 a.m. and the alarm was going off. And you were still there."

"I didn't want to slip away while you were asleep. I thought it might make you worry."

"It would have. Thank you. Thank you for being you. Pour me a glass of wine, would you darling?"

Alice went to see Henry about John—and for that matter about Fred. "We have more business than we can handle," she said. She assumed he knew what she was really talking about.

John was no problem. He could keep the beard. "I assume he's got a new woman to go with it," said Henry. "Is she a lawyer?"

"He says she's a 'risk professional.'"

"How appropriate. Anyway, I never cared for old Cheese. That's what we actually called him when we were associates."

"Hard to imagine you as an associate, Henry."

"You think I'm getting old, Alice?"

"Not in the least, Henry." She looked straight at him as she said it, so he'd know she was telling him the truth.

"Well, when you decide to make your move, be sure to kill me. I am not a good loser."

Alice couldn't decide if that was a warning or advice.

"So, regarding Fred," said Henry.

"Yes?"

"There isn't a rule, as you know. Not written down anywhere. We've just always felt that being law partners was challenging enough without there being personal relationships as well."

"You put people together and they tend to develop relationships," said Alice. "Sometimes they become rivals, sometimes lovers."

"Rivalries are fine. They make people work harder. Dislike can even be useful. Look what some of our partners accomplish because Oscar makes them angry."

"He's mellowing."

"Bad news."

"Not for Oscar. He's in love."

"Hard to imagine," said Henry. "Don't tell me she's a lawyer. Or if she is, at least tell me she doesn't work at a rival firm."

"What's wrong with a partner at a rival firm? I thought you wanted to promote Millie."

Henry got a sheepish look. "Well, I do, actually. But how do you know that?"

"We don't have to talk about things to know things, Henry."

"Anyway, Mike Forrest's firm isn't really a rival."

"Don't try to tell him that," said Alice.

"So who is Oscar's girlfriend—and is she a lawyer at all? I assume she doesn't practice in the same field. It's too narrow for two people to sleep in."

"You're pretty frisky this morning, Henry," said Alice. He liked it when she teased him. "For an old fart," she added.

Henry bristled for a fraction if a second. Alice saw it. He saw that she saw it. Neither of them said anything.

"Oscar's girlfriend, as you call her," said Alice, "is a federal judge. He thought someone in management should know that, though he doubts any matter he touched would ever come before her. Very correct of Oscar, to give him his due. Anyway, he goes to Cincinnati every other weekend to be with her. She comes to New York . . . '

"Not *that* judge?" said Henry. "She's going to be nominated for the Court of Appeals next month. That's confidential, of course. She could wind up on the Supreme Court eventually. She's approximately the third best federal district-level judge in the country."

"He says he didn't realize who she was," said Alice. "And by the way, who ranks first and second?" Henry considered himself a connoisseur of judges. And liked his Washington connections to be known.

"They're too old," said Henry. He mentioned their names.

"And they're men," said Alice. "I don't think Oscar would want to sleep with them."

"Hard to imagine anyone wanting to sleep with Oscar. But give him my congratulations."

"Why don't you speak to him yourself, Henry? I'm sure he'd appreciate it."

"Why didn't he come to me in the first place, then?"

"He's afraid of you, Henry."

"Really?"

Alice knew Henry knew that most of his partners were afraid of him, so she didn't answer his question. "He spoke to me two weeks ago," she said, "right after they 'formed a relationship,' as he reticently put it. You were in Europe, Henry. On a 'marketing' trip."

"Umm. So I was. And yes, I'll speak to him."

Alice suspected he wouldn't get around to it. "And about Fred?" she said.

"I think I've expressed my views, Alice."

Alice was suddenly exasperated. "So it's all right to have an affair . . ."—she paused for half a second—". . . and with a judge, even, but it's not all right for members of the same household to work here? You realize Thomas will have to leave?"

"I thought the 'librarian girl' quit," said Henry.

"Harriet. She did. They got married. You and Elizabeth came to the wedding. You gave them a soup terrine. But Leonard's mother has died and Thomas and Harriet are becoming his legal guardians."

"Leonard the messenger?"

"Yes. I think under New York family law he is now essentially their child, even though he's fifty-seven. Or something like that."

"Thomas will have to leave," said Henry with a straight face. "Leonard has been with the firm far longer than he has."

Alice laughed. But she'd accomplished nothing, she realized.

The following Friday, Alice and Charles had a serious conversation in the bath. "You can get the rule changed," said Charles. "Most of our partners would agree. But if it benefits you, it will undermine your moral authority to have done so."

Alice listened. "Put your arms around me, please," she said.

"The issue won't arise until we get married," he continued.

"Because Henry is an 'old fart,'" she said. "I called him that this week, by the way. He didn't like it. I was a bit surprised. I thought it was a joke. Anyway, as far as he's concerned, *irregular* relationships don't count. They're off the books."

"Be careful, Alice."

"Well . . . I'm right."

"You know that doesn't matter. He's an old lion but he still has teeth. And old friends all over the profession. And to be fair, he ignores our irregular relationship, so you shouldn't use Veronica against him."

"Also, it wouldn't be fair to Veronica," said Alice.

"Or to Elizabeth," said Charles. "You cannot tweak one part of a network without affecting every node."

"True. But since when are you studying engineering?"

"I ran into an old playmate," said Charles.

"Do I want to hear this?" said Alice.

"Walking up Park Avenue. I was going to lunch with Stephen again. I'm doing due diligence on him, as requested. He was president of his class, did you know that?"

"At Yale?"

"Oh, probably. But I was talking about the secondary school he want to. Here in New York. He took me to see it. I met the headmaster. The line about nodes and networks was hanging in the auditorium. It's part of their 'sustainability initiative,' he told me."

"Stephen?"

"No, the headmaster."

"And the woman you encountered on Park Avenue?"

"Sigrid. Hadn't changed in twenty years."

"You'd slept with her in your youth."

"And her screwy roommate, Stephanie."

"At the same time?"

"Approximately. But don't worry. It was the last time I ever did that."

"Is it important that I hear this?"

"I date my adulthood from the day I left their apartment. I wrote them a note full of pompous advice, and by the time I got home I realized I should take it myself."

"I seem to remember some other things you claim to have done."

"Oh, *those* things," said Charles.

They both laughed. "What was the advice?" Alice asked.

"To take their emotions seriously."

"Did you get an update on Park Avenue?"

"Stephanie died in a car crash. Sigrid's unmarried. She's still good-looking and still an actuary. *Carpe diem*, she said."

"Latin," said Alice.

"Go to the head of the class."

"I'm Irish, remember—and therefore a Roman Catholic."

"So what does it mean?" said Charles.

"Put a crown on a goldfish? Sorry. I don't actually know any Latin. What *does* it mean?

"Seize the day," said Charles.

"You told her about us," said Alice.

"I said there was someone. I didn't say who, or where you work."

Alice thought about that for a minute: Charles on the sidewalk in front of the Racquet Club, telling a stranger about Alice. Well, not a stranger—a woman he'd played with once. "So what does sexy Sigrid have to do with sustainability?"

"Networks," said Charles. "She and Stephanie moved into separate apartments. She said they were trying to follow my advice and find husbands. But it never worked. Without Sigrid to argue with, Stephanie got into arguments at work and lost her job. Started to drink. Drove into a tree one night."

"Go on," said Alice. Charles for some reason needed to tell her this story.

"Stephanie's death unsettled Sigrid. She refused to go out with anyone. Now it's too late to have a relationship, she told me."

"Were they lovers?" said Alice.

"No—and that's the point. They *sustained* each other. They were part of a fragile network of weakness and support. My stupid advice disturbed it. And the node called Stephanie was destroyed."

"Silly girl," said Alice.

"No need to get jealous," said Charles. "She's dead."

Alice didn't say anything for a while. "Sorry, darling."

"Me too," said Charles.

"And the point of this is?"

"Our relationship is important to me. I don't want to screw it up."

Alice could have asked a lot of follow-up questions, but she decided not to. "Could we skip dinner and make love right now?" she said.

Charles liked that idea even more than Alice expected him to, which probably told her something. Seeing that woman with whom he had done foolish things in his youth had unsettled him. Charles was the handsomest, funniest, most considerate man she had ever met, but he was afraid of getting old, losing his edge, losing Alice. "Could we start with a lot of kisses?" she said.

Nothing, her partners said later, could have prevented Alice from seizing power eventually. She just made her move a little sooner than anyone expected, which demonstrated confidence, which made the move successful.

Henry kept coming to "Second Friday" late. Those partners who were in town—those who came to Second Friday at all, that is—would show up at five, and wind up chatting aimlessly for ten or fifteen minutes. This annoyed those who had a lot to do, which was all of them, and especially those who had promised their wives they'd be on a particular train, and home in time for family dinner that night. It annoyed Oscar enough that, on those weekends when Miriam was coming to New York, he came late himself. "Phone call from Cincinnati, Oscar?" Paul or George would say as he took his seat. "Phone call from a *client*, George," Oscar would say. George was effectively a utility outfielder, who could do the work but had no "marquee value," meaning that he didn't originate much business.

"The boys are getting on each other's nerves," was Sandra's opinion.

"Everyone is tired," said Alice. "Too much work is a high-class problem, but some of our partners are sleep-deprived."

"And I'll bet you none of them is sleeping with a twenty-eight year old," said Sandra.

Alice considered speaking to Henry about the matter, but in the end she didn't. "I'm going to raise the non-existent nepotism rule," she told Charles.

"The *unwritten* nepotism rule," he said.

"Yup," said Alice.

"OK," said Charles.

So at exactly five o'clock on the second Friday in November, Alice walked into the big conference room and sat down at the head of the table. "I've asked Jane to take minutes," she said, nodding in the direction of her secretary, "so that those who are unable to attend will know what we discussed and what we decided. Jane has been with the firm for fifteen years, and I have complete confidence in her discretion. Does anyone have a problem with her being in the room?" She paused.

"Very good." She ignored the whispered questions about Henry being home with a cold or out of town.

"There's an issue we need to focus on," she said, "and I thought we might turn to it first. The projected full-year financials will be circulated on Monday. Nice of you to join us, Oscar. And we will be considering invitations to join the partnership next weekend. That meeting will start at eight-thirty, by the way."

"Paul has never been here before nine," said someone further down he table."

"I've been getting in at eight," said Paul. "You'd think I was an associate."

"You were an *excellent* associate," said another partner, to brief laughter. Paul's attention to detail was famous. He liked to describe himself as inefficient but reliable. Everyone loved him, from Alice and Sandra to the boys in the mailroom.

"The issue," said Alice, "is partners being married to partners—or for that matter to associates . . . '

"Or employees," Thomas interjected. This was probably the first time he had ever spoken at a Second Friday. He'd started coming after Alice told him he should.

" . . . or to children of active partners," Alice continued. "The anti-nepotism rule. In all its permutations."

The table got quiet.

"The most immediate issue is Fred and Mary," Alice continued. "When they got married, we didn't address the matter because Mary was about to take maternity leave. Since the third month after the birth of their son, Tyler, Fred has been taking paternity leave and Mary has been working. I understand that she has been doing very good work."

Voices down the table muttered agreement.

"Next weekend we need to address the question of offering her a partnership," Alice continued. "The complication is that Fred is ready to return to work. He called me a couple of weeks ago.

"I think we had assumed that one or the other of them would transition to a less demanding role somewhere else. Good afternoon, Henry..."

Henry paused at the door of the conference room, looking around.

"We needed to get underway," said Alice, in a voice that was neither a rebuke nor an apology.

Henry said nothing.

"There's room next to me," said Paul.

Henry walked around the table and sat down. "Do go on," he said.

"It seems that is not the case," Alice continued, offering no summary of what she had said already. "I have reminded Fred that Mary is likely to be under consideration this year..."

"Rather have Mary than Fred, to be honest," said Henry. "Smart girl. And I worry that Fred is losing it. Couldn't understand a man wanting to take *paternity* leave. Still can't."

"With the greatest respect, senior partner," said Paul slowly. "You don't have children."

If there was going to be an explosion, Charles said later, that's when it would have happened. But it didn't. Henry didn't have an answer.

"Fred has told me," Alice continued, "that if the anti-nepotism rule remains in effect, he will resign his partnership immediately, so that Mary has a clear shot, as he puts it."

"I think he loves her," said a voice down the table.

"He'll probably resign if we don't make her a partner," said another.

"But we will," said one of the men who had already spoken in Mary's support. "I suppose that's a decision for next weekend, though. Sorry."

"So, the question is," said Alice, "are we willing to affirmatively end the anti-nepotism rule, or do we lose Fred no matter what we decide about Mary?"

The question was just complicated enough, and delicate enough, that no one immediately spoke. "They were thinking about it," Alice said later, "as partners should."

"Perhaps I should say a few words," said Charles. Everyone turned in his direction, in doing so making it obvious how carefully they hadn't been looking at him. "As some of you know, Alice and I are fond of each other."

No one spoke. It was common knowledge.

"Making the proposed change would make it possible for us to marry. Strictly speaking, under the existing rule, we shouldn't be . . . seeing each other. We shouldn't be fond of each other. But one's emotions have a mind of their own. So, I must thank you for your indulgence.

"But I also need to tell you that I have decided to leave the law. With the greatest respect to you, my partners, the law no longer does it for me."

Several of his partners spoke at once. "What do you plan to do, Charles?"

"I think I'll be a high school English teacher," he said. "We'll see. I have to go back to school and get a teaching certificate. In the interim, I'm hoping Alice will marry me. The point I wanted to make, however, is that effective with my resignation at the end of this month, I no longer have a *personal* interest, nor does Alice, in how you decide on the anti-nepotism rule."

"Thank you for making that clear," said Oscar.

There was more Alice could have said, but instinct told her not to. The room had backed her even before Charles spoke.

"Well, I think you all know I'm not comfortable with the change," said Henry.

No one spoke.

"So, perhaps I should retire too."

No one spoke.

Henry got up and left the room.

"It wasn't that he cared about the rule," Sandra said later, when they talked it over. "He cared about not being deferred to."

"As he should," said Alice. "Sad, though." Just because she understood power didn't mean she thought it was pretty.

After Henry had left the conference room, the meeting started to break up. There was more on the agenda, but no one had the appetite for it just then. Alice stood up, walked over to Charles and kissed him on the mouth.

"I'll take that as a 'yes,'" said Charles.

Their partners began to clap.

Alice wrapped her arms around her fiancé and put her head on his shoulder for a moment. "Take me home," she whispered.

"Go see Henry right now," said Charles quietly, drawing her toward the door and then out into the hall. "You mustn't let him resign."

"He's an important node, I guess you're saying," said Alice.

"And he's given the firm nearly forty years. And you don't want today to be remembered as the meeting when Alice killed Henry."

"He told me to kill him, remember? I told you about that."

"Yes, and what he meant was, 'Don't drag it out.' He was asking you to be merciful. He knew already that you'd won.

He's a wise old lion, Alice. I wouldn't be surprised if he knew you'd won the day you came into the gym and started to unbutton your dress."

"Did you know?" said Alice, genuinely surprised.

"No. I was very excited, but no. I'm not into politics. Just sex and poetry, it would appear."

Alice laughed. "Are you planning to teach both in high school?"

"Prose composition will be sufficient," said Charles with mock stiffness. "But we can talk about my plans later. They'll take care of themselves. Now, you go see Henry before he goes home. Don't let Veronica keep you out."

"And I tell him his partners want him to stay?"

"Tell him *you* want him to stay. He could care less about Oscar and Thomas and Andrew and those others whose names he does probably remember but rarely talks to. What the new lion thinks is all that matters to the old lion."

"I could give him Millie."

"Is she up this year?"

"Next year, really. But he'd like to see her promoted. I could ask him to stay around for that—or until the President asks him to do something for his country."

"Which he will do after you talk to him," said Charles.

"Henry?"

"No. The President. You call him next week and tell him Henry has passed the baton to you, making him available."

"I'm supposed to call the President of the United States?" said Alice. "I'm not sure I'm ready for that."

"It appears to be in the job description. But go talk to Henry now. Save the President for next week."

Henry was packing his briefcase when Alice got to his office. Veronica was sitting at her desk noiselessly sobbing. Alice walked right past her.

"This isn't right," she said without preliminaries. "You haven't finished teaching Millie how to be a partner. You haven't made provision for Veronica. You haven't let Elizabeth think this was her idea. And you're not being fair to yourself."

Henry said nothing.

"You told me, a while ago," Alice went on, "that you weren't a good loser. I don't see why that needs to be true. Stay another year. Let us give you a grand party. With enough notice, the President will probably come."

Henry just looked at her.

"And to be honest, Henry, I could use another year of your advice."

"You don't always take it," said Henry.

"Of course not. You're not always right. *I'm* not always right. That's why lawyers practice in partnerships. You told me that when I was a first-year associate. I suppose you don't remember that time. I'd misunderstood something rather badly, and you caught my mistake. I was very close to tears."

"I do remember," said Henry.

"Catch my mistakes for another year."

Henry said nothing, and neither did Alice. She knew there was nothing more to say.

"All right," he said. "Veronica will like that. See you Monday. You'll talk to the others?"

"I will," said Alice, realizing as she said it that "the others" included the President of the United States.

"So, when will you have a better excuse to call him?" said Charles.

"Thank you for telling me," said the President. "And haven't I met your mother?"

Coming soon in November 2015

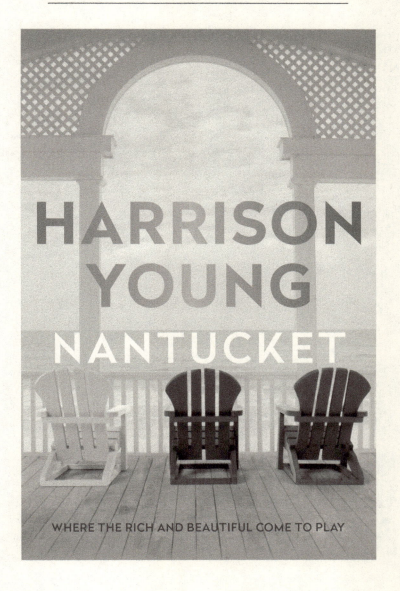

HARRISON YOUNG

NANTUCKET

WHERE THE RICH AND BEAUTIFUL COME TO PLAY